TOM STONE

ONE SHOT, ONE KILL

DON SIMKOVICH
LON CASLER BIXBY

CARVED IN STONE MEDIA
WWW.CARVEDINSTONE.MEDIA

Tom Stone: One Shot, One Kill
Copyright © 2019 Don Simkovich, Lon Casler Bixby

ISBN: 978-1-694156-51-8

Story based on characters created by Lon Casler Bixby for an original screenplay.

Cover Artist: Ben Southgate
Interior Book Design: Bob Houston eBook Formatting

Published by Carved in Stone Media
www.carvedinstone.media

ACKNOWLEDGEMENTS

Special thanks to our Beta readers for their input, honesty—and finding the typos we missed:

Grace Harrell, Lars Nilsson, and Chrisia Johnston.

And another thanks to our technical consultant, Moses Beltran.

We're grateful for Ben Southgate and his fabulous cover design. He was able to create the art exactly as we had envisioned.

We also appreciate the encouragement and support of our family and friends, and in turn, we acknowledge and value those who put their lives on the line to help others.

CHAPTER ONE

Brushing the weeds aside allowed for a perfect view of the backyard. His laser rangefinder registered eight hundred and eighty yards. Exactly a half mile. An easy shot. A white-haired man, the target, was relaxing poolside as expected. After setting the rangefinder down, his movements were subtle, blending into the brown grasses and green bushes as he positioned himself behind the rifle. He made slight adjustments to the riflescope, and readied himself with the weapon, a Barrett .50 caliber equipped with a sound suppressor. It rested on the bipod, ready for action. The scope brought the details into focus. The man by the pool wore swim shorts and was wrapped in a robe that was partly opened. His chest and stomach were quite flat for a man his age. Probably spent thousands every year on a personal trainer.

The target held a fluted wine glass and chatted with a few other adults who looked like old Yuppies. A woman sitting next to the man wore a halter top and a wrap around her waist. A real beauty. Maybe an actress in her early thirties, although he didn't recognize her. Or, he scoffed, maybe a former lingerie model past her prime. Children splashed in one end of the pool and a middle-age couple sat in a bubbling hot tub.

The mission was clear. Take out only the white-haired man. Having a few people around was fine since it would add to the excitement. This was the third trip back to the ridge, waiting for the perfect moment. Take the shot. One shot. One kill. And then softball in the rec league that played in Griffith Park. The team needed a win to get a good seed in the playoffs.

His finger was set on the trigger and he breathed deeply, but the woman in the halter top ruined it by sashaying in front. He kept breathing gently, rhythmically ready for when she stepped away. Take a deep breath. Slowly. Poetry in motion, feel the rhythm with the finger on the trigger. A kid jumped out of the pool and ran past the man who got up out of the chaise lounge. Breathe. No problem. Just wait for the right moment. Patience. You were trained for this.

Brown weeds covered the hillside down into the luxury home development and the city of Los Angeles rolled beyond to the ocean. The pool was nicely situated behind the house and the setting sun illuminated the target. Once the round was sent, there was plenty of time to disassemble the rifle, slither away through the weeds, and walk back to the hiking path. The sunset promised to be beautiful and he could admire it among the health-conscious joggers and lovers entwined in each other's arms. And getting to the ballfield for warm-ups would be a cinch. The team needed him with his .375 batting average and ability to drive a fly ball to deep center field.

Another look in the scope. The woman was extra chatty. Maybe had too much to drink. A barbeque grill sat in one corner of the patio with something sizzling on it. This was like when he was a kid and stumbling upon an ant hill, with the ants moving neatly in one line after another until he took his foot and kicked the dirt to scatter the critters. Watching them instantly transform from an orderly community into a panicked dizzying pack of insects always made him laugh. Take that. And that. One kick and another kick. It didn't bother him because the ants would re-build. And sometimes he'd let the ant hill alone, and just observe.

This was no different. This guy's wife was good looking enough to remarry and he had multiple millions in life insurance and stocks. She and the kids would get over missing him. For some, money solved so many aches and pains. She turned, took off her wrap, and revealed a gorgeous body with a marvelous bikini. She stood on the edge of the pool and the kids scurried back into the water. Playtime with mama. The white-haired man sat back down in the chaise lounge and smiled at her. Older man. Younger woman. And there was always a jilted ex-wife, or two, sitting in some luxury condo smacking lips with their own lovers. Idiots. All of them were idiots.

The crosshairs were aligned on the man's forehead. Perfect. The finger on the trigger felt so good. The vibes from hundreds of yards down the slope made their way up the ridge and he could soak them in. Los Angeles had so many wonderful canyons with crevices and ridges and everything fit together perfectly. He watched, waited. And then it happened. The woman with the gorgeous figure leaned forward, sprung from her feet, and as she arched into the water he released his breath and in between heartbeats he squeezed the trigger. The shot sounded wonderfully quiet and, in an instant, the white-haired man's head vanished into red mist. The sniper smiled.

Thanks to the breeze rolling in from the ocean and the marine layer drifting over the hills, the screams and shrieks from below were practically inaudible. Just like kicking an ant hill. The people scurried in panic and the woman clambered out of the pool. But there was no time to watch and enjoy the unfolding pandemonium. *Time to go.* Shock would engulf the group and it would take at least a couple of minutes for them to gather their wits and call 9-1-1. The call itself would take at least one minute. And it would take another three or four minutes before police cars rolled to the scene and even longer for the stupid police and news helicopters to swarm the area, flooding the property and surrounding hillsides with their angry-sounding rotors.

He moved methodically, breaking down the weapon and removing the brass catcher that caught the spent round, and then concealing it all in a backpack by his side. He pulled a cloth patch out of his pocket and set it where he was laying as a message, his calling card and personal touch put on the scene. He scooted backward on his stomach through the weeds, balancing the backpack to minimize disturbance to the area. He stood and lifted the pack on to his shoulders, adjusted the straps, walked to the main trail and headed along the ridge toward the parking lot. Time to shift gears. Batting practice. Catching fly balls, running, and then leaping with his glove outstretched, spoiling a rally and driving in runs with the bases loaded—the hero who got his team into the playoffs.

A man in white cap, T-shirt, and running shorts huffed up the trail, holding the leash to his Irish Setter, a friendly-looking dog who was wagging its tail. A woman dressed in a stylish sweat suit walked quickly, pumping her arms. Before he reached the steps to the parking lot, he passed a bench overlooking the city where a man and woman embraced and kissed. He was black. She was white. Los Angeles was such a great place to live with people from so many different races and languages mingling and mixing. He held his backpack steady and walked carefully down to the parking lot. The couple kissing made the man smile wistfully as he remembered his wife. He missed her so much.

CHAPTER TWO

Jake Sharpe raised an eyebrow like he couldn't believe what he just heard. "What do you mean you don't want to be here?" Lights shining on the ball field at Griffith Park in the evening were as gratifying to Jake as lights on a movie set were to an actor.

"I'm not big on softball," mumbled Tom Stone, tying his cleats with his ball glove by his side.

"Since when?" Jake, Stone's partner on the force, grabbed a bat from along the protective fence separating the field from the benches. He flexed his muscles, a body kept in decent shape from working out except for softness around the middle.

"Never really cared for it."

"Man, you can work with a guy for years and still learn something new about him." Jake stretched. "You like baseball."

"Baseball's not softball. And I played enough of it." Stone was an All Star in high school and played into his sophomore year of college.

But that was more than twenty years ago. He leaned and reached for his toes to stretch his lower back muscles.

"Well, you never cease to amaze me," sighed Jake. "What about when we played, and finally won, against the Hollywood division? I saw you smiling and enjoying yourself."

"They had some great women playing on their team. Of course, I was smiling. But truth be told, I'd rather go running. It's more freeing."

"Dude, you are so weird."

Stone laughed. "Takes one to know one." He looked across the field where the opposing team was gathering. The players were city firemen from several different stations.

Jake stepped away from Stone and the others who were sitting on the bench and took a hard practice swing.

"Whoa, feel the wind," Stone laughed and acted like he was falling down.

"Just visualizing knocking the ball a good four hundred feet or more." Jake looked at the cop sitting at the end of the bench by himself. "What about you, Brian? Doesn't it feel good to smash a home run?"

Brian Kilbraide had four years on patrol and recently became a detective. "You can say that." A former military vet and an African American man like Jake. Muscular. Spent most of his off-hours at the gym or the shooting range and, except for softball, never mentioned that he had a life outside the department. He was a disciplined and a by-the-book kind of guy.

"We should call you killer," chuckled Jake. "Killer Kilbraide."

"I'd rather not. It's nothing to joke about."

"Whoa. Excuse me and lighten up. It has a good sound." Jake wondered why his remark hit a nerve with Kilbraide, but then let the thought go. "You can bat third."

Detective Matthew Wildman made his way to the bench and dumped his cleats on it.

"Who bats fourth?" asked Kilbraide.

"Me. I've been assigned the privilege of hitting clean up." Jake took another swing through the air.

"Actually, Kilbraide is clean up. I've got you batting seventh," said Wildman.

"Say what?" Jake was astonished. "Come on, don't you want me at clean up? I've earned the right."

The opposition was forming into their groups for warm-ups.

Stone chuckled. "This is why I come, Jake. Watching you is cheap entertainment."

Wildman continued with a serious look. "It just makes the most sense. I was up last night figuring this all out. There's always someone left on base when we get midway through the lineup. I see you batting seventh—it's like a second clean-up position. I think it's a better chance for you to get some RBIs."

"Come on, Wildman. That's a demotion." Jake, who played a couple of years in the NFL, flexed his biceps. "You need muscle power."

Kilbraide laughed.

Wildman sat, took off his running shoes, and put on his cleats. "Come on, bro. This is a recreational softball league. Sometimes you smash home runs. A lot of times you strike out and other times you get a base hit or a double. This has nothing to do with your ability."

Jake's face fell. "It really sucks."

"Let's just try it out, okay? I actually think you'll get more RBIs. Like I said, there's always guys left on base in the middle of the lineup. Kilbraide's not an automatic home run when he's up."

"Thanks a lot," remarked Kilbraide.

"You're not. You're consistent, though." Wildman pointed toward the outfield where a few of their teammates were tossing softballs to warm up. "Snyder hits singles and doubles. He's going to be fifth after Kilbraide."

"Where am I?" asked Stone, scratching his perpetual five o'clock shadow. He grabbed his bottle of Gatorade, took a swig, and spilled some on his jersey.

"You're going to lead off. You're more likely to get on base than anybody here."

"Seventh?" Jake looked depressed. A handful of spectators were shuffling into the stands. He could see his wife Tasha and three kids making their way from the parking lot and waved to them. He'd been bragging about hitting high in the lineup. How humiliating. "Hey, Stone? Is Alisha going to make it?"

"Nope." Stone stood and grabbed his glove and ball. Having his girlfriend in the stands would have been nice. "She's got some new cases."

"Wow, she's busy. Has she hired another paralegal to help handle the load?"

"Not just yet," said Stone.

"Heck, wish I was a busy ballplayer. But I'll be sitting on the bench for a while longer tonight."

"For crying out loud, Jake," Wildman laughed and patted him on the shoulder. "I've got myself batting eighth. I don't even show myself favoritism." He picked up his glove. "Come on, let's warm up."

"All right." Jake set his bat aside and Stone tossed him his glove.

"Remember, there's no *i* in team."

Jake laughed. "Yeah, but you can't have a team without *m-e*. Me."

"Hey, listen," said Kilbraide. "I'll bat seventh."

"No, don't worry about it. I know us *brothers* got to help each other out, but you go ahead and hit clean up." Jake moved his arm slowly in a circle to loosen up. "Let's see if Manager Wildman's plan is going to work."

"It'll work just fine." Wildman sounded reassuring.

Kilbraide snagged his glove and headed onto the field.

Stone's phone vibrated on the bench and he picked it up. "Stone here."

"Hey, Stone. It's Captain Harrell. Where are you?"

"Getting ready for a critical league game."

"Put it on hold for now. Is Jake with you?"

"Yeah. He's on the field."

"It's got to wait. We got a shooting victim. Took a bullet in his skull and I need you over there." Harrell gave the address, discussed a few known details, and then hung up.

Stone called the guys over. "Hey, Wildman. Jake. Kilbraide. Come here."

They trotted in. "What's up?"

"Jake and I have a crime scene to visit. Some guy at a house in the hills got his head taken off with a shot between the eyes. You'll have to play without us tonight."

Jake shook his head and frowned. Tasha and the kids finally came to watch him play, but he had to skip out. Crime never slept.

"Where'd it happen?" asked Wildman.

"Out near Coldwater Canyon."

"That sucks."

"It most certainly does."

Jake plopped on the bench and changed his shoes. "Let's go, Stone. Damn." Jake looked at Kilbraide. "Here's your chance to bat fourth *and* seventh."

Kilbraide saluted. "Good luck, guys."

Stone looked across at a fireman taking batting practice and spoke to Wildman. "Think you can handle things while we go mop up a crime scene?"

"Sure can. We'll mop 'em up here, too."

CHAPTER THREE

Stone and Jake exited the 101 freeway, sped on to the streets of Studio City, up Coldwater Canyon and crossed the winding Mulholland Drive. They followed Coldwater down the hill toward the backside of Hollywood and as the street narrowed and flattened out, turned left at a traffic signal where homes with neatly trimmed hedges and solar yard lights looked peaceful. An official department car with flashing lights guarded the street and beyond.

Stone pulled up in his Jeep and rolled down his window. An old flame, Monty Tusco, was looking athletic in her uniform and putting the brakes on potential lookie-loos. "Hold on, hold on." Her brunette hair was tied up in a bun beneath her cap.

"You're not going to turn me away are you?"

She smiled. "Never." Her jaws were working a piece of chewing gum that snapped and popped. She acted every bit the Montana horse wrangler that she once was.

"Hey, Monty." Jake waved from the passenger seat.

"Hey ya, Jake."

"Do I need to show my badge?" Stone smiled back.

"Oh, sweetie, you're good." Monty leaned in the open window. "How's Alisha doing?"

"Doing okay. Battling a mountain of cases as always."

"When you get a chance, tell her I said, 'Howdy.'" Monty flashed her eyes. "Hey, if you ever want to sow your oats and ride in another rodeo sometime—"

"That was a long time ago, Monty," Stone smiled. *Monty Tusco.* You can take the girl out of the country, but you'll never get the country out of the girl.

"The offer's always open. Hey, wait 'till you get a load of what happened up the hill."

"They let you up there?"

"You know me, they couldn't keep me away. Love that gruesome stuff. Just wait 'till you see—"

Stone held up a hand. "We'll see for ourselves."

"Okay, Detective Stone." She winked. "Maybe I'll catch you on the way back down."

"And if not, another time."

She patted the side of the Jeep. "Git along, lil' dogie."

Stone pulled away, leaving Monty beneath the flashing traffic light. He followed the winding road, rising higher above the city lights.

"We should've ridden a mountain goat for this one," remarked Jake.

"Keep the belt fastened." Stone pulled to the summit and reached the circular driveway. A two-story creation stretched east and west, one of several mansions that were custom-built into the hillsides only several years earlier. The lights of Los Angeles that glittered below were overtaken by flashing lights from police cruisers, the headlights of other official vehicles, and floodlights erected to search the surrounding hills. Stone and Jake parked and showed their badges to the officers as they were directed through the front door of the house. The plush carpeting, curved stairs leading to the second floor, over-sized chandeliers, and recessed lighting showed just how new and opulent the home was.

Wracking sobs from the dining room ruined the charm. Stone looked and saw a distraught woman cradling a child on her lap while someone who spoke softly like a counselor sat and consoled her. Another man and woman leaned back in their chairs, looking like they were in shock and dabbing at their eyes with tissue.

The detectives walked through a den with a large entertainment center to the back patio and swimming pool.

Crime scene activity was in full swing with the medical examiner on site, a police photographer busy, and investigators combing the surface of the patio, the pool area, and walking freely in and out of the house.

A uniformed patrolman stood on the deck, jotting notes.

Stone got his attention. "Detective Tom Stone."

Jake introduced himself. "Detective Jake Sharpe."

"Officer Clint Browell." He looked drained and acted like he was catching his breath. "Pleased to meet you guys."

Lights in the pool cast an eerie glow.

"So were you the responding officer?" asked Jake.

"Sure was." Browell pocketed the small notepad he was writing on.

Stone surveyed the patio. A body on the chaise lounge was covered with a white sheet, stained with blood. He studied the area as a medical examiner knelt and put markers around the patio furniture and barbeque grill. Pieces of bone and brain ripped from the victim added to the macabre setting. A trail of blood marked the grill area and flagstones.

"Obviously, that's him under the sheet," said Browell. "I was cruising the canyon when I got the call. A shooting. A maid let me in the front door. Guess they were having a little get together. The paramedics came soon after. The family was going crazy. A few friends were over and they were having a cookout. Wife and kids were swimming in the pool. Next thing they know his head exploded. They didn't hear anything."

"Thanks," said Jake.

Stone and Jake walked to the body as Browell followed behind.

The medical examiner called out to them. "Hey, Stone. Jake. How you doing? Heard you guys were playing softball. Sorry to interrupt your game, but here's what we got."

"Mind if I take a look?" asked Stone.

"Go ahead. It's not pretty."

Stone pulled the sheet back and Jake took a deep breath. The man's face was nearly intact except for a hole just above the eyes. A closer look showed the power of what had struck him. The back of the head was missing so that the face was covering nothing. A mess of blood and brains splattered below the chair to the area behind him.

"Jesus," whispered Jake. "For once, I've lost my appetite."

"Looks like one bullet. Obviously high caliber," said the examiner. "A hell of a shot."

Stone looked at Browell, the color had drained from his face. He acted shaky. "Do you know anything about this guy?"

"So far, just the usual. His name was Charles Scott, aged sixty-four. Was in good shape. Had a lot of money. The wife kept crying that he was a good man. You might have seen her. She's inside with their kids and friends." Browell motioned to the house and wiped sweat from his forehead. "Apparently, Scott is chairman of his own financial consulting firm. *Was* chairman. Damn, that changed fast."

"Did they know where the shot might have come from?"

"No, this place is secure. Like its own little fortress on a hillside." Browell inhaled. "Hey, do you guys mind if I step to the front of the house for a change of scenery?"

"Go ahead," said Jake, reaching in his pocket. "Here's my card and make sure to email me your notes. Thanks."

"Sure will." The patrolman wobbled away.

Stone glanced around. The patio was situated partly behind the home facing east. It was perched on a level spot above a cliff. The lights of Hollywood stretched like carpeting toward downtown Los Angeles.

There was no place for a gunman to run up to the fence and shoot. Behind the property a hillside rose toward a ridge that looked about several hundred yards away. A few small trees and scrub brush covered the steep grade. There was no trail or steps leading down.

Jake glanced at the ridge where the floodlights created a glare and he walked toward the railing that marked the back boundary of the property. Below the fence was a gully about fifty feet deep. The hillside was steep enough that finding a spot to shoot accurately seemed impossible. "Hey, Stone." Jake called to his partner who wandered over. "I'm thinking something."

"Good to know. What is it?"

"Unless the gunman was hovering in a helicopter over the canyon, the only place I could logically see where a shot would come from is up there." He shielded his eyes from the floodlights and pointed to the ridge.

Stone followed the line of sight. A hiking trail ran along the crest of the ridge, a popular spot off Mulholland Drive that had different lookout points to gaze over the Hollywood Bowl to the east and Century City's high rises to the west.

"Let's get a team over there right away," said Stone. "And since we're going to be here a while, let's plan on getting up there first thing in the morning."

"I'd like to bring our resident expert along."

"Oh?"

"Yeah, Brian Kilbraide," said Jake.

"From his experience in the Army Rangers?"

"Yep, as a sniper. He was a damned good one from what I've heard and I'd like his perspective."

Stone studied the steepness of the hillside. He squinted through the lights and followed the ridge line from east to west and then back. "A sniper, huh? Damn. That'd be one hell of a shot."

CHAPTER FOUR

Mexican flags fluttered green, white, and red over the archway of the newly constructed elementary school. Dignitaries from the town and state government posed for pictures and shook hands after giving their speeches at the podium set up in the courtyard. A student orchestra took their cue from the band leader and struck up a song, celebrating the school's opening.

Teachers, parents, local shopkeepers and business owners, hoping to catch a picture with or share a grievance with a local official, got up from their seats. They mingled at tables filled with carne asada, salad, tortillas, horchata and plenty of punch. One man, muscular with tattoos decorating his body, towered behind the podium where he had finished a speech and kept greeting well-wishers. He watched his pregnant wife and two stepchildren make their way to the food and tried to join them, but an old woman stopped him. He knew her and she took pride in her roots that she traced back to the Aztecs. Her long black hair was tied neatly with a bow. She shook his hand and smiled, lines from a hard life were etched deeply in her tan skin.

"*Gracias.*" She spoke and her teeth showed decay from years of chewing cocoa leaves. Speaking in Spanish, she said how his investment in the town was like water refreshing the parched mountains. She hoped that her grandchildren would be able to learn, grow up, raise families in the town, and not have to live in fear of being killed. She prayed for peace and was thankful that someone was finally standing up to the drug cartels. Her dusty dress was likely one of only a few she owned.

"Thank you," said the man, grasping her hand and looking in her eyes. "Without your courage and the help of the other families, it would never have happened." He glanced away and then back at the woman. "If you'll excuse me." He wore new blue jeans with a freshly pressed shirt and moved quickly to his wife. She brushed her flowing brunette hair aside and helped her children fill their plates. "Marta, rest your feet." He pulled a chair out for her. "Enjoy yourself."

"You're not sitting down?"

"I've got to meet with someone in a few minutes."

"Too bad, Arturo." She whispered in his ear while her son and daughter moved along in the line. "I had hoped to send the children to mother's so we could celebrate this special day on our own."

He smiled. "We'll have time, soon. I promise." He kissed her on the cheek.

A man with a bulging stomach beneath a loose-fitting dress shirt and tie greeted them both.

"Thank you for making this day possible."

20

"You're welcome," said Arturo, warmly shaking the man's hand, calloused from years of labor. "Are you excited about the new school?"

"Yes. I was waking up before five A.M. every morning to drive my children to school in Zacatecas. Criminals never sleep. I feared we would get pulled over and they would take my girl and I'd never see her again. Now, with this *escuela*, we can have a normal breakfast together and get them home before dark. Thank you."

"I'm glad I could help."

The man thanked him again and moved to the food table where he grabbed a plate, his jeans held up by a worn belt.

"You have so many meetings lately. Who are you meeting with now?" asked Marta, keeping an eye on her children.

"Senator Lopez. He sounded concerned about something."

Marta's eyes filled with worry. "Is everything okay?"

"I'm sure it will be. He said it will be brief. And no worries. I won't be leaving your sight." He caressed her stomach. "I can't leave you and our little *nino*."

She smiled and corrected him. "*Nina*."

Murmurs rose from the crowd that was finishing up the food as Senator Carlos Lopez approached. "He's here," said Arturo.

The senator was flanked by three men, his bodyguards, made necessary by his stance against the cartels and his work at weeding out police officers who were on the take. "Arturo, nice to see you."

"Senator, I see you're well." He glanced at the men.

"I got delayed, but I was eager to stop by and see the commotion that you're creating." He looked at the school. "Obviously, this is the kind of commotion that we like."

Arturo beamed. "I'd like you to meet my wife, Marta."

"Congratulations." The senator smiled and looked at her pregnant belly. "I had heard you were recently married. Sorry I couldn't attend the ceremony."

Marta smiled. "Arturo says good things about you. He's lucky to have met you."

"That's kind. I feel the same way about him. If you'll excuse us. Arturo, give me a tour of the school."

"Certainly."

The senator spoke to Marta. "We won't be long, I assure you."

"Of course, senator."

Arturo led the way across the plaza toward the school's entrance while the bodyguards followed behind.

"This is quite an accomplishment," said Lopez.

"It's just the first of many schools."

"Still, it represents hard work on your part."

Arturo agreed. "It was difficult. But the families knew it was time to build a school here and keep our kids safe."

"It's like you've always been in Zacatecas," remarked Lopez.

"My heart's always been here. Living in Los Angeles has its good side, but this is where I belong."

"Do you ever think about going back to LA?"

"Sometimes. For now, I like traveling back and forth. I'm trying to get my father to move back here again." Arturo glanced over at Marta and the children who were enjoying their lunches.

"You certainly know how to get things done," said Lopez. "Getting approval from the local authorities and then donating the money was nothing short of a miracle."

"A labor of love. And—"

"Yes?"

"A move to beat the cartels at their own game. Senator, I know you didn't come down just to chat? What's going on?"

Senator Lopez looked directly at Arturo. "Charles Scott was murdered last night."

Arturo shook his head as the grim news sunk in.

CHAPTER FIVE

A wide, trodden path ran like a finger along the spine of the hills. Others veered from it like tributaries of a stream, including a fire road that wound down into West Hollywood. This was the eastern edge of the Santa Monica Mountains, leading to the Hollywood Bowl with spectacular views of downtown Los Angeles, the CNN building on Sunset Boulevard to the west, and the urban sprawl extending to the Pacific Ocean.

Stone surveyed the entire area where a trail zig-zagged down a ravine on the north-facing slope, toward the San Fernando Valley. "Do you see it?" He squinted at the properties below as Jake narrowed in using binoculars.

"Yeah." Jake stood off the trail, about knee-high in a patch of brown, wavy grass. He lowered the binoculars. "The crime scene in all its glory. But we have to move east a little more. Man, it's hard to walk around in this brush. No wonder forensics didn't find anything last night."

Walking slowly toward them was Brian Kilbraide, quietly studying the landscape.

"Hey, Kilbraide. You're lagging. I heard you got thrown out at home plate last night," said Jake.

Kilbraide studied the homes down the slope. "That dirt around third base was as slippery as ice. I had a lot on my mind. I wasn't really into the game."

"Sounds like it wouldn't have mattered if you did score since we lost by seven runs," remarked Jake.

Kilbraide and Stone followed as Jake moved along the trail, adjusting the binoculars. The men, with the aid of their GPS, zeroed in on the estate below where workers were removing police floodlights used the night before.

Jake stopped and looked closely. "Okay. I see it fairly well. The patio." He stepped forward into the weeds. "There, that's better. Stone? You want to take a look?"

"Absolutely." Stone took the glasses, adjusted them, and brought the patio into view. Directly below where he was standing there was a smaller ridge and hillside running southeast. He was surprised the line of sight was so clear. "Yeah. I see it."

On the chaise lounge, the team had erected a dummy target to reconstruct how the body might have been sitting. The patio and adjoining house were built on a westward facing slope to catch the late afternoon sun. The property was well protected by fencing, and the hillside leading up to the ridge was a natural barrier against attack. That made sense since normal people never expected to be shot in their own backyard.

Stone handed the binoculars back to Jake and yawned. A night of studying notes and reading up on high caliber bullets had sucked him in. There'd be no time to nap because in a few hours he'd be visiting Andrew, a nine-year-old boy who lived at Ivy Acres, a group home in the San Fernando Valley. Stone had met him more than two years earlier while delivering Christmas presents with Jake, had developed an on-going relationship, and had become like a father figure.

"Hey, Kilbraide." Jake motioned to the former military vet and handed him the binoculars. "What do you think?"

He looked. "Steep but steady descent. A clear shot."

"Possible?" asked Jake.

Kilbraide nodded. "No problem."

"How hard?"

"For a civilian it'd be a tough shot, but for a highly trained marksman, doable."

"So you think the guy was trained?" asked Stone.

"He'd have to be. You don't just go practice at a shooting range for a few months and then come up here and shoot somebody." Kilbraide spoke like he was piecing it together in his mind. "You got to have what it takes."

Jake spoke up. "Is that luck or skill?"

"Totally skill. You said he only did one shot, right?"

"Yep. No evidence of any more, and ballistics confirmed it was a .50 caliber round."

"Wow, .50 cal." Kilbraide muttered. "One shot, one kill. He's trying to get noticed. Maybe sending a message?" Kilbraide had served as a sniper in Afghanistan and Iraq. "It's like one shot is bagging the big prize. You know, winning a hundred-million-dollar Power Ball Lotto or something like that." Kilbraide eyed the canyon and lifted his face to the breeze. "Very few people could pull that off. Had to be military." He spoke quietly, as though muttering to himself. "He could have double-tapped him one in the chest and one in the head."

"Why didn't he?" asked Stone.

"Don't know. No need. He got him on the first shot. I'd do it, too." Kilbraide knelt in the grass and pulled it aside. "A lot more fun that way. Plus, the other advantage to taking the guy down in one shot is no wasted rounds. Your job's done and the mission's complete. And you're gone before anyone notices. Back to the barracks, time for a beer, and no one's the wiser."

"God, that's cold." Jake shook his head.

"Yeah? And so's the beer," quipped Kilbraide.

"So what really goes into making a shot like this?" asked Stone. "We're a half mile away."

Kilbraide surveyed the scene. "You got to take into account not just the distance but the rate that the bullet is going to fall. Wind, position of the sun, temperature and humidity all play a role. And patience is the key. You have to wait for the right moment."

"Complicating things was that there were people running around the patio," said Stone.

"And that's where patience comes in. That's what makes us unique."

"So you got good training in the military?" asked Stone.

"The best." Kilbraide continued taking in the surroundings. "And I'll bet this guy did, too."

"How much did you guys practice?"

"Enough."

"Did you shoot targets this far away?" asked Jake.

"All the time."

"Maybe he wasn't military. Maybe he was a cop. Or a damned good hunter."

"Could be," said Kilbraide. "Some amazing shots have been made on the battlefield, though. Longest known sniper shot is about two miles."

"Seriously?" asked Stone.

"Yep. By an elite Canadian sniper and spotter. They were in Special Forces. Took out an ISIS militant. Three-thousand eight-hundred and seventy-one yards. The shot took almost ten seconds to make its kill."

"Wow," said Jake. "You're kidding?"

Kilbraide looked down, took a breath, and calculated. "One-thousand-and-one—" he snapped his finger. "Bam. The bullet hits Mr. Scott."

Stone studied him. He watched Kilbraide's steady breathing as though the guy was living the moment.

"So much wrapped up in one shot," muttered Kilbraide.

A kid's squeal shattered their concentration. Stone turned to see a boy straining to hold the leash of an Irish Setter, but the dog yanked free. A man followed behind as the dog came and stopped by Stone, sniffing his leg.

"Come back here, Red," yelled the kid.

"You got him, Robbie?" The man in his running shorts and T-shirt was breathing hard. He looked at Stone, Jake, and Kilbraide. "Sorry, guys. Excuse us." The man was ready to run on, but the dog had different ideas. "Come on, boy. Get him, Robbie, we don't want to bother these men."

"It's okay." Stone lowered his hand for Red to sniff it. "He must smell my dog. I've got a Silver Lab. I ran him out early this morning."

"Nice trails up here, huh?"

"Yeah, do you come up here often?" asked Stone.

"All the time."

Red, who had been sniffing, noticed a bird flying past and leaped after it.

"Red, get back here." The man looked embarrassed. "Got to get him back into obedience classes." He motioned to the boy. "Robbie, go get your dog."

The boy dashed, caught up with the animal, and grabbed the leash. "Come on." Robbie grunted and strained. The dog returned to sniffing in the grass.

"Curious dog," said Jake.

"Always. I think he has Attention Deficit Disorder."

Stone laughed.

The man pointed several yards away to some grass that was obviously trampled down. "On our way up here this morning, he had gotten off the leash, again. Ran for that spot there. Might smell a coyote or something. Looks like one was lying in the grass."

"It does?" Jake walked toward the spot. "Kilbraide, Stone, look at this."

Kilbraide knelt, taking a picture with his tablet.

The man tilted his head. "You guys cops?"

"Detectives," Stone replied.

"Oh, yeah. I thought so. You have that look. Hey, I heard about the shooting. I mean, who hasn't? It's all over the news." The man looked over the ridge. "Is the house right down there?"

"We're investigating. You said you come up here often. Did you happen to come up here last night?"

"Whoa, wait a second. I've never fired a gun in my life."

"Sure," Stone assured him. "I was wondering if you had seen anyone acting suspicious. Or noticed anything unusual."

"No." The guy looked puzzled and peered below. "How could they shoot from way up here?"

"They could do it." The boy spoke up. "Happens all the time on my video game. There's a sniper who fires from like a mile away and takes out the suicide bomber. But if he misses, then *ka-boom*, he gets taken out by a grenade."

"Robbie, I told you to stop playing those games."

"Yeah, yeah." The boy was as antsy as the dog. "Can we go now?"

"All right."

Stone handed the man his card and brought him back to the point. "If you can think of anything, no matter how small, please call right away."

"Yes, sir." He looked at the card. "Detective Stone. We sure will. This is really scary. I hope you get the guy."

"Thanks. We're working on it."

The man and Robbie started walking off, but then the boy stopped. "Hey," he shouted to Stone. "Maybe this can help you. I thought it was cool. It's like the logo on my video game." He reached in his pocket and pulled out a cloth patch that was embroidered with a slogan that gave Stone a chill.

Stone called to his partners. "Look at this."

"What's up?" asked Jake. He sauntered to Stone who pointed to what was in the boy's outstretched hand.

Kilbraide sounded concerned. "Where'd you get this?"

"Red found it when he was sniffing. Over there in the grass."

Stone spoke to the boy. "Do you mind if we keep this? It could help us."

"No, I found it."

"Robbie," said the dad, "give it to them."

"But—"

"No *buts*. Give it to them now."

The boy hesitated. "But it looks so cool." He gave it up.

"Thanks, son," said Kilbraide as Stone carefully lifted the patch with his fingers on the edges.

Embroidered in the center was a picture of a skull with a phrase encircling it: *One Shot. One Kill. No Remorse. I Decide.*

***

Frank DeVito grabbed his bag of golf clubs and hoisted them into the trunk of the Mercedes S-class. He liked handling them and didn't want an assistant to touch them. Made him feel part of the game that lay ahead. He was dressed in golf slacks and a polo shirt, size XXL to accommodate his beer-laden stomach. His hairy chest was adorned with gold chains. He shut the trunk while his driver got in behind the wheel. His new head of security, Ryker, stood and waited for his boss.

DeVito was about to get in as a sedan sped from the guard gate, up the driveway, and stopped behind his car. It was Denise, his office assistant, in her Prius. She leapt out. "Mr. DeVito."

"Good morning, Sandy."

"It's Denise, sir."

"Of course. Denise." He looked at the car. "Why do you drive that thing?"

"It's environmentally sound."

"But it's got no *oomph* to it. No class. With what I'm paying you, you could afford a—"

"Mr. DeVito. Thanks, but I like it."

"Suit yourself." He sounded disappointed, pulled a cigar from his pocket, bit the tip, and spit it out.

"Did you hear?" Denise sounded excited, almost panicked. "Charles Scott was killed." She caught her breath.

DeVito narrowed his gaze and wrinkled his brow. "Really?" He looked over at Ryker, a muscular man with wiry hair. "Did you know anything about this?"

"Nothing." He shrugged. Ryker was a smart guy, and he was tough: boxer as a kid, served in the military as a MP, and had gone on to earn a business degree with a specialty in surveillance technology. He ran his own security firm before DeVito bought the company and hired him as his personal head of security.

Charles Scott. DeVito's first thought was that the man was a smug bastard who loved nothing more than showing off his trophy wife and little clean-faced kids who were spoiled brats. DeVito looked at Denise. "What happened?"

"Gunshot. Killed at his home. Murdered in front of his family."

"He should have hired me for security," quipped Ryker.

"Hmm?" DeVito scratched his nose. *Interesting.*

"Yeah. The *Times* just identified him this morning." Denise scanned the Internet 'round the clock for DeVito and his operations.

"Did they catch anybody? I mean, any idea who—?"

"No, sir. Rumors say it was a sniper. I was able to confirm it. He was shot right between his eyes. Large caliber from a long ways off." Having connections inside the LAPD was nice.

"Damn." DeVito was suddenly filled with intrigue. "Thanks, Denise."

Charles Scott had a successful financial firm. He had been focused on building an investment empire and managing a portfolio of properties and businesses. The way the man did it was a method that DeVito found boring as hell and, frankly, DeVito had his own style and never did like dealing with the man. He liked the idea of managing business operations hands-on and the feeling of cold, hard untaxed cash in his fingers. The blood and guts of making money, just like his father taught him.

DeVito's empire was an eclectic mix of consumer goods and entertainment. He had a packaged dog food operation that was fascinating to watch in action as the robotic equipment filled the bags and prepared them for shipping. But nothing felt as nice as walking into his bowling alleys, dive bars with their pungent beer aroma, and newly acquired casinos. Counting the cash made him feel invincible.

Beyond all that, his prized operation was one that he liked to keep hidden below the radar: smuggling drugs into Los Angeles and throughout the U.S.

"Anything else?" he asked Denise. His Mercedes was waiting.

"No, sir. I wanted to make sure you knew. I'll see what else I can find out about it."

"I'll look into it on my end as well," said Ryker, lifting his phone.

34

"Good. Hey, Denise?"

"Yes, sir?"

"Set up a massage appointment for me this afternoon. I'm sure my back's going to be tight after my eighteen holes."

"Certainly."

"Call and get that new Thai girl. The one with the tiny hands, always makes me feel more like a man."

"Consider it done." Denise reached back in her car for her purse and file folders.

DeVito still didn't get in the car. "Oh, Denise?"

"Yes?"

"The coffee you bought, you know that Blue Mountain shit— where's it from? Hawaii?"

"Jamaica. The Kona blend is from Hawaii."

"Yeah, whatever. Anyway, it's really bitter."

Denise turned her head at an angle like she was trying to problem solve. "Maybe the beans weren't ground just so?"

"Maybe. I don't know. Look, just stick with Maxwell House. Good to the last drop, as they say."

"Yes, sir."

He got in the back seat, Ryker slid into the front, and the driver pulled past the gate and onto the streets of Encino with its sleepy, weekend morning stillness. They headed to the freeway and a country club so exclusive that there was never any waiting at the tee. *Scott was killed. Shot at his home.* DeVito simply couldn't imagine who did it. After a moment, he didn't care as he pictured keeping his back swing low and smooth.

CHAPTER SIX

The vantage point from the hillside was clear with the old-fashioned steam locomotives and box cars from Travel Town directly below. The popular destination was located along the northwestern area of Griffith Park. It was one of the few places in Los Angeles that families could go for free and turn back the clock to an earlier era of transportation. A roadway cut a path between the local tourist attraction and a well-traveled equestrian path with riders in jodhpurs and helmets walking and trotting their mounts.

When the war on terror started after September Eleven, Two-Thousand and One, then-president George W. Bush announced that many heroes in the struggle would remain anonymous and the public would never learn their names.

Smuggling drugs and ruining men and women financially was just as cruel and evil as a suicide bomber attacking innocent civilians. The government was failing miserably in its battle against drugs, and it was necessary to be an anonymous warrior. Leaving the patch gave a clue that someone was brave enough to battle it on their own. It took research, lots of it, to identify the responsible parties for the havoc being wrought on Los Angeles and throughout the United States, hell—the whole world: needles in the veins, coke snorted up the nose. It all came down to following the money. Month after month of looking up facts and figures, following trials of arrested drug dealers, and connecting the dots revealed each of the players and the fortresses of wealth and luxury that made them look like upstanding citizens, role models. But their wealth was gained by poisoning the lives of men and women craving euphoria.

That's why there was no mistaking the rider in the teal tank top, brown leggings, and dark helmet who was riding English saddle with two other women.

Nothing but the best. A one-hundred-thousand-dollar Hanoverian warmblood trained and shown by top-dollar professionals. The rider in the front was her teenage daughter and the one behind was her personal assistant. They moved slowly at this point as they always did, week in and week out, exercising their mounts kept at the equestrian center. A tunnel beneath the freeway connected the stables and the riding path through the park.

The bullet was taken out of its case and loaded into the weapon with precision.

Two boulders and manzanita bushes about five feet high provided the perfect cover. And it was time to breathe steadily, slowly, to inhale and exhale, emptying the mind and feeling the trigger, the pressure ever so slight as the trio made their way toward the zoo at Griffith Park. The riding helmet posed a slight challenge, while the side of the face remained totally exposed. The jawbone, just below the ear, was perfect.

They emerged from the tunnel and made their way along the path in the sunshine and warm weather. Cars and bicyclists passed on the street. Other horsemen were moving toward the trio from the opposite direction. But they weren't any problem since they were still a good thirty yards away.

The crosshairs in the riflescope marked her well.

She was a real beauty with her red hair flowing from beneath the dark velvet helmet and contrasting with the soft teal of her clothing. *Wonderful.*

A quiet euphoria took hold, as pleasurable as relaxing by a mountain lake and all it took was breathing in—and out—sensing the moment like a conductor of an orchestra. He focused so deeply that the sounds of traffic on the street and freeway faded into quiet. The only sound he heard was the slow beating of his heart as she pulled into view a few hundred yards below. He squeezed the trigger and within a split second the exact position where her body was on the horse vanished beneath a splash of red.

The screams didn't happen instantly. They almost never did. A surprise shot took several seconds for reality to awaken the bystanders. How perfect. His camouflage shirt and khakis blended in with the trail of scrub brush while the boulders acted like a wall of concrete, making for an easy getaway. The screaming started and then was drowned out by the noise of the 101 Freeway. It was tempting to want to stay and watch the riders jumping off their steeds and wailing for their mortally wounded friend. That was a luxury and there was no time. Not now. Not in war.

A battle by an anonymous lone soldier was going to achieve what corrupt law enforcement failed to do. There was no way to launch a full-scale attack with an actual army, so surgical strikes would have to do, picking off the leaders one-by-one—the wealth creators. As each one crumpled and died, there would be fewer investments made to bring the shipments into Los Angeles and up the coast. Little by little the cartels would get the message.

Military experience made it second nature to break down the rifle and fit it into the pack. Pulling a small round patch out of the pocket was even more satisfying this time, laying it on the dirt clearing where the shot was fired from.

The hillside curved so dramatically that the getaway on the bicycle was an easy ride down the steep road. It led west toward the famed Forest Lawn cemetery and the movie studios. He merged into traffic and by the time the police and news crews arrived at the scene he was simply one more cyclist enjoying the afternoon.

The backpack fit well over the shoulders while pedaling along. Staying in shape was a gift whether it was biking, hiking, or playing softball in the park. It was a damn shame about being alone in a city that had so much to offer. Stop for a cup of coffee and relax. Remember her and don't ever forget.

CHAPTER SEVEN

"What the hell is going on?" Frank DeVito held court in his boardroom and slammed his hand on the table. He had no problem venting in front of his three associates: Ryker, Denise who worked tirelessly, and Lewis Banali, his lawyer with a sharp wit and legal mind.

"That's what we're trying to find out, Mr. DeVito." Denise's face was pale.

"This is total bullshit." He fiddled through his cigar box, pulling one out and then another, laying them across each other like Lincoln logs. It didn't make sense. Taking out Charles Scott was fine. The jerk was a rival, but Darlene Cutchins was different. He had deals with Darlene who had a network for filtering his money. She was cautious and handled it expertly, making sure there were no ties back to him. Her sophisticated demeanor was a perfect complement to DeVito's style, not to mention that she was excellent eye candy. She and Scott were in opposite camps. "Denise, have you heard anything from inside the department?"

"No, sir. I've got calls in but there's nothing new to report." She had done well joining the Chamber of Commerce and linking up with the LAPD's community liaisons. Extra cash bought information when necessary.

"Damn. Stay on it."

Darlene buried herself in financing for film productions, worked closely with the executive producers, and was always happy to never have her name in the credits. She liked the anonymity and how it provided her with power to move effortlessly through the circles of the ultra-wealthy. Now she was dead.

Shot while riding a fucking horse. Unbelievable.

DeVito couldn't wrap his mind around what happened. "She was just picked off?"

"Just like Scott." Ryker sipped from a water bottle.

In a flash, DeVito pictured himself on the golf course or on his yacht and—suddenly life goes black. "So you're putting in new security measures?"

"Yes," said Ryker. "But the first step is doing a new security analysis on all your properties and taking a sniper into account. Trying to figure out who is behind it is puzzling, of course. From what I gather, Scott's people didn't owe money to anyone. No one I spoke with, from here, south of the border or across the Pacific, even hinted that they knew anything. No one's taking responsibility."

"Shit." DeVito tried to mask his concerns. He felt like his money and his many assets couldn't keep him secure. He grabbed the cigars and in frustration threw them back in the box.

Banali spoke up. "Whoever did it put in a lot of effort. The shot at Scott's was fired from one hell of a distance and, in Darlene's case, the gunman must have known her riding schedule and habits."

"And how in the hell would someone know that?" bellowed DeVito. "Taking down Scott. I can see that. He loved having all those interviews about investments and the economy. I saw him one time and he asked me if I had read his interview in Forbes magazine. Like I'd give a shit. The man always sounded like a prick with a stick up his ass. He could be tracked down easily enough. But Darlene?" DeVito looked at Ryker. "You search every corner on this property for any security issues."

Ryker sounded confident. "We're doing that now."

His tone reassured DeVito. The estate had plenty of barriers with thick hedges and trees that shielded the buildings from random views. The pool was in a courtyard and completely unassailable.

Ryker considered all angles. Security was part of his life starting with the experience he had gained in the Navy. He did well enough to enter Navy SEAL training but suffered hypothermia while wading overnight in the surf off San Diego. He lost his chance to serve in an elite force, but ended up as a master-of-arms. Determination was at the core of Ryker's personality and he wasn't satisfied with a title and rank. He handled security at the most important naval bases in the world.

DeVito was thankful to have come across him.

"Any pushback from trying to arrange for a new shipment?" asked Banali, who sipped a cup of coffee and wore his trademark bow tie.

"I'm sure not aware of any," said Ryker.

DeVito wished he had hired Ryker a few months earlier, before he lost three tons of coke in a shipment that had made the way from South America, through Mexico, and finally into California.

Banali touched his glasses like he was searching for answers. "Scott loved his high profile, that's for sure. It seems strange because there are less dramatic ways to have him knocked off. A staged car accident, a poisoning that would take weeks to figure out. Something that wouldn't get splashed across the news and put so many people on edge. Maybe he was getting greedy and skimmed something off the top."

"Possible. But why Darlene? She never made a move without consulting me." DeVito was perplexed. "We had a distribution arrangement. Whoever it was knew very specific information about her. Cut down while riding a horse."

"Both happened when other people were around. A built-in audience."

"Maybe I won't be playing golf again for a while."

"Playing golf?" Banali smiled. "Is that what you call it? I always thought you were digging up gophers."

"Very funny." DeVito looked increasingly worried. "All right, Ryker. It's on you to make sure everything's covered. The yacht, the restaurant. The perimeter of this property. Double check staff clearances and backgrounds."

"Take it easy, Frank," said Banali. "You're well respected. Everyone around here has pledged their loyalty to you."

"Loyalty can be bought, and I hate being taken by surprise."

"The good news is that you've got one less competitor," said Banali.

"And one less associate."

"Someone will fill her shoes soon enough," Banali smiled.

"What's up with you? This is nothing to smile about."

The old lawyer's eyes danced. "You know I've been stopping at a new coffee shop in the mornings?"

"Yeah? So?"

"Truth be told, Frank. I may be in love again. After three marriages, I didn't think it was possible."

"You're kidding?"

"Not at all. There is a wonderful barista who works there and we just struck up one conversation after another and – well, I've taken her to dinner at the club a few times."

DeVito looked at his friend and was puzzled. "All right. I've got to ask—"

"You mean how old she is?"

"Yeah."

"She's young enough to be fun, but acts real mature. She likes talking about important things, unlike my daughters who are all wrapped up in the latest celebrity gossip and fashion trends."

Ryker smiled. "Congratulations."

Denise agreed. "How nice to hear."

"Thank you," said Banali.

DeVito smirked. "When she gets tired of you, or when you get done playing with her, don't forget we have a whole stable of young girls who just came in from Bangkok."

Denise frowned at the remark.

"That won't happen any time soon," said Banali. "She's fresh out of college and has been asking me lots of questions about law and what kind to practice. Said she looks forward to learning as much as she can from me." He winked. "I told her I have years of experience and it'll take quite a while to share it all."

DeVito laughed.

"Perhaps I can bring her around some time."

"If you do," said Ryker, "I need to clear her."

"Of course."

DeVito drummed his fingers on the table. "After that big fiasco in Santa Monica a few months ago, and the little shit Angelino screwing me over, the last thing I need is someone new walking in here who we don't know anything about." He looked at Banali. "Hopefully, she's not cozying up to you to get near me."

Banali furrowed his brow like he was insulted. "Frank, relax. She knows nothing. She doesn't even know you exist."

"That hurts," said DeVito.

"The only thing I've told her is that I have important corporate clients and she can meet one of them sometime soon."

"I won't be important if we keep losing cocaine to the DEA. Sure eats up the profits. Two tons gets captured by the Feds and who knows where in the hell the third ton went."

Ryker spoke up. "I've been following up on things and connecting the dots. I found out there was a colleague of Angelino's who never made it to the warehouse. His name was Arturo and was a member of a small gang that operates in Van Nuys, the Victor Boyz. He was the last known person seen with the missing ton of coke, and we believe he's in Mexico."

"Follow up on that, too." DeVito waved his hand, annoyed. "A bunch of small-time shits." His face twisted in frustration. "What a pain in the ass. You set up systems and businesses, you think you're all powerful and mighty and then you get mixed up with some stupid asshole who robs you blind and gets killed in the process. Angelino was a real piece of work." DeVito bit the tip off a cigar and clenched his teeth on it. "Stupid social media. That's where the problems lie. We were happy to kill people and make our money in private, but these new kids want to brag about their drugs to the whole world. Idiots. I don't know about this business anymore. I miss the days of cutting up people in places like bowling alleys and empty warehouses."

DeVito paused and lit his cigar. "The whole thing humiliated me. During the Christmas Party at the Los Angeles Athletic Club, I bumped into Charles Scott and the man laughed in my face."

"Which brings us back to *the who and why* of someone killing Scott and now Darlene," said Banali. "We're dealing with two different issues. A missing ton of coke and two people murdered."

"Enough," groaned DeVito. "I'm getting a headache. Ryker, make sure our phone lines and Internet connection are secure."

"Of course, Mr. DeVito."

"Denise, stay on top of things."

"I will."

DeVito looked at Banali. "And as for you—"

The lawyer looked at his watch. "As for me, I'm out of here. I have a hot date."

CHAPTER EIGHT

Softball fields, golf courses, the Los Angeles Zoo, and the Gene Autry Museum were among the attractions in Griffith Park, one of America's largest urban parks. The 4,310 acres also remained a destination spot for visiting the Griffith Park Observatory. The Hollywood Sign stood on a nearby ridge, announcing its presence to the tourists and residents below.

But there was more. Miles of hiking trails wound through thickets and open spaces in the park with roads twisting along the eastern edge of the 5 and 134 Freeways. On the western edge off of Los Feliz Boulevard, streets passed by older stately homes and the Greek Theater.

The focus today was on Travel Town, highlighted in yellow in the image projected on the police station's conference room wall. It was located in the northwest corner of the park giving the gunman a few different options for escape.

Pictures of the victims showed how the grim reality of homicide intruded on this otherwise innocent recreational area. Darlene Cutchins' body lay on the packed-dirt bridle trail covered in blood. The side of her face was blown off. In another image, Charles Scott's body lay twisted on his carefully landscaped patio, his face sunken from the bullet's impact that tore open the back of his head.

The map showed the proximity of the two killings. Stone and Jake studied the victims with Captain Kyung Harrell, a Korean-American whose father was a Marine once stationed near the DMZ. The rigors of growing up in a military family along with his years of experience on the force made him able to endure scenes like these.

Jake had been compiling his notes. "The second attack was far more difficult than the first."

"How so?" asked Harrell.

"The timing and zeroing in on a target with plenty of bystanders in the area."

"Whoever it is likes a challenge," said Stone.

"And is able to handle the challenge," Jake agreed.

"So far you guys have determined that both victims handled money, albeit in completely different ways," said Harrell who changed his tone.

"Yeah, Cutchins owned Mountain High Studios along with a few others. She was chairman of—"

"Chairwoman," said Jake.

"Chairperson," noted Harrell.

"Let's just say she financed some big projects," mused Stone. "Both she and Charles Scott had access to wealth and were themselves in a class of super-wealthy." Stone always felt the difference between the rich and the truly wealthy were that the rich had money, but the wealthy created money and never worried about where the dollars would come from to pay for what they needed or wanted.

"Both of them appear clean," said Jake. "No outstanding debts, and from what we can tell, no business partners pissed off at them and certainly no prior records."

"Their businesses weren't connected," remarked Stone. "But they must have known each other. Even in Los Angeles, there aren't a lot of people with that kind of money."

"We've got some real tough homework to do," said Jake. "We didn't see any footprints in the brush above Travel Town. There were no trails there, either. It's like the shooter skipped along some random rocks. We found an identical patch on a dirt clearing, just a few feet from a boulder."

Harrell drilled deeper. "We've got some info back on the patches. A small manufacturer in Georgia made them as military replicas and sold them via old-school magazine ads like the old *Soldier of Fortune*, but now they sell almost exclusively online and in huge quantities to Army-Navy Surplus Stores. They're a big seller at gun shows and at flea markets, apparently."

"Crazy world we live in," muttered Stone.

"Video game suppliers also give them away as promotional items," Harrell continued. "You know, those first-person shooter games that kids like. The real bloody ones. The patches you guys recovered were in good condition and the lab didn't find anything unusual in the fabrics. No traces of blood, hair, saliva or viable touch DNA."

"Makes it tough to track," said Jake.

Harrell looked back at the map. "The two victims didn't live far from each other."

Darlene Cutchins had her main residence up the coast in the town of Montecito, a wealthy enclave near Santa Barbara. She owned a second home in Studio City, on the northern side of the ridge facing the San Fernando Valley. Scott lived on the southern side facing Los Angeles.

Harrell pointed at the equestrian center on the north side of the 101 Freeway and noted where the tunnel ran below the traffic and carried horses and riders into the park. "To pinpoint the moment that she appeared from beneath the tunnel and on the trail is incredible."

"Whoever did it knows something damned intimate about the people," remarked Jake, "and must have a hell of a lot of time on his, or her, hands. My Dad used to go deer hunting back east and said the toughest part was waiting for the right moment."

"So the shooter is a very patient person, just like Kilbraide said." Stone studied the maps.

"Patient? More than that," Jake responded. "I have to have patience when I'm waiting for Tasha to take a pie out of the oven. I'd say the shooter is highly disciplined and focused, willing to wait for long periods of time. Definitely did lots of research."

"So there are no witnesses whatsoever?" wondered Harrell.

"Only bystanders who saw the deaths and they all check out clean," said Stone.

"Scott's wife is completely at a loss for a motive," said Harrell. "She can't comprehend who would have done it. And Cutchins was a divorced mom, living with her daughter. Her Ex lives in the Bay Area and was stunned. And there's no way he would have done it. Said he's never so much as loaded a BB gun in his life. Not only that, his whereabouts at the time of the shooting are well-accounted for. She paid him a huge alimony with all kinds of stipulations. Lots of paperwork drawn up that if he started scheming and anything ever happened to her then he'd get nothing, which now seems to be the case. She was very careful."

Stone considered the various angles and pieces of information. "Let's move him to the side but not rule him out completely. Not yet anyway."

"Fine," Harrell agreed.

"So Cutchins was riding on the equestrian path that, at that point, runs parallel with the freeway?" asked Stone.

"Yep," said Harrell. "Here's the 101 with the fence separating it and the park. And here's the horse path, and then the park road. This leads east from Forest Lawn Drive and toward the zoo. The shot, as we've seen, hit her in the jaw, down the cheek bone, and blew out the other side of her face. She fell toward the freeway, directly off her mount."

"Next on the list is looking at the local gun clubs," said Jake, "and seeing who's on the rosters."

"Where the hell can you shoot a weapon like that around here?" wondered Stone. "Where's our resident expert?"

"You mean Kilbraide?" asked Harrell.

"Yeah, he'll know."

"He said he needed time off—had something to take care of. Personal reasons."

"He was in here this morning," noted Jake. "Going over all this stuff." Jake motioned to the maps and pictures.

"What can I tell you?" Harrell shrugged. "He looked a little pale. Maybe just wasn't feeling well."

***

Kilbraide sat back in a large cushiony chair, popped open a can of beer, and closed his eyes. Despite being on the fourth floor of an apartment building in Hollywood, memories of Afghanistan flooded him. He could still see dust kicking along the streets of Kandahar from his perch while his spotter kept watch with binoculars. He became engulfed again with the shrill screams of incoming rounds bursting in the air then focusing, squinting, and clearing his mind. Nothing else at that moment mattered. His world consisted of his finger on the trigger and lining up the target in the crosshairs.

As Humvees pursued the enemy, he calmed himself and waited patiently on the rooftop. All he needed was one shot to end the chaos— get the right guy and the carnage would stop. Momentarily. One shot placed just right. Breathe, take it in, feel the weight of the trigger and how easily it pulls back, get lost in the sensation and think of nothing else.

Music helped him focus as much then as it did now. He sunk into the chair while his mind played *Story Of My Life* over and over again. It was a song from Social Distortion, a punk-rock group from the *90s* that still spoke his language.

He took another sip of beer that suddenly felt stale on his lips and thought about the lyrics. *Ain't that the truth?* He needed to right the wrongs that he had witnessed. The police department was an extension of his military service. The beer made its way through him and he got up, used the bathroom, and stood in the doorway of the second bedroom that doubled as his office.

Maps pinned to the wall brought him back to the moment. Mulholland Drive with the hiking trails was on one map while another centered on Griffith Park and Travel Town. He mulled it over. The military was definitely a prerequisite for pulling off the shots.

And below the maps was a .50 caliber weapon perched on top of his dresser. *Hardly the kind of thing to have around a wife and kids—if that day ever comes again.* He was so focused on the war that he couldn't let it go and his personal relationships fell apart, including his marriage.

More music. The meaningful lyrics of Everlast's *What It's Like* flooded his thoughts. *How appropriate.*

Kilbraide ran his hand over the barrel. Talk about the power to mess up someone's life forever. The ridge off Mulholland came into full view in his mind. Walking along the trail, slithering through the grass, and taking in the target.

Stone and Jake could never understand. They didn't live his life and they couldn't feel the things he felt. Kilbraide caught his image in the mirror. His eyes reflected the seriousness of life and death. You have a job to do, so do it better than anyone else in the world. Because you are the best.

CHAPTER NINE

The small room was dark, a little dusty, and the cool night air of Zacatecas flowing through the open window was starting to warm as dawn approached. Arturo lay with his arm around Marta. The hormones of pregnancy had taken their toll, but for the first night in a long time she was sleeping soundly. Arturo wasn't. He hadn't slept much since the news of the murders. Charles Scott assured him that there would be no problems, now he was dead. Murdered by an unknown assassin.

The sleepless nights were wearing on him. A new wife, two stepchildren, and a child of his own on the way. He just wanted to provide for them and give them a good life. Be a father. He thought back about his childhood growing up in the San Fernando Valley. *The SFV*. He remembered his mom. She was a good woman with a big heart. But she couldn't deal with his dad's womanizing, and she turned to drugs. After years of abuse, she eventually OD'd, leaving him and his dad on their own. Being raised by a single hard-working parent was tough. His father taught him a good trade, construction, but otherwise, he was never there. He was always out drinking and chasing after his next one-night stand while leaving Arturo on his own.

Arturo thought about how he searched for a new family and eventually found one, Angel, Ronaldo, Lil' Jo and the rest—The Victor Boyz. Angel stood out because he bragged about big dreams and how they could all become rich and powerful. He made it known that he was the most qualified to run the show.

They became the best of friends – but like all kids with no direction, they looked for something to do. It was fun at first – tagging, petty vandalism, taking cars for joyrides. And when that wasn't enough, drugs came into their lives. First it was just weed, but it turned into ecstasy, coke and then everything else came so fast and spun them out of control. Crime, real crime, drug smuggling, murders. Arturo thanked God that he never killed anybody, but he sure put a few in the hospital.

But that was in the past and now, finally, he left all that behind. A sad smile crossed his face because he had to steal a ton of cocaine from his friends in order to get out and live the life he wanted. But if he hadn't, he would be dead like Angel and Ronaldo. Poor Ronaldo—he only wanted to take care of his mother but had gotten caught up in Angel's schemes. Or he could be in prison like Lil' Jo. He had made the right decision. With the help of Charles Scott, he sold the coke to help his community and now he was going to be a dad. Life had promise.

The floor creaked. Arturo rolled over to see if one of his stepkids was coming into the room wanting a glass of water or fleeing a bad dream. Nothing. He sat up as he heard another creak that sounded like a door opening. Not wanting to wake Marta, he carefully slipped out from beneath the covers and stepped quietly into the hall. He listened, then opened the door to his kids' room. Both were twisted up in the blankets, but they were sleeping soundly.

Arturo closed the bedroom door then stepped into the kitchen to get a drink of cold water. As he opened the fridge, he heard the creak again. This time behind him. He turned and came face to face with a bad dream – evil, black-eyes staring at him.

***

Arturo lifted his head as a sack was roughly pulled off of it. He sat on a chair in the middle of a vacant warehouse, wrists bound behind him. His bruised, battered, and bloodied lips stung every time he inhaled, and his eyes, beaten black and blue, were nearly swollen shut. His ribs ached and made taking deep breaths excruciating. He tried to look at his surroundings, but every movement was painful.

A heavily accented voice welcomed him back to consciousness. "Finally awake, *pendejo*." It was a statement, not a question.

"Where am I? Where's Marta?"

A couple of men stepped into view. Almost every square inch of their skin was covered in tattoos. Foot soldiers from some Mexican drug cartel.

"Who the fuck are you?" moaned Arturo.

One of the men leaned in close, eye to eye. The whites of his eyes were tattooed black. *Ojos Negros.* Black Eyes. The newest and one of the most violent cartels fighting for control of the drug trade in South America, Mexico, and now the U.S.

Arturo knew he was dead. "Am I such a big shot that *Ojos Negros* sends a couple of errand boys for me? What the fuck?"

The foot solider smiled with amusement and stepped back as the other black-eyed man dialed a smartphone.

"Someone wants to talk to you."

"Kind of hard for me to hold a phone right now," quipped Arturo.

The black-eyed man listened while the phone rang, then spoke into it. "He's awake."

He waited a moment, then switched the call to video, and held the screen in front of Arturo's face. Arturo was shocked. Lil' Jo, wearing an orange jumpsuit and sporting her usual close-cropped hair, was staring back at him.

What the hell? "Lil' Jo?"

"Arturo, *buenos dias.* How was your trip?" She smiled and spoke casually as if they were just two friends sitting down for a meal. Behind her were the starkly colored walls of a cell. California state prison. Tattoos ran from beneath her sleeves, along her toned biceps, and down to her wrists.

"What going on? Where's Marta? My kids?"

"Yeah, I heard you got married. Thanks for the invite that you never sent me. And you're going to be a Papa. Congratulations." She laced with her voice with compassionate-sounding sarcasm.

"I swear to God, if you've hurt Marta—"

Her toned changed. "What? What are you going to do? I don't think you can do anything right now. So you should just shut the fuck up and listen." She spoke to the black-eyed man. "Javier, we're old friends here. Cut him loose and let him hold the phone."

Her orders were followed without question as the man brandished a box cutter and slit the zip ties that bit into Arturo's wrists. He rubbed the soreness from them as he took the phone. He started to stand and stretch his muscles, but Javier pushed him back onto the chair. Arturo looked closely at the screen and saw Lil' Jo reclining on her bunk.

"Did you do all of this? And where the fuck am I?"

"Look around. Don't recognize the place?" asked Lil' Jo in mock surprise. "Maybe that's because you never showed up there like you were supposed to."

Arturo thought about it. "Santa Monica?" So this was her revenge.

"You got it. Welcome to America, *vato*. Yeah, that's the warehouse that you were supposed to deliver the coke to. But instead, for some reason you double-crossed us. Did you know that the *pendejo* Angel was dealing with turned out to be a DEA agent?"

Arturo fought a sick feeling in his stomach.

"Now Angel's dead and I'm in prison, although, as you can see, I'm making the best of it." She scanned with her phone and showed bags of chips, butts of cigarettes, and books with torn covers. "I got food and books, what else do I need? Oh, hold on." She smiled, reached under a corner of her bunk's mattress and pulled out a familiar looking bag. "I even got a little King Moses OG Kush. This stuff's getting harder and harder to find."

"You can't leave home without it, can you?"

She opened the plastic baggie and inhaled. "Why would I want to?"

"If I would have come here that night," protested Arturo, "I'd probably be in prison or dead, too."

"Oh, no. You would have surrendered right away to save your sorry ass. You still might get dead. That depends on you. And the only reason that you're still breathing is because we're friends. You're my homeboy, bro. And even though I'm in here and you're living your life, helping kids, and building schools—"

Arturo's eyes widened.

"Don't look so surprised," Lil' Jo continued "I know all about you. I do have to say that what you pulled off was brilliant. Really? Never thought you could do something like that – didn't know you were that smart, or maybe you're just really stupid. That's yet to be determined. But I'm pissed off at you about it, too. Why didn't you tell me? We could have done it together and got even more coke. I didn't give a shit about that little *pendejo*, Angel. Arturo, we been homies since we were kids, dawg. Why you do me like that? It hurt worse than getting shot and ending up in here."

"Looks like you're living the life. Cell phone and all. Got a good deal?" asked Arturo.

"Dude, I fucking run this place. I get whatever I want and use whoever I want. Like all the fish around here, I get their families to smuggle in shit, and in return their little minnows stay safe and under my protection. Plus, I get them to give me good head whenever I want."

"You're sitting pretty, just like a queen. Always in charge, huh, Lil' Jo?"

"Maybe. It's not like I want to spend much more time in here. I got my sights set on better things which is why I hooked up with Angelino's scheme in the first place. He was just a stepping-stone. Arturo, I always trusted your judgement. Figured you were level-headed and could balance out Angel's craziness. And I was right. Nice job getting the school built in Zacatecas. You probably don't give a shit about the Victor Boyz anymore, even though we're family and we always had your back. But you screwed us over and sold off the coke because you wanted a nice place for your kids to get all smart."

Arturo quietly protested. "You leave my kids alone."

Lil' Jo smirked. "Don't you tell me what to do or not do. Javier's box cutter does a damned good job on flesh. Honestly, *vato*, I'd rather keep you alive but only if I can trust you. Which I'm not sure I can. Look, you know as well as I do that people who got their shit together got the power. Something's up in LA. You've heard about it, right?"

"Yeah."

Lil' Jo smiled. "I know you're still connected. Stealing all that coke felt good, huh?"

Arturo stayed silent.

"Well, two major sources of financing have now been killed. Funny thing is, they were rivals. I don't know, maybe that DeVito dude did it. Had Scott taken down and did a power grab by knocking off his partner Cutchins. Hell, I'd do that, too. Now the dealers are going crazy. A lot of supply's been cut. You know what that means? Opportunity. Cut the head off and people rush in to fill the vacuum. There's going to be a lot of shit soon. Everyone's going to try and replace them—fucking power struggle. I'm sitting pretty in here thanks to my uncle, *mi tío*, the shot caller in Mexico for Ojos Negros. He set me up in the safety of my cozy cell to handle all of Southern Cali. It's time for me to make another move. These clammy-skinned addicts need their hits, and I need their money. Now tell me, do you know anything about Scott and that cute bitch Cutchins being knocked off?"

"I don't know a thing. Nothing."

"Hey, Javier, help him remember."

Before Arturo could react, Javier punched him in the stomach.

Arturo yelled and gritted his teeth. "I'm telling you, I don't know anything so fuck you and your black-eyed errand boys."

"That's too bad. Looks like you're no use to me." Lil' Jo was calm. "Hey, Javier, show him your box cutter up close."

Javier held the tip of the cutter to Arturo's throat.

"Now, Arturo. Homie. Listen to me," said Lil' Jo. "I don't have much time. They're doing a cell check soon. If you want to stay alive and have a chance to see your kids attend that nice little *escuela* and be there to hold your wife's hand when she pops out your new kid, then you do what I say. And you'll be free to go. Or, since no one else knows you're here, you can disappear."

Fear and anger mixed like a molten cocktail in Arturo's gut. "Where's Marta?"

"She's fine for the time being. So do what I say, or she'll be dead, too."

Arturo hated the feeling of powerlessness.

"I know you dealt with Scott for getting rid of the coke. So *numero uno*, you owe me money and lots of it. And *dos*, I also know that you didn't sell all of it. Where's the rest of the coke, dawg?"

"I don't know what you're talking about. Scott took it all so deal with him."

"Oh, great suggestion," said Lil' Jo in a mocking tone. "I can't *pendejo*. The dude's dead so it all comes back to you."

"I don't know what to tell you. It's gone."

"I'll give you some time to think about it. I want my share. Oh, *and tres*, you know that pretty black bitch that got Angel out, his lawyer, what's her name? The one dating the cop that killed him? I've written and called, but she's not answering. My little soldiers don't blend in too well around Los Angeles so I want you to pay her a visit. You got it?" Lil' Jo glanced away from the phone. "Cell check. Got to go."

The line went dead.

CHAPTER TEN

Stone pulled around the corner and drove toward a three-bedroom house in Van Nuys where some of the neighborhoods never changed. Homes in the area were built in the mid-fifties by men and women working in the old General Motors plant, a memory that the younger generation knew nothing about. For Stone, Mary Ann Bostovich, the owner of the house, and her fiancé, Marty Brannigan, were friends and crime fighters.

Brannigan, a retired police officer, told Stone he was doing research on the two victims and called him up. "Got something to show you, Tommy Boy."

The name grated on Stone's nerves, but Brannigan had often proven useful and Stone wondered how they uncovered their info. Brannigan and Mary Ann had started their own detective agency, B&B. It worked perfectly for them since they had few interruptions in their day.

With time on their hands and their nosy natures, they had built quite an informational network around Los Angeles and found nifty surveillance equipment to use. The duo had solved smaller petty crimes around the neighborhood, and on bigger projects they had their own home-cooked approach that sometimes overstepped legal boundaries.

Brannigan and Mary Ann had met a couple of years earlier after Brannigan was wounded while on a call with Stone a few houses up the street. It had been the residence of Angelino, a suspected cocaine dealer, who was being pursued by a mobster. There was a shootout and Brannigan had taken a bullet in the shoulder. Mary Ann, a do-gooder who had worked tirelessly to start a Neighborhood Watch, visited him in the hospital. Love blossomed and—they stayed together.

Stone pulled into the driveway and walked into the house which always had an aroma of baked goods. Mary Ann's specialty was baking pies and homemade chocolate chip cookies. Brannigan sat at his laptop while a police scanner crackled above the gas fireplace.

"Cookies?" called out Mary Ann from the kitchen.

"No thank you."

"Take some." She carried in a tray from the kitchen. "My son's coming down from Sacramento with his family this weekend so I'm practicing."

"I'm sure they're fine, Mary Ann." Stone grabbed a handful. Chocolate chips oozed from the dough. Stone took a bite and chocolate dripped from his chin and onto his shirt. He tried wiping it away, but it smeared. He licked his fingers clean. "You got my vote."

"I used apple sauce to make these. Decided to cut down on sugar," she said, handing him a napkin.

"They're great."

"Put in a little cinnamon, too."

"Hey, Mary Ann," interrupted Marty, "Stone's a busy guy. Stop making him fat, like you did to me." Brannigan leaned back, laughed, and patted his stomach before turning serious. "We got stuff to show him."

"Go right ahead." She retreated to the kitchen and then brought out a tablet, clicking the screen and pulling up a chair alongside her fiancé. She was a natural at transforming from a housewife to a professional private eye.

Brannigan made the most of having Stone's attention. "All right, Stone, it was a known fact that Scott had more money than an orange has Vitamin C. He loved talking about it."

Stone agreed, unimpressed. "That took us about two minutes to establish."

"But Darlene Cutchins stayed out of the spotlight. Even though she made movies."

"That's odd. Most producers like the limelight," replied Stone.

"True," said Mary Ann. "She and Scott ran in different circles, their money never crossed paths, but they had something they both liked to do with their riches."

"And what was that?"

"Give it away by the truckload. Or boatload as you'll find out." Brannigan clicked on the keypad and brought up a spreadsheet on the computer in front of him. "What all the wealthy like to do. This is a listing of all the little community newspapers from Santa Barbara to San Diego. And you know what they do?"

"Run massage parlor ads. We've busted a few places that way."

Mary Ann laughed. "That's not all. Each of these has a little society page that reports on charity balls and fundraisers."

"Look." Brannigan pulled up an article. "Two years ago. One of the rare public photos of Darlene Cutchins. She held a dinner for wild horse rescue."

"There's such a thing?" remarked Stone. "I like horses."

"And then this one for troubled youths. This comes close to home, Stone. They've donated to Ivy Acres."

Stone immediately thought of Andrew and that he hadn't spent much time with the boy lately.

Brannigan brought up a more recent article that was only a few months old. "And then look here."

A photo showed Cutchins and Scott smiling together in a group of people who were all holding champagne glasses.

"Who are these other people?"

"We're working on it," said Mary Ann.

Although the picture was in black and white, it was obvious that the setting was outdoors with clear skies and a few puffy clouds. The caption read, *Financial Wizard Charles Scott and Darlene Cutchins of Mountain High Studios at the Every Kid's Dream Wine Tasting.*

"How is wine tasting every kid's dream?" asked Stone sarcastically.

Brannigan laughed. "That's a good one. It really is. The article says they had local wineries from Temecula to San Luis Obispo display and offer their wines. Tickets were one-thousand dollars each for the evening."

Stone smiled and nudged his friend. "How come you weren't there?"

"Because you hadn't lent me the big bucks," Brannigan responded. "Personally, I'm fine with the Two Buck Chuck from Trader Joe's."

"Except I watch him closely," said Mary Ann, looking at Marty. "Liver problems."

"I'll stick with my beer," said Stone.

Brannigan and Bostovich both smiled like they were unveiling something new and exciting. "Study the picture. Can you guess where it might have taken place?"

Stone looked closely. "The buildings in the background were all one story high and were slightly lower than the photo's location. It had an open-air feeling. "Are they at a marina?"

"Keep looking." Brannigan crossed his arms over his chest.

The game was annoying, but Stone humored his friends. He noticed the background to the left and saw a name that was blurry— *Gentle Cove*. The only business he knew by that name was the Gentle Cove Restaurant and Yacht Club in Marina Del Rey. Stone had been to the restaurant where he scuffled with Anthony Angelino. His interest was piqued. "Are you kidding me?"

"Nope."

"Are they on Frank DeVito's boat?"

"Yacht." Mary Ann corrected Stone.

"Mega-yacht," exclaimed Brannigan.

A few months ago right before Halloween, DeVito invited Stone for lunch on the yacht and wanted to make a deal. DeVito hinted that the clumsy, wanna-be drug dealer Angelino had intercepted *inventory* and the mobster wanted Stone to look the other way in the case of capture. Brannigan had fitted Stone with a wire and hidden mic to get evidence on DeVito's wrongdoings, but one of the thugs on board found it and threw it into the water.

"We were there." Stone thought through the history.

Brannigan laughed. "We sure were."

Stone felt amused and frustrated. He knew DeVito had plenty of shady dealings, but was also skilled at covering his tracks with an endless mix of business formations and high-priced lawyers. He was brazen enough to have his men follow Stone and his family during the ordeal with Angelino.

Mary Ann read with a flourish. "Here's what the article says: This late fall outing on the Gentle Cove yacht was graced with temperatures that were warm enough to make the guests cozy, but cool enough to chill some of the finest wines the Golden State has to offer."

Brannigan piped up. "Scott and Cutchins were drinking on DeVito's boat. This was just a few months ago."

Stone skimmed the article. "Ol' Frankie's name isn't mentioned."

"But we know this is his boat and he always hosts charity fundraisers on it. See one of the sponsors? Perfect Blend Dog Food. That's one of his companies," said Brannigan.

"Why is a dog food company sponsoring a wine tasting to benefit kids?"

"Who knows what rich people think," was Brannigan's answer.

"We spent hours and hours digging up all this intel," said Mary Ann.

"Yep, quite a bit of time," agreed Brannigan in a low voice.

"You sure did. Thanks. Let me talk to Jake. Maybe we can rustle up a gift certificate to a Sunday brunch or something."

"Oh that'd be great, Stone. We don't want to put you out. I mean, cash would be great, too."

"I've got five bucks in my pocket." Stone smiled.

Brannigan returned the grin. "Well, I guess we won't be going to any expensive wine tastings soon."

"Marty, Mary Ann. You know I love you. I appreciate the help."

"Of course, you do, Tommy Boy. Just a reminder that I've put my life on the line for you more than once. Seems like every time I'm with you, I take a bullet. The house down the street and then when we were staking out the warehouse for you."

Stone reached in his wallet. "Hey, look here. Forty dollars." He started to hand over the bills.

"Aw, thanks, Tommy Boy," said Marty.

"Just don't call me that."

Brannigan suddenly had a change of heart. "Just kidding, Stone. We can't take that from you."

"Yes, we can," said Mary Ann, slipping the bills from Stone's grasp and depositing them down her bra with a sly smile.

Frank DeVito's yacht. The place sure had plenty of action. Time to pay him another visit.

CHAPTER ELEVEN

Coffee was something Arturo's father would make before the sun came up and the truck was loaded for the job site. An aroma of thick grounds filled the air every morning, and the first time that Arturo tasted the blend he nearly choked. But he had gotten used to the bitterness and later learned to welcome the taste as he gulped it down. Coffee signaled the beginning of the day for both him and his father—and ninety-nine percent of Americans.

Now he sat waiting in the middle of smart-looking people on laptops, pecking away with little earbuds connected to block out the world around them. His eyes and lips were still swollen from the beating and he felt self-conscious. He ordered his coffee in a ceramic mug to show he was going to stick around and not try to walk quickly out the door. He made the show for the two *soldiers* with their eyeballs tattooed black, sitting in the corner and watching him intently. The arrangement was clear. He would sleep in the warehouse at night under surveillance and was given a car to get around in during the day. Even though the gang-bangers shadowed his every move he had to text his location once an hour to Lil' Jo. His prized low-rider was sitting in his dad's garage in Van Nuys but there was no way he could safely retrieve it.

In Zacatecas, Marta was told to stay quiet and say her husband had an urgent matter in Los Angeles. But he wasn't allowed to have any contact with her by phone, Skype, or any social media. He had to take *their* word that she was safe.

He drained a cup of coffee and got a refill when Alisha walked in. Angel had shown him a picture of her, an attractive black woman with caramel skin. He said she was cool and knew her stuff. She was like his hero, even though she was dating Stone, who busted Angel's ass a couple of times and got him tossed into prison. But Alisha got his convictions overturned through technicalities and good lawyering. She didn't come across as a hard-charging attorney, but as someone determined, in control of her emotions, and with a personality that invited conversation.

Arturo was ready to weave a tale to convince her that Lil' Jo needed help. Getting Alisha on the case was the first step toward getting Lil' Jo out of prison.

He held up a hand and motioned. Alisha noticed him and sat down. Arturo almost stood to greet her but decided against it. He wasn't trying to impress anyone, just stay alive and get out of the mess.

"Hey, Ms. Davidson. Thanks for coming here."

"Arturo?" She squinted like she was trying to recognize him.

"Yes, that's me."

She reached across the table and shook his hand. "I'm not really sure what's up and I've got plenty to keep me busy. But you got me curious. Ooh, looks like something nasty happened."

"Yeah, I just used my face to hit someone in the fist."

"Looks like you hit him a few times."

"Guess I did." Arturo didn't want to play his hand too early. "You want coffee?"

She glanced to the counter. This was one of those independent shops that was tucked into an old video rental store, but it was still larger than a Starbucks where people were usually smooshed. "Yeah, sure." She smiled. "I'll get it." She walked to the counter.

Arturo considered his approach. Ask questions. Get the other person talking. Angel taught him that. It wasn't going to be easy. Alisha had eyes that were like laser beams, ready to uncover uncertainties and see through people's lies, including those of her own clients. Arturo felt more relaxed when she returned with her cup of coffee. Had she noticed the guys in the back? He hated people looking over his shoulder. The relaxation vanished as quickly as it had arrived.

She sat with a to-go cup and set a honey packet and lid on the table. She blew softly on the coffee and her eyes invited Arturo to speak first.

"We never met, but I knew your client, Angel. Anthony Angelino." Arturo paused. "And his girlfriend Sara."

She narrowed her eyes. "How so?"

"I worked with him."

"In what capacity?" asked Alisha.

"You probably knew he had a house not far from here in Van Nuys."

"Yes. You mean one that he used for growing marijuana?"

"Yeah, that's the one," said Arturo. "I fixed it up for him after he got out of prison and now that he's dead I went to court and bought it."

"Keeping it a grow house?"

"Nope, no interest in that." Arturo answered honestly.

"Good. How well did you know Angelino?"

"Pretty well. We grew up together and then kind of hung out over the years."

"Were you good friends?"

"I can't say we were always the closest, but we had each other's backs." Arturo smiled. "Angel was a real dreamer. But he wasn't just a talker, he also got things done and that's what I liked about him."

"You knew Sara?" asked Alisha.

"Yeah. She was a good woman. You tried to help her, didn't you?"

"I got to know her situation and did what I could. Sad."

"It certainly was," Arturo agreed. Sara was a good friend and he was hoping that she'd graduate and get her nursing degree. But it didn't happen. "Doing drugs and pressure from the cartels ruined him, and her."

Alisha sipped her drink. For a moment, Arturo thought she might ask more questions about Sara and how Angel had gone crazy on her and put her in the hospital with multiple injuries. But Alisha relaxed and simply commented on Angel's fate. "Seems like he got caught up with the wrong crowd. What do you think?"

Arturo nodded. "I'd say he did."

"How else did you work with him?"

She was turning the tables.

"Let's say that I tried to talk him out of his schemes. I know you were well aware of the marijuana dispensary and that it was completely legal."

"Yes, I knew all about it ... along with the cocaine raid at the warehouse."

"Real sad. The cartel wanted to snatch him up and do him in."

Alisha spoke quietly. "He tried to out-maneuver some dangerous people."

Arturo had his opening. "True. But they wouldn't leave him alone. Or any of us."

"Any of you?"

"Angel envisioned a whole line of products made with CBD and hemp. Stuff that was cool with the law."

"I know. And the point you're trying to make?"

"This whole damned network of, well, I don't know how to say it. They wanted to smuggle drugs and knew Angel still had close family ties in Mexico. All this started a few years ago when he wanted to be his own boss and they sold him some candy machines. Quite a few, in fact. He worked hard and was making enough to support him and Sara."

"You don't do coke?" asked Alisha.

"I don't touch the stuff."

78

Alisha mulled over the past. "Angel was responsible for her death."

"I know, but if the cartel hadn't been involved in the first place—"

She stopped him. "People face all kinds of pressures but there's no excuse for beating someone to death." She paused. "But that's not what you want to talk about, is it?"

"No, it's not."

Alisha looked attentive. "Go on."

"You see those two guys back in the corner? The ones covered with tattoos?" Arturo lowered his voice and motioned over his shoulder.

"Yeah?"

"They're the fists I ran into."

Alisha practically recoiled as one of them lifted a coffee cup and acknowledged her presence. Their eyeballs were tattooed black.

"They're foot soldiers with the Ojos Negros Cartel, and, guess what? They're holding me hostage."

Alisha took a breath. "Looks like they've just stepped out of hell. Have you called the police?"

"You don't call the police with these type of people. But this is why you're here. You know the night Angel got killed?"

"Of course."

"Well, there was a crowd of people in the warehouse when the Feds raided the place."

"Were you there?"

Arturo was matter of fact. "No, I wasn't. Missed out on the excitement."

"It's so hard when you can't stop people from destroying themselves," sighed Alisha.

"Turned out it was a big win for the Feds. The government scooped up some quality coke and a lot of people are pissed off about it. One of my friends got shot and arrested."

"You're talking about Lil' Jo?"

"Yeah. Said she's been writing to you, but you haven't answered her letters."

"No. I wrote her back and told her I wouldn't take the case."

"Well, she never got your message."

Arturo knew the events of that night all too well. On the night of the warehouse raid, Angel held Alisha hostage in a standoff on the Santa Monica pier until he was shot and killed by Stone.

"Lil' Jo doesn't deserve to be locked up."

"Why doesn't she?" asked Alisha. "She knowingly committed crimes."

"I've known her for a long time. She was just following orders and was in the wrong place at the wrong time."

"It's a case I can't take."

"Why not? You helped Angel."

"That was a different circumstance."

"But you have to help Lil' Jo. People's lives depend on it, including your own."

Alisha straightened up quickly like someone jabbed her with a thumbtack. "Excuse me? I have to go."

Arturo put his hand over hers.

"If you leave now, you'll never make it home."

Alisha stopped. "What the hell are you talking about?"

"Our lives are on the line, just like the lives of my pregnant wife and kids in Zacatecas. Look, Ms. Davidson, hundreds of millions of dollars arc at stake and that's just in the next one or two years." Arturo spoke quietly. "I'd like to fill you in on everything, but the main thing is that you've got to get Lil' Jo out of prison."

"I told you, I'm not taking the case. It's open and shut. They got Lil' Jo dead to rights."

"If you can find some type of loophole then I'll tell Lil' Jo you're thinking about it. That'll buy us some time."

Alisha scoffed. "I don't like people telling me what to do."

Arturo locked her in his gaze. "You don't have a choice. If you say 'no,' we're both dead."

***

Kilbraide hit a nice stride rounding the curve in the road. He had parked near the LA Zoo and jogged west toward Travel Town, needing to put his extra energy to use. Trying to concentrate on details in the station was impossible when adrenaline was coursing through his veins.

The equestrian trail ran parallel and he slowed down when he spotted the wreath, flowers, and candles at the exact spot of the death. The crime scene was described so clinically: *on the mount and fell toward the freeway.* There was more to it. She would have been looking straight ahead and down the trail with her mind on so many other things. Perhaps business or chatting about her daughter's schoolwork. The bullet struck without warning and she wouldn't have had any time to react.

He picked up speed and ran toward Travel Town. The locomotives and old-fashioned passenger cars had school age boys and girls climbing in and out of them followed by doting moms and dads. No one at the attraction would have even heard the shot. One bullet fired in hiding held such power to change the course of a family's life, the business dealings of a company, and even the fate of a nation.

Kilbraide finished his run, toweled off, and headed back to the station with its maps, buzzing phones, and controlled chaos. He walked by Stone's desk. In the corner was a trench coat and fedora that Stone's grandfather wore when he was a detective decades ago in Buffalo.

"Hey, Kilbraide. Where you been?" Stone waved a file.

"Out. Just needed to go for a run."

"We missed you the other day," Stone furrowed his brow, "when we talked about the cases."

"Yeah, sorry about that. Wasn't feeling well."

"Are you better now, I hope?" Stone gave him the files. "I got some new data. I want you to look into this. The financial guys are following the money trail. I want you to catch up on what you missed. Check it out and don't miss a day again."

Kilbraide leafed through sheets of paper showing charitable donations.

"Sure." He saw the various charities that Scott and Cutchins had each donated impressive amounts to. He tried to crack a joke. "Maybe they should have just given to the United Way. A lot safer is what I hear."

"Maybe." Stone let the humor slide and turned away to log on to his computer.

"I'll go over these." Kilbraide walked to his desk and set the papers down.

Money isn't always a motive. That was something Stone and Jake didn't understand. You're good and have the talent as a sniper and then you train day in and day out until the shot becomes an extension of yourself. Just like it was in the military with wind whipping dirt and sand in your face. You're not there because you want to make a shitload of money. You're there to do a job. Get it done. It's your mission. You dedicate your life at that moment to bringing down the enemy.

Kilbraide picked up one of the evidence bags from his desk and inside was a patch. *One Shot, One Kill. No Remorse. I Decide.* The mindset of a sniper. An idea caught Kilbraide. Adjusting to civilian life wasn't as easy as he had thought. Why was military life so different? Because in the military, soldiers were trained to carry out missions against the enemy. Kilbraide knew the police department was good for him because it gave him structure and purpose.

What about the shooter? What mission does he think he's on?

CHAPTER TWELVE

Gently rolling waves lifting the Jet Ski felt relaxing. Early morning broke from the east with light finding its way beyond the beach and just starting to touch the ocean. Fortunately, only a few walkers, runners, and bikers were on the path that ran along the shoreline. The water was calm like the whole scenario was meant to be. Like God was smiling down and giving approval.

The battle was going well, according to plan, and the intelligence gathered was high quality. If you wanted something done right, you had to do it yourself. A jogger went along the asphalt trail not seeing the patch that was placed as a marker. Light mingled with the marine layer and illuminated the area in a diffused haze. But over the ocean and beyond the breakwater, just enough inky darkness remained as a natural camouflage.

The water was like a lullaby, soothing arms giving him the freedom to breathe. The waves rolling toward shore made him feel like he was floating in the clouds. He researched the spot and time perfectly. Commercial fishing boats toiled farther out to sea, surfers chased larger waves a mile north, and recreational boaters didn't frequent this area.

He chambered a round, lifted the rifle, and peered through the scope. A man entered view. Heavy. Moving slowly. He stopped and knelt to tie his shoe. Too close to the patch. *Keep breathing. Let it happen. Don't force it.* And then the man stood and went on his way. He looked at the time and as another minute ticked past, he wondered. *Would it happen this morning? Such a perfect scenario.*

Only several minutes more and he'd have had to abandon the post since the light was spreading. He focused the scope and brought a jogger into view, heading past the heavy man and going south. Like an answer to a prayer there she was. Her long black hair pulled back in a ponytail. In good shape for a woman entering her fifties. She made her way down the street from her home in Pacific Palisades and onto the beach path, her exercise regimen that she described during the interview in the *Wall Street Journal*. Lithe in stretch pants and a form-fitting sport top. Jogging as her Golden Retriever ran free several strides ahead. She conducted business from her estate above the ocean and traveled back to her native Shanghai up to six months a year. The Journal showed a picture of her recently constructed home in China that was adorned with two Red Tibetan Mastiffs who added to the display of wealth.

She was the link between the west and the east, overseeing a global shipping conglomerate, Mingyun Shipping, that transported containers across the oceans. The Pacific was the busiest route. She inherited the company that was started by her grandfather and run by her father. She had the fortune of expanding it as China welcomed western businesses and prospered economically.

Hidden in the ocean-going cargo containers was more than raw materials, consumer goods, and recyclables. She was a global link in the supply chain and was so adept at finding new businesses to grow and expand that her holding company was among the richest in the world.

Pacific Palisades was a closed community just north of Santa Monica where the newest Teslas, Bentleys, and classic Jaguars were common sights. It gave her a sense of security so that she often jogged alone without the presence of bodyguards.

He dialed her in through the riflescope and didn't need to check distance. All was measured and accounted for in previous trial runs. He enjoyed how the sunlight played on her hair. She wasn't a fast or serious runner, but was known for exercising to clear her mind. That's what she had said at the latest business forum where so many admired her wealth. If only they really knew. That was all the motivation he needed as he rested the weapon against his shoulder, in sync with the motion of the waves. *Breathe, relax.* He held the rifle as though he was reaching from the water, up the sand, and onto the trail to grab and take her away.

She reached the patch and that's when the time was right to fire. The suppressor did its job when he pulled the trigger, the sharp crack sounded more like an ocean wave hitting gravel on the shore than a killing machine. The brass catcher did its job, keeping the ejected cartridge from sinking into the water. In the instant the bullet struck her temple, her one-hundred-pound frame was thrown backward and her feet lifted high in the air like a soccer player doing a bicycle kick. She landed violently onto the path while her dog trotted innocently on. The only other person nearby was a cyclist who hopped off his bike and ran to investigate.

Time to go.

So much confusion erupted on shore that he was completely unnoticed. He sealed the gun inside its waterproof case. No one heard him turn on the engine and gradually open the throttle on his watercraft. For extra security, he had painted it with gray and light blue stripes to blend in with the ocean.

The marina was a fifteen-minute ride south of Santa Monica and the cool spray was refreshing. *It's too bad it had to come to this, but maybe the message will become clear.* No signs of the harbor patrol and if there were then the weapon case could simply be dropped into the water, sink, and be retrieved later.

He passed the breakwater and by now the paramedics were likely on the scene and soon the woman would be splashed all over the news as a "victim." *Such bullshit.* She was as much an oppressor as the world's most vile dictators, but now her reign was over. This was a perfect shot that was like poking a hornet's nest. There were so many others involved; just had to keep checking them off the list.

CHAPTER THIRTEEN

The morning sky had just started breaking through the marine layer that had rolled in overnight. It wasn't thick, but it gave a slight glow as the sunlight's early rays streamed through. Stone yawned and looked out the kitchen window. He was dressed to go jogging with Silver, his Labrador. But Alisha had called in a panic saying she was on her way over. She pulled up in the driveway, gathered her things, and hurried to the back door.

Stone opened it. "Moving in? You're getting serious about our relationship all of a sudden."

"I figure the only place safer than sleeping in a police station was staying in a cop's house." She balanced a few blouses, small overnight bag, her laptop, and files from the office.

Stone grabbed the clothing and set it on the kitchen table while Silver wagged his tail and greeted her. "You kept me up all night, Alisha. You didn't return my calls. I was worried."

"I told you I was at my mother's."

"You just thought you told me. I had to call her and find out where you were, and she told me you were asleep and she wasn't about to wake you."

"Yeah, I was exhausted." Alisha leaned against the kitchen counter. "I've never been threatened to take a case before."

"Always a first time. You could play along with it." Stone wrapped his arms around her.

"Play along?"

"Make them think you're going to take it and do a little surveillance while you're at it."

Alisha gave a nervous laugh. "Oh, a double agent?"

"Exactly."

"You want me to be bait?"

"I want to understand what's going on. And then put a stop to it." Stone poured a cup of coffee. "Want breakfast?" Daylight was in full swing.

"I snarfed a power bar on the way here." She eyed the back door and then walked toward the front. "How well are your locks working these days?"

Stone smiled. "Hey, Monty Tusco is offering a free self-defense class. This Friday evening, the community room at the Burbank Library."

"Friday may be too late."

"Okay. You stay here and you'll be fine. The locks are great, Silver will protect you, and you know where the guns are." He stopped and smiled. "Hey, I've got an idea."

"What?"

Stone leaned in to kiss her, but his phone rang. "Stone here."

"Glad you're up." It was Captain Harrell.

"I was about to get a little exercise. What's up?"

"I need you and Jake at Will Rogers State Beach. There was a shooting on the bike path about an hour ago. And take that new guy, Kilbraide. The victim was shot in the face and the responding officers think it was another *one shot* killing. I'll text you with the info."

"All right." Stone hung up. Rush hour meant it would take a full sixty minutes to get to the beach.

"What is it?" asked Alisha, pouring water in the teapot.

"Possibly another sniper attack." Stone dialed his phone.

Marty Brannigan answered. "B&B investigations. A fine day to crack a crime. This is Marty Brannigan."

"What the hell kind of a greeting is that?" asked Stone.

"Hey, good morning, Tommy boy. Mary Ann and I went to a seminar yesterday and they said we needed a catch phrase."

"A fine day to crack a crime? Come on, Marty."

"We're trying. What do you want?"

"I got to take off. Alisha is at my house and I need you guys down here to watch things and keep her company. She can explain more. Can I count on you?"

"Absolutely. Mary Ann was just starting some cookie dough but I'll tell her to wait on it. Better yet, I'll have her bring it and bake at your house."

"That works. Can you be here in thirty minutes? I'll make sure you guys get a little something."

"That's mighty kind of you. We'll be right there."

Stone hung up and held Alisha. "I'm glad you're here."

"Me, too."

***

As Stone pulled his Jeep into the beach parking lot, he thought of how mass shootings at nightclubs and schools were so different. They were done openly and caused panic and terror among hundreds of people. But this third killing would make people paranoid and wondering if they'd be next. And the media, feeding on the public's fears, sensationalized the story at every opportunity.

Jake and Kilbraide drove in and parked alongside. "I'd thought we'd beat you." Jake got out from behind the wheel of the department's Crown Vic and Kilbraide emerged from the passenger side.

"I figured you'd get here before me, but I guess not."

"Accident in the carpool lane," remarked Jake.

The scene from the parking lot leading down to the beach was chaotic. A Mobile Command Unit was already in use.

A fire truck that accompanied the paramedics called earlier to the scene was now pulling away. Several patrol cars plus vehicles from forensics and the medical examiner filled the lot. Yellow caution tape kept the public away while journalists crawled everywhere. Four different news vans each had a cameraman and reporter telling the story before they knew the facts.

"Hey, guys, about time you got here." Monty Tusco looked sharp in her uniform, flattering her figure.

"Monty, are you at every crime scene?" Stone glanced around, taking in the surroundings.

"No, just the cool and gory ones." She smiled at Stone. "I thought you might be called."

"Tragedy brings us together again."

She pointed across the lot. "Sergeant Sanchez is the guy in charge. Over there." She winked. "Certainly good to see you again, Tom."

"And you, too. It's a fine day to crack a crime." Stone smiled.

Jake rolled his eyes. "Sounds like you were talking to Brannigan."

"That obvious, huh? See you later, Monty."

"'Bye, Tom. See you later, Jake, Kilbraide."

The three detectives made their way to the Mobile Command Unit.

"How are you gentlemen?" Sanchez greeted them. "Lousy reason to come to the beach."

"I'd say so," Stone remarked.

"I've had better days here." Jake looked at a folding table with coffee and helped himself. Kilbraide followed behind and poured a cup.

"You've turned this into a full-blown operation," said Stone.

"Absolutely." Sanchez remarked. "Take a look at the victim and you'll see why. Another high caliber blast to the head."

"What do you know so far?"

"Lots of information to scour but we've got a jump on it. The woman didn't have any identification, but she had a dog with an address on its collar. Checked it out and it was her home. A maid there said the victim's name is Helen Zhuang. Did a quick Google search and saw that she ran an international shipping conglomerate. My immediate thought was about the other shooting victims you're investigating. They had similar traits. Thought we better set up shop and dig into this quickly. We've got a witness. He was close to her when she got shot." Sanchez motioned to a man dressed in a colorful biking outfit who sat on a picnic bench. A racing bicycle was propped near him, and a paramedic sat taking his vitals.

"What'd he say?" asked Stone.

"Poor guy's been shaking like crazy. In shock and distress. Can't say I blame him. We think he's beginning to settle down."

"All right, I'll talk to him." Stone walked toward him. Jake and Kilbraide tossed away their coffees and followed.

Stone flashed his badge. "Detective Tom Stone."

"Don Donnelly."

The paramedic finished up and was hopeful. "You're sounding better now."

"I'd hope so." Donnelly looked pale but was regaining his composure.

"It's never easy," said the medic. "Thanks for what you did."

"Did what?" His hands began shaking. "She was already gone."

The medic patted the man's shoulder. "But you called for help. That's a bigger deal than what you realize." He grabbed his equipment and headed to join his unit.

"Mr. Donnelly, I hear you had a tough morning," said Jake, pulling out his tablet.

"Horrible."

Stone spoke softly. "So you saw the victim go down?"

"You can call it that. I was riding up the path, just relaxing and I was, I don't know, thirty or forty yards away and all of a sudden she looked like she lost her footing."

"Lost her footing?"

"You know, thrown backwards. Like someone invisible gave her an uppercut to the jaw and toppled her."

"Did you hear anything or see anyone?" asked Stone.

"No. I had my earbuds in."

"Listening to music?" asked Jake.

"Yeah. Spotify. Just pedaling along. The tires just kind of hum on the asphalt. Seagulls were squawking and landing up on the rocks."

Kilbraide shuffled from one side to another.

"You see anyone up there?" asked Jake.

"No. Just looking around. I didn't see anyone. Especially anyone with a gun."

"What happened once you got to where she fell?" asked Stone.

"I saw her flattened out and not moving. Totally still. I stopped, jumped off, ran to look and—got sick. I mean, I threw up." He looked down. "Still got puke on my riding shorts. I called 9-1-1. Then others came. I couldn't hold it together."

"Of course not," said Stone. "So you didn't see anyone on the beach?"

"No. I don't recall anyone."

"Okay, we'll be in touch. And in the meantime, if you remember anything at all, no matter what, please give me a call." Stone handed him his card.

The man took it. "I think I'm in shock."

Stone motioned for the paramedic to come back over. "That's understandable. We'll get them to check you out again."

"Thanks," replied Donnelly as the detectives headed to the beach.

Stone, Jake, and Kilbraide followed the yellow caution tape down to where the body lay. In the distance, onlookers with smartphones jockeyed for position. Someone turned, held up a phone—a selfie at a murder scene. Too far away for anything to show up, but Stone thought the action was disgusting.

The medical examiner pulled back the sheet and revealed the utter destruction of a human face and head. A jaw ripped apart, eye sockets obliterated. A massive exit hole in the back of the skull.

"My God. Might as well have used a rocket launcher," said Jake.

Bits and pieces were scattered far and wide. The examiners were placing numbered markers along the path and in the sand where skull and bone fragments had landed.

"We found this right near her," said one of the team, bringing out a plastic bag. Similar to what was found twice before and was now a link forged into the chain of evidence. The patch. *One Shot. One Kill. No Remorse. I Decide.*

"What the hell?" Stone muttered.

The examiner spoke up. "We're waiting on forensics, but it certainly looks like the bullet was large caliber. I bet it matches the other two."

"It was a .50 cal," Kilbraide spoke up, "and ballistics will match."

"You sure about that?" asked Jake.

"Definitely."

"She ran a shipping company?" Stone sifted details in his mind. "What did she do to deserve this?"

"That's the question of the day," said Jake. "Shot when the guard is down. When life is good. Scott, relaxing poolside. Cutchins out riding her horse. And now a morning jog along the beach."

Kilbraide spoke up. "It came from off the water."

"What do you mean?"

"The shot. Whoever did it was on the water."

Stone glanced toward the ocean. "Maybe."

"Maybe?" Kilbraide huffed and looked agitated. He walked off the path, trudging along the sand toward the water's edge.

"What the hell's wrong with him?" asked Stone.

"Just trying to piece things together, I guess," said Jake.

"Just like the rest of us, but he's acting like something bit him in the ass."

"A sand flea?" quipped Jake.

Kilbraide looked out over the calm water.

Stone tried to picture a shooter on the ocean. On what? A speedboat? He began walking down the path looking for clues. Jake joined him.

"So how's Alisha? You get in touch with her?"

"Yeah, she's moving her things in."

"Oh, yeah? Congrats. You guys are finally getting serious."

"It's not what you think it is."

"Then what is it?" asked Jake.

"She's freaked out. Anthony Angelino's influence is lingering."

"What're you talking about?"

"You remember that guy, Arturo?"

"Angelino's buddy, the remodeling guy? Yeah."

"He's resurfaced and met with Alisha about taking on a new case. He talked to her about Lil' Jo, the woman who was in the warehouse the night of the shootout. He's pressuring Alisha to get her out of prison."

Jake huffed. "No way could she get her out. That was a slam dunk case. She's doing fifteen to twenty for her role. Easy."

"According to Arturo, Alisha doesn't have a choice."

"What? He's threatening her?" Jake asked in disbelief. "Sure doesn't sound like the guy we know."

"Apparently, he's in deep shit himself. Alisha said a cartel is threatening him. *Ojos Negros.*"

Jake whistled softly. "Damn, those are bad *hombres.*"

They wandered about thirty yards down to the point where the biker would have spotted Helen Zhuang.

"What's she going to do?"

"She's not taking the case, but she's looking over her shoulder a lot. I asked Brannigan to keep an eye on her." Stone surveyed the scene. The only building in the area was a lifeguard station and tower. There was no place to be concealed. No concession stand, restrooms, or pier. Maybe Kilbraide was right and the shot did come from the water. He wanted to discuss the possibility with Sergeant Sanchez. "Let's go back up."

"Sounds good." Jake shouted to Kilbraide who was pacing slowly through the sand. "Hey, Kilbraide." He bellowed again, this time louder. "Kilbraide." Jake got his attention and motioned to the command center. Kilbraide gave a thumbs up and Jake continued the conversation with Stone. "I can see why Alisha wouldn't want the case."

"The only thing in it for her is a major headache."

Jake thought it through as he and Stone walked up the steps to the parking lot. "Damn."

"What?"

"Just think if she did take it. I'd love to be on that side for once. It's a whole '*nuther* world. All that information a defense attorney gets."

"She wouldn't, and couldn't, tell us anyway."

Jake persisted. "Not even little bits here and there?"

"Nope. She's the ultimate professional."

"Yeah, I know." Jake sighed. "Guess I couldn't moonlight as a defense attorney. I'd be telling everybody everything."

Stone laughed. "I don't think that'd be practical."

"What if she did take it? I mean, she's got the background for it since she worked for Angelino and got him cleared."

"That's what Arturo's thinking. But Ojos Negroes puts a different spin on everything," said Stone. "They're behind it all and she doesn't want anything to do with them."

Stone and Jake reached the command unit. The man on the bike was gone, but Jake noticed that there was a familiar face talking to Monty Tusco.

"Your favorite person."

"What the hell?"

Special Agent Wally Lightfoot smiled at Tusco, accentuating the high cheek bones of his Native American heritage. He gave her a playful salute and walked toward the command center.

She rolled her eyes.

He had broad shoulders and matched Stone's height inch-for-inch. He and Stone had butted heads while trying to capture Angelino the night of the warehouse raid. He strode to the unit in his leather cowboy boots as though the entire federal government was at his disposal. He greeted Stone and Jake with his jet-black hair in place. "Gentlemen. I didn't expect to see you here." His turquoise bolo tie contrasted with his bronze face and his cowboy hat made Stone think of a man with a strong, independent streak. Too bad he was such a jerk.

"Why not?" asked Stone. "Our expertise goes a long way."

"I'd say you should keep it in the Valley then," said Lightfoot.

"You were looking quite friendly with Officer Tusco."

"Of course. We've seen each other a few times since you introduced us at Thanksgiving dinner."

"I didn't introduce you."

Lightfoot seemed amused. "What's the matter, Stone? You jealous that I'm dating your ex-girlfriend?"

"She said she went out with you once," said Stone, "and then she was done with you. That's not dating. And jealous? I'm not jealous."

"Looks like Monty's standards have dropped," remarked Jake. He smiled at Lightfoot. "She said you're good for a full sixty seconds."

"Personal insults aside, I can assure you that you won't be needed on this case now."

"What're you talking about?" asked Stone.

Lightfoot continued. "I don't want you screwing this up like you did with Angelino's case. Do you know who this woman was?"

Jake looked at his tablet. "Yeah, we've got her name right here and her address."

"Screwed up Angelino's case?" growled Stone.

"We've been tracking her for two years. She was international. Drugs of all kinds. Cocaine, heroin, fentanyl. Sending it right into the Port of Long Beach and Los Angeles. And on to the rest of the United States. This is a federal investigation."

"I didn't screw up Angelino's case. If you had the intelligence or respect for our hard work that you're supposed to have then we could have cooperated."

"Or maybe if you had a sense of common decency," added Jake.

Lightfoot ignored their protests. "Thanks for all you've done. Hand over your notes and you can be on your way."

Stone puffed up his chest and was ready to protest.

"What's going on here?" Sergeant Sanchez stepped from the command unit.

"I'm Special Agent Wally Lightfoot, DEA. Your victim down on the path is a woman who we've been investigating for the past two years."

"And we're just finding out about that now?" Sanchez sounded bewildered.

"We do what we do for a reason." Lightfoot addressed everyone like inferior subordinates.

"So what got you interested in her?" asked Sanchez.

"The shipping containers that she sent back and forth across the ocean had enough illegal substances to make her one of the wealthiest women in China. Not to mention the paper trails and money laundering. Everything was hidden in a global network of commerce. She was good at what she did."

Stone mumbled. "Better than you are at what you do."

"What?" asked Lightfoot. He looked toward the ocean. Kilbraide was at the water's edge, crouching, then standing and looking from land to the water and back again. "Who's that?"

"He's with us," said Stone.

"Of course he is," quipped Lightfoot.

Kilbraide walked quickly across the sand and toward the parking lot.

Lightfoot addressed Sanchez. "We've got a lot to go over." He waved off Stone and Jake one more time. "Anything you guys hear, I'd appreciate if you let me know. Other than that, have a safe drive back to the Valley. You're dismissed."

"We'll see who hears from who," said Stone as Lightfoot joined Sanchez in the unit.

He and Jake made their way back to the car. Stone looked over at Monty Tusco. "Hey, you, uh, with that guy—?"

"Just once," she said and then she smiled. "Want to go bowling sometime?"

"Sure, I'll see when Alisha's available."

"We'll make it a party." She winked. "See you guys later."

Kilbraide caught up with them and his shoes were caked with wet sand.

"How was it playing on the beach?" asked Jake.

"She was in the photo." Kilbraide was matter of fact.

"Who?" asked Stone.

"The victim, Helen Zhuang. She was in the photo with Cutchins and Scott."

CHAPTER FOURTEEN

Red wine always fit the occasion, according to Frank DeVito. It had a calming effect and offered a special moment within a mundane meeting, or, like tonight in his estate's dining room, added a richness to a gathering of friends. The caterer cleared the salad plates and wheeled out what was left of the Caesar salad and a walnut-spinach creation, passing behind one of the bodyguards on duty who was casually strolling the hallway. The homemade croutons had all been gobbled down and there were only a few strips of anchovies left.

Denise sat attentively with the party, making sure all details were cared for.

Harold Mortensen, CEO of Capital Lending Corporation, sat between his wife Charisse and DeVito. Mortensen leaned over to his host. "What the hell is it with these murders?"

"Now's not the time, Harold. I'll update you."

"I'm getting a little nervous here." He studied the unique table.

"Relax. We're looking into it."

The table had rounded edges at both ends and curved slightly inward like an hourglass. DeVito always thought it represented a luscious, curvy woman.

"This is quite the set-up," remarked Harold, running his hands over the smooth surface.

"Bought it while in France. On a whim," said DeVito. "In Provence. Some woodcarver had just made it. Cost me a pretty penny, but it cost even more to ship it over."

Harold laughed. "Reminds me of a long maple bar doughnut, but with curves in it."

His wife who was dressed in a form-fitting red dress took a playful exception to the remark. "I thought you'd say the table reminded you of me."

"I guess it was because of what I ate at the doughnut shop this morning." Harold shook his head and gave a remorseful look. "But it was after my run, so I just replaced the calories I lost."

Lewis Banali laughed. He wore his ever-present bow tie and leaned back in his chair with his arm around his date for the evening, a young barista, Kelsey Johnson. She was an attractive black woman who had moved from Cleveland two years earlier and was, as she put it, an auditioning actress.

"Speaking of calories, we got our walk in at the beach this morning," said Banali, patting the young lady's shoulder.

"And then I hit the gym at noon." Kelsey clapped her hands together and wiggled in her chair.

Dinner was a slow-roasted lamb with mint jelly. The aroma filled the dining room as the caterers wheeled in the main dish. Harold raised his glass of wine in a spontaneous show of camaraderie. "Frank, thank you for being a gracious host, a wonderful business partner, and bringing good friends together."

"Here, here." Banali held his glass high and clinked it with Kelsey.

"You're quite welcome. These little get-togethers are nice." DeVito sipped from his glass.

"Where's the missus?" asked Harold.

The server sliced the lamb and gave a portion to each guest.

"Off to Italy. Visiting some of her cousins." DeVito lied casually. His wife traveled the world, doing her thing like she had for the last couple of years, and was now traipsing around Italy with a wealthy businessman that DeVito secretly screened and approved. He was harmless.

The marriage turned into one of convenience that was for tax purposes. Their love had died a slow death. She was addicted to DeVito's money and would never leave—until someone better came along and the wealthy businessman was looking promising. He had often reneged on his agreement not to see anyone, but he enjoyed the naughty tension and his wife no longer pried into his private life. He considered it a necessary effort to display some affection for his spouse; at least until his paid companions showed up after everyone left.

There was certainly enough to occupy him in her absence. Ryker was searching for more details on Helen Zhuang's murder, but only came up with what the police already knew. And that wasn't much. Denise's contacts in the department were tight-lipped about the investigations. No help there, either.

The most pleasant element of the evening was that Banali's antics and cooing over his young girlfriend kept the table entertained. Kelsey Johnson. She had landed a role on a cable reality show and DeVito could see that she had a certain innocence and flirtatious way with her eyes that made Banali smile. As long as the man was happy, although DeVito would have preferred that Banali had submitted her name for a background review earlier in the week. He had waited until the late morning and Ryker didn't have a chance to do more than a cursory check.

DeVito cut a piece of lamb. Zhuang was the third victim in three weeks' time. Ryker, working with Banali and his legal team, scoured DeVito's friends and foes but drew a total blank. Nevertheless, Ryker took precautionary measures and shut down the yacht and advised DeVito to stay close to home. Kelsey was enjoying herself with yet another glass of red wine.

"Are you old enough to drink?" smiled Harold Mortensen.

"Of course. I've been legal age for the past month," she replied. "And I like my men the same way I like my wine. Aged and with plenty of sophistication."

"So tell Frank about the game show audition." Banali laughed, relaxed in his chair and wiped his mouth with a napkin, fine linen imported from Belgium.

Kelsey smiled and tried to wave off the suggestion.

"Oh, come on, Kelsey." He patted her shoulder.

"Okay. Los Angeles is such a crazy place. The concept of this show was having contestants live at actual estates around the city. This one was in Beverly Hills."

"What do you mean having contestants at the estates?" asked DeVito.

"We literally went into someone's home and it's like a remodeling trivia game. Winners get cash along with select valuables from the home. Appliances, chandeliers, rugs. Could be anything."

"This thing actually airs?" DeVito thought pop culture was just getting weirder by the day.

"It did. On the Game Show Network and House and Garden. I made it through three rounds." Kelsey stopped long enough to cut a piece of meat. She glanced at her phone and kept a wide smile plastered across her face.

Denise interjected. "I saw it. It's such a great concept and I'm surprised it hasn't been done before."

"I thought the same thing." Kelsey's comments were always bright and bubbly.

"They probably pay the homeowners nicely." Harold took a bite of meat and looked at his wife. "We should rent out our home."

"Hold on. It sounds like this production sells valuables out from under a family." She laughed. "They get rid of things in the home."

"That'd be fine with me. We've got so much crap in the attic and garage," moaned Harold.

"You made it through three rounds, huh?" DeVito took another bite of lamb.

"I did. Got a bunch of valuable things that I sold and gave away as gifts."

"I should be careful with my place," joked DeVito. "With such a full acting schedule, how do you get time to work as a barista?" He asked with a hint of sarcasm.

"I'm not as busy an actress as I would like." Kelsey patted Banali's arm. "Fortunately, though, that wound up being a good thing or I would never have met this doll."

"You're too kind." Banali grinned. "Keep at it sweetheart and your big break will come."

Kelsey shrugged. "You keep saying that." She glanced at her phone again.

DeVito noticed her fidgeting.

"Because I know it's true," affirmed Banali.

DeVito tried to imagine the pair together in an intimate setting and found it amusing and a little heartwarming. It gave him hope that love was always available.

The meal proceeded cordially and Kelsey checked her phone again.

"Your fan club?" asked DeVito. She had picked up the phone quickly, set it back down, and acted casual.

She laughed. "My mother back in Cleveland."

Banali chimed in. "She's quite funny. I heard them talking once. The woman's full of wit."

"Wit?" DeVito queried.

"I see where the little kitten here gets her personality." Banali chuckled.

Kelsey straightened up. The phone's screen glowed with activity. She spoke softly. "If you'll excuse me for a moment. I need to freshen up."

"Don't we all," smiled Charisse.

"Be right back," nodded Kelsey.

DeVito caught Denise's eye and tipped his head toward the door as Kelsey left. *Watch her.*

But Harold caught Denise off guard. "How did you find out about that show?"

Denise gave a nervous laugh, not wanting to offend someone like Harold Mortensen while trying to follow through on DeVito's orders. "I saw it while scrolling through the lineup. And it caught my eye."

"I hear you're very observant. Frank speaks highly of you," said Harold.

"Why, thank you." She cast a helpless look at DeVito who shrugged and waved a hand to indicate *relax*. Denise sat back in her seat.

DeVito grabbed his phone and texted Ryker. *The girl walked into the hallway. Watch her.* Banali saw what was going on.

"Relax, Frank, she's fine." He spoke quietly.

"I'm sure she is."

***

The sounds of the dining room faded quickly as Kelsey hurried down the breezeway, smiled at a bodyguard, and stopped outside the bathroom. Her phone lit up again with another text message that contained a blueprint of the estate. She gave the bodyguard a flirtatious smile and he smiled back.

"Hey, would you do me a little favor?"

"What's that?"

"Where can I take a quick smoke?" She giggled.

The bodyguard pointed down the breezeway. "Out the front and to the left. You'll be fine there."

"Thank you, so much," she answered in a syrupy voice.

He smiled. "Don't get lost."

"I'll be right back."

Her heels clicked along the tile floor. She glanced around. No one. She went toward the front entrance, past bushy potted plants that gave cover. Instead of heading left toward a patio overflowing with baskets of flowers, she stopped to check her phone and confirm the layout. She turned right through a doorway, into a garage and crept along a wall that was softly lit by a string of small LED lights on the floor. It was just enough to guide steps but conceal faces.

The risk was enormous. She agonized over the decision for several nights and then decided the high stakes gamble was necessary. Her sister was hostage to one of the most notorious inmates at the state prison, Lil' Jo—a woman controlling a cartel from behind bars. Meeting Banali was one of life's awful coincidences.

Lil' Jo had informants listen in on visitor calls and had heard the sisters laugh about Kelsey dating the sweet, older gentleman. When it turned out that Banali was DeVito's lawyer, opportunity presented itself and Lil' Jo couldn't pass it up. Then the last time Kelsey visited her sister at the prison, the girl had a deep gash beneath her left eye and bruises along her arms. That was the warning. *Help shut down DeVito or your sister dies.*

Kelsey held her cell phone and the bluish-green light revealed a fleet of the most expensive sports cars she had ever seen: a Lamborghini Veneno Roadster; a Bugatti; and an Aston Martin. Time was speeding along and she couldn't gawk. To the right and toward the back wall there was a row of metal boxes. Her phone's light was almost too dim. It buzzed with a new text message. *Where are you, darling?*

Shit. Banali. Poor guy. He was so trusting. She texted back. *Anchovies in the salad didn't agree with me. Lol. Hang tight.*

Another few minutes and she'd be found out. Probably caught on a surveillance camera by now. But what would happen to her sister? Jeanine didn't deserve prison anyway. She got hooked up with the wrong friends and went along for a joy ride that turned bad. Jeanine didn't know her girls were going to hold up the check cashing place.

The master breaker box. Kelsey fingered a metal box and held her light to reveal the same schematic that was sent. *Yep, the switch.*

Just pull the switch and slip out the breezeway into freedom. Nightmare over. She pulled the lever and the estate was plunged into darkness.

She turned to escape, but instead came face to face with Ryker.

"That was rude."

Suddenly, explosions and shouts engulfed the compound.

The structure shook and a beam fell in, smashing onto the Aston Martin.

Kelsey screamed and cowered. Ryker grabbed her and headed toward the door as shouts rang out. A loud blast and flash of light, then the rattle of automatic gunfire made Ryker take cover inside the door frame. He pulled Kelsey in front of him as a shield and held her by the neck. She scraped her face on the wall. She wanted Jeanine. *Why the hell did they ever come to LA?* She wanted Cleveland and home.

Suddenly, it was quiet.

Ryker pulled a gun from inside his suit coat and charged with Kelsey across the breezeway. An intruder clad in black knelt, lifted an assault rifle and aimed while another combatant scampered past the garage, fired, then took a hit from Ryker's men. He fell dead.

Ryker kept one arm tight on Kelsey as he turned, fired, and cut down the man with the assault rifle.

DeVito's guards shot from the rooftops toward the front gates. An explosion blasted one man into the air. Windows shattered from automatic rifle fire.

Kelsey's tears broke through and she cried from terror and remorse while Ryker pushed her into the library. He grabbed a handle on a bookcase as another black clad assailant fired. The shot tore at Kelsey's shoulder and stunned her. Ryker hit the floor and shot back, striking the shooter while gun fire raged outside.

Kelsey noticed blood pouring from her shoulder and started panicking.

"Shut up." Ryker slid the handle to one side, revealing a hidden doorway and pushed her into a metallic hallway. He sealed the door behind them and pushed her forward, causing her to stumble. Her shoulder felt like it was on fire. Ryker forced her into a room on the right where DeVito stood with his shirt torn and stained red. Banali lay on a cot, bleeding. Kelsey noticed she was in a *safe room* with medical supplies and rations of food and water. Weapons lined one wall while Denise checked a bank of security monitors that were installed on another. They showed grainy images of Ryker's guards with guns at ready, making sure the compound was buttoned down. The battle was short but fierce. A radio crackled with sporadic gunfire before going silent.

Ryker wore an earpiece and had a mic on his coat lapel. "Medic's on his way? Good. Yeah? All clear? Let's make sure. Search room by room." He reported to DeVito. "We're counting six dead. Two of ours, your two guests and then a pair of the assassins. We gave chase but they made it back beyond the perimeter and took off. We also have a few wounded staff members.

"Shit," DeVito exhaled and sat in a chair.

Banali spoke weakly and motioned to Kelsey. "Sweetheart, you're hurt?" He was barely able to lift his arms.

Ryker spoke up. "Hang in there, Lewis. The doctor's on his way."

He gripped Kelsey's neck tighter and she recoiled from his fingers digging in. "Ouch."

"Ryker, what're you doing?" asked DeVito.

"She was in on it."

"What?" DeVito bolted up like electricity shot through him.

"I caught her in the garage where she had shut off everything."

DeVito's expression turned from exhausted to furious. "What the hell?"

"I'm scared." Her throat was dry as cotton.

"You sure as hell better be," growled DeVito.

Banali groaned. "No. Baby?"

"She used you, Lewis," yelled DeVito. "I fucking warned you about this. Now my business partner and his wife are dead."

Denise turned with her eyes wide with terror, facing Kelsey. "Oh my God. Why?"

"I'm so sorry. I was just supposed to kill the power. I had no choice. I didn't know. I was just trying to save my sister," Kelsey pleaded.

"From what? Who the hell is your sister?" DeVito grabbed a gun from off the desk and pointed it at her.

Kelsey held her shoulder and tried to stem the flow of blood. "Jeanine. She knows Lil' Jo." She stammered. "She's in prison. And said Ojos Negros would kill her, me and my mom—everyone unless I—" the tears fell hard.

"Lil' Jo? That bitch. You set me up?" DeVito raised the gun and rested it against her forehead. "You disrespect me in my own house?"

"Frank, wait." Banali's voice was weak.

"Please, don't." Kelsey cried out as urine ran down her leg.

"Ojos Negros? You work for my rivals?" DeVito's voice rose with fury and anger as he pulled the trigger.

CHAPTER FIFTEEN

Hedges rose above his head and when Stone pulled back the greenery, he discovered a cement wall topped with spikes. DeVito's place was like a fortress. Jake walked along looking for discarded ammo, clothing or anything that could give answers to the carnage.

"The city allowed this?" asked Stone, looking at the wall. He had parked the Crown Vic down the street, away from the news vans and cameras. Police cruisers clogged the residential area.

"Maybe he got an exemption." Jake surveyed the street. "Or he paid off code enforcement to look the other way."

"Yeah. Routine for someone like Frank DeVito." Stone glanced ahead to the driveway. "Ready?"

"No, but let's go anyway." Jake and Stone walked to the car and then drove beneath the hedges and trees that made an archway above DeVito's driveway. A bullet-riddled guard shack sat several feet back from the street.

"Wow, look at this," said Stone.

"Yeah, a forest right here in Encino." Jake looked at the trees.

"No, I'm talking about the shack. Look at all the holes. Christ." Neighbors initially called wondering if the explosions and gunfire were effects for a movie.

"Damn. Looks like a full assault," said Jake.

Encino was one of the wealthiest and quietest neighborhoods around Los Angeles. The San Fernando Valley enclave often went unnoticed, unlike its more glitzy cousin, Beverly Hills, to the south and San Marino to the east. Yet, the zip code that DeVito lived in had its share of celebrities and wealthy entrepreneurs.

The lot was sprawling by urban Los Angeles standards, a few acres. The house sat down the driveway like an estate in the countryside.

A prickly native California oak tree with a wide trunk rose above the property and shaded what looked like a garage and the side of the house. Stone could see that the house was built deep toward the back of the lot with tiled steps leading down a breezeway. A dead body sprawled across the steps ruined the southwest Hacienda look. Crime scene investigators, photographers, and journalists created a chaotic scene that was decorated by yellow caution tape and flashing lights.

Stone pulled behind police cruisers and vans. The neighbors had to be stunned.

A medical examiner greeted them and pointed to a corpse that was clad in a black T-shirt and dark jeans and full of bullet holes. Holsters crisscrossed his chest and an excessive amount of ammunition was strapped to his body. His mouth and torso were stained with dried blood.

"Take a look at the eyes," said the examiner, going about his work.

Stone and Jake peered more closely. Eyeballs dyed black with eyelids tattooed *Ojos Negros*. A drug cartel shooting up DeVito's place.

In the last few months, Stone had met Frank DeVito twice. Once on the yacht in Marina Del Rey and the other was in a dive bar that DeVito owned. Both times Stone was trying to track a flow of drugs, but nothing ever turned up.

The garage roof was partially caved in and blackened. Straight ahead a breezeway led back to the main house.

Stone and Jake followed the walkway past the courtyard where a small crater was blown in the patio. They were shown the dining room. On the table lay a man in a suit and white shirt soaked in blood. Diamond cuff links gleamed in the light. *Who wore cuff links anymore?* Only someone who was quite formal and had some money. A woman in an evening gown lay on her back, her face disfigured. A purse lay in the corner.

Stone imagined the situation. Bullets would have been flying everywhere and the guests were cut down while sitting or turning and trying to hide, yet near the door there was a young woman sprawled on the floor. She was black and had a minor shoulder wound. Draped across her legs was an older man wearing a bow tie. Both the man and woman had taken shots to the forehead. *Execution style.*

Along the wall there was a door with a window. Inside was a kitchen. A few men and women were dressed in white shirts and black slacks talking to uniformed officers. Some were wiping their eyes, crying from fear and terror. They looked like hired help. Serving-plates and food were scattered across counters and over the floor. The catering staff.

Jake came alongside Stone and eyed the employees. "I'll go talk to them."

Where was DeVito? Stone stepped back into the breezeway, walked through a courtyard, and past the pool where fresh blood was starting to congeal on the tiles. Working the chain of command, he was led to a sliding glass door. Inside, there were several people and in the middle of the group, seated at a conference table, was Frank DeVito adorned in gold chains, sipping a glass of red wine. He was wounded.

A man wearing hospital scrubs was dressing DeVito's shoulder.

"Well, Detective Stone." DeVito sounded surprised and amazingly calm. "I'd offer you a glass of wine but you're on duty, aren't you?"

"I am. I just happened to be in the neighborhood and thought I'd stop in. Of course, the sounds of machine gun fire and explosions had something to do with it as well."

"Yes, it was all quite unexpected." DeVito looked at the man wrapping his shoulder. "This is my good friend, Doctor Thomas."

"Got a guy on call that fast?"

"He was doing his rounds at St. Joseph Medical Center and, my good fortune, had just gotten off duty."

The doctor glanced at Stone but said nothing and went about his business.

"Looks like the party got out of hand."

"Denise," DeVito said to a woman in a shirt and blouse standing nearby, "can you get a bottle of water for our good detective?"

"No, thank you," replied Stone. "I'm fine."

"Then get one for me. This wine has suddenly lost its taste."

Denise grabbed a water bottle from a small refrigerator and handed it to him. Her hair was disheveled, and her blouse had a red stain on it. *Blood?* The one who looked the most calm and together was a young professional-looking man in a button down shirt who sat a few seats away from DeVito. He had a yellow legal pad and pen. He had dark wavy hair and olive-toned skin.

"And this nice man," DeVito nodded, "is my lawyer."

The man rose and handed Stone a business card. He wore khaki slacks. Real preppy. "I'm Eric Rossi."

"Detective Tom Stone, LAPD." Stone handed his card to the man.

DeVito moaned as the doctor finished. "Being ambushed is certainly no fun. Creates heartburn."

"And kills the guests, too." Stone pulled out a chair opposite DeVito.

"Unfortunately, yes."

Stone looked at DeVito. "I saw four poor souls in the dining room."

"Yes. It was terrible. My business partner and his wife along with my lead attorney and his young girlfriend. Her life cut short."

"I got a lot of questions for you, Frank."

"I'm sure you do, Detective. I have a lot of my own as well."

"Starting with the assailants. I noticed a couple who were dressed in black and tattooed from head to toe, including their eyes."

"Yes, very stylish."

"Obviously, someone was angry enough to invade your party. This wasn't some kind of random home invasion."

"Very observant, Detective Stone. And when you find out who's so pissed off at me, I'd kindly ask you to let me know."

"Because you don't?"

"No, I don't know."

"And you don't have any idea why?"

DeVito took a sip of water but remained silent.

Stone pressed for answers. "So you didn't skim money from someone else's books? Try and wipe out key employees from a competitor? Smuggle in underage girls for your massage parlors?"

"Excuse me, Detective, that's not appropriate." Rossi the lawyer frowned.

"I'll say it's not," said Stone.

"It's okay, Mr. Rossi, let the man do his job," muttered DeVito.

Stone continued. "That's Ojos Negros out there. Did you try and rip them off, perhaps?" He sounded casual and didn't mind if he was getting on DeVito's nerves.

"As a law-abiding citizen," replied DeVito, "I pay taxes for the police to protect me and not treat me with scorn. I was having a dinner party and a bunch of killers swarmed us. That's what I know."

Stone turned to the lady. "What's your name?"

"Denise Everett."

"Where were you when all this went down?"

"In the dining room. We were eating roast lamb, talking, and suddenly—gunshots rang out. There were some explosions. I hit the floor immediately."

"And then?"

"I stayed low. The shots came fast ... and then they stopped. There were lots of shouts and yelling. A lot of confusion and blood everywhere."

"Fortunately, I have a top-notch security team and they cleared out the intruders before any more damage was done." DeVito set down his water.

"No kidding?" asked Stone.

"My pride has definitely taken a blow." DeVito reclined back.

"Not to mention the dead bodies."

"It's no fun to feel like you're vulnerable and that an attack can hit at any moment."

"You're telling me this was totally unexpected?"

"If I had known it was coming, do you think I would have just sat there and risked my life, Detective, and the lives of my guests?"

Stone thought of the picture from the yacht. "Frank, I know you like hosting parties. We came across a photo that was taken a while back during a charity event held on your yacht. Were any of your guests that were here tonight in that picture?"

"What the fuck are you talking about? I don't know who had pictures taken on my yacht. We hold a lot of charity events there –

photographers everywhere. *Jesus*, Stone – how about a realistic question?"

"Like I said, Frank, I have a lot of questions for you." Stone narrowed his gaze. "Have you been to the yacht lately?"

"No. We've had it buttoned up tight for renovations."

"What kind of renovations?"

DeVito rolled his eyes. "More stupid questions. What do you care?"

"Humor me."

"There's all new carpeting and the restrooms have had to be tidied up. There, you happy?"

DeVito was tight-lipped and drawing facts from him was going to be a long process.

"Tell me about your guests here tonight," said Stone.

"Mr. and Mrs. Harold Mortensen? I've known them for many years." DeVito paused and teared up. "And then a dear friend of mine, Lewis Banali, and his young girlfriend Kelsey Johnson. He was retiring and this was a farewell party for him. One hell of a way to say goodbye."

Stone circled back. "Tell me, Frank. Did you know Charles Scott or Darlene Cutchins? How about a woman named Helen Zhuang?"

"You mean the ones who were shot by some type of sniper?"

"Yes."

"Of course, I did. They were guests on my yacht, and Darlene was not only a business associate but a friend as well."

"You seem to be losing a lot of friends. And I know this just happened and you need some time to get your wits together. But here's an idea. Could it be that whoever killed them also came after you—or one of your guests?"

"Detective Stone?" Eric Rossi interrupted. "I'm curious. Is my client a suspect here? Or would you like him to make an appointment and come in for questioning?"

DeVito looked unconcerned and waved his counselor off. "It's okay. I don't mind." He had a poker face extraordinaire and spoke to Stone. "The tactics were quite different."

"True. Maybe they decided to change it up."

"Possible." Anguish came over DeVito's face. "But why me, Detective?"

Stone wanted to laugh. Frank DeVito never pitied himself. He was more than happy, from what Stone knew, to chase down whoever got in his way. "If you're going to start crying, let me know. I have tissues back in the car."

"I thought you were a compassionate man, Detective. I lost a few dear friends tonight and nearly entered eternity myself."

"Yeah, but what did you do to piss off Ojos Negroes?"

The lawyer spoke up. "Detective, I'm sure you have lots more questions. As Mr. DeVito said earlier, we do as well. Since this is going to take a while, how about if we arrange a time to put everything out on the table? My client's traumatized and needs his rest."

Stone looked at DeVito and his lawyer and stood to leave. "I'm sure you do. I'll be in touch, Frank."

CHAPTER SIXTEEN

The images of bodies ripped apart by bullets looked artistic in the glow of a computer screen. He gazed at them in the comfort of his home office. *Especially Harold Mortensen.* Another one down in a rather surprising way. One side blaming the other now. *Perfect. That's how it should be. Makes the work so much more efficient. Makes my work so much easier.*

A sheet of paper lay on the desk. Charles Scott was written first with a line crossed through it. Next was Darlene Cutchins and a line crossed through her name. Then, Helen Zhuang and another line through hers. Time to write. H-a-r-o-l-d M-o-r-t-e-n-s-e-n. Once it was written, a line was drawn through the middle. Almost perfectly, as though the edge of a ruler was used to guide the pencil.

But the work wasn't done. Far from it. There were still more rocks to throw at the hornet's nest to create the deadly buzz that would finish them all off. Cut off the money flow and send everyone into a panic. That's how wars were fought in the old days—the Civil War and the World Wars. Blow up train tracks so food and ammo couldn't reach the troops on the front lines.

This was similar. *How satisfying to wreak havoc.* So far it was wonderful to see the moneyed people who only cared about themselves cowering in panic. A local television reporter was already connecting the dots, estimating the net worth of each individual killed and then trying to figure out why DeVito's place was assaulted. *And the kicker, calling me the One Shot Sniper.* The TV gal was smarter than the police or even the newspaper reporters. Good journalists were a dying breed.

Time to scour the map. *Timing is critical.* Surprise is so powerful. Not knowing where and how to have one's guard up creates such wonderful vulnerability. That's why the governor of California and the mayor of Los Angeles placed more police around their mansions. *Laughable. Jerks.* The politicians are running scared. *You're safe. Unless— you're a piece of rat shit like the rest of them. And if you are, then you'll find yourself on the list.*

Now's the time to become even more strategic. Keep the skills sharp. Don't get dull. Get some practice in. He turned to the floor where a stopwatch lay near his Barrett .50 caliber. He clicked the watch, flew into action and within seconds had stripped the gun and put it back together. *Feeling it now.* Again. Gun stripped. Put back together. Five seconds. A feeling of invincibility rose within.

Where are the drug financiers most likely to let down their guard, to think they can relax? They think they're so much better than everyone else. They think they're untouchable. Like they're God. *I'll show them that they're mortal.*

***

"You're taking too damn long getting an answer from the attorney." Lil' Jo snarled through her phone.

"I'm working on it." Arturo pulled over to take the call. "Why the hell did you attack DeVito's house? That really screwed things up." Arturo had driven to get dinner for the thugs at the warehouse. Buckets of fried chicken sat on the seat next to him teasing his nostrils.

"My momma always told me to think big and aim for the top. DeVito and Scott were rivals so it's a good bet that one would knock off the other," mused Lil' Jo.

"So you really think DeVito took out Charles Scott?"

"Fuck, yeah. And that Cutchins chick, too."

"Why would he take out Cutchins? His own partner?"

"Why not? It's more money for him. Shit, Arturo. Loyalty's cheap when there's *bank* to be made. You know that." Lil' Jo looked bored, eating from a bag of chips with the gray walls of her cell as the backdrop. "Thanks for the care package, by the way."

"Eat slowly. One stupid box of chips cost me thirty-five dollars to send you."

"It takes a lot to incarcerate a woman like me."

"I thought you had people waiting on you hand and foot."

"I do. I just wanted you to get it." Lil' Jo was matter of fact. "So that's up with the attorney? Is she going to get me out of here or not?"

"I've spoken to her a few times. Saying she's busy, but she'll consider it. Says she may come pay you a visit and discuss matters."

"She may?" Lil' Jo tensed. "She better get her ass up here in a hurry. Hiding out at that Detective's house isn't going to do any good. She better see, just like you better see, that no matter where she is I can take her life. Didn't you fucking learn anything?"

"From what? You blowing up a guy's place? DeVito's still alive but you killed a few of his friends. You get a few of your own people killed in the process. What the hell? I don't call that successful."

"A shitload more successful than you've been."

Arturo held his anger in check. "All right. I know you don't give two shits about it because you're moving up in the world, but I've been thinking about it. Who the hell is the sniper dude? I don't think DeVito would take out his own partner. So who's the sniper? Is he going to come after me?"

Lil' Jo laughed. "Dawg, you're a nobody."

"Maybe, but who the hell would cut down the top people? One by one? Someone who's pissed off. Maybe someone who got a bad deal. Got sold some real poor shit. Got ripped off in a big way. Or saw someone get ripped off, maybe a life snuffed out. So this is the ultimate revenge. Cut off the supply before any more shit goes down. Could be a threat to you. Maybe. Maybe not."

"You're just now thinking that up?"

"I have been Lil' Jo. But it's damn hard to get your thoughts together when you've got these murderous fuck-ups dressed in black following my every move. Do you know how ugly they are?"

Lil' Jo laughed. "They look cool."

"They're weird. Every one of them. And they stink. Tell them to take a shower."

"If that makes you happy. You can thank me later. But in the meantime, I got word that we can get another shipment on the way, but only if we can get the money together. And with me still in here, it doesn't look like it's going to happen. So it's up to you, Arturo. You can be the hero. Or die. And don't worry about your lovely new wife and kids. They can join you in heaven. Or maybe I'll spare her and play with her myself."

Arturo wanted to reach through the phone and choke Lil' Jo. But not possible. He could lose his mind or get back to thinking. He came up with a few possible suspects who could have been the killer. He got excited but each thought had gone nowhere. One was an informant for the police. Another nearly died of an overdose. And another was an alcoholic who had the shakes so badly that he couldn't hold a shot glass steady, much less a rifle.

The only good thing is that Lil' Jo finally stopped questioning him about the missing coke. Did she believe him? *Who knows?* Arturo was worried and frustrated. What would it take to drive back to Zacatecas? No way. He had to check in at least twice a day at the warehouse. If he didn't, all they had to do was make a quick call and someone would stop in and kill his family. Shit. What a mess.

***

Desert stretched east and west. The drive from Los Angeles really wasn't all that bad. Kilbraide stopped at a mini-mart off the freeway. He got a thirty-two ounce soda for a dollar, filled up the car with gas, and drove off to visit a shooting range out in the Mojave Desert near Barstow. Back in the hills and over the rutted roads was the only sanctioned place in Southern California to practice, the only range with enough distance that would allow weapons with the capability and power of a .50 caliber. Shooting calmed him and made him think clearly, just like meditating.

It was where off-duty soldiers, policemen, and weapons enthusiasts went to sharpen their skills. This little corner of the United States resembled Iraq and Afghanistan more than most people would ever realize. Skipping out on softball was more than worth it. Target practice. He'd register, sign in, answer all the questions and then take his shots. And look around to see if he could connect a familiar face with the hunch that was brewing in his soul.

CHAPTER SEVENTEEN

Driving back to Los Angeles through the curvy roads in the high desert made Alisha feel like she was navigating a lunar module. Something about the land north of Edwards Air Force base and just west of Mojave reminded her of moon craters. The view fit her mood. Vacant and cut off from an oxygen supply. Questioning Lil' Jo in prison sucked the air out of the room and left Alisha emotionally drained and fearing for her life.

Even with the threat of harm, taking the case had been a distinct possibility and there was a glimmer of hope for a retrial. The DEA had swept away key evidence and Alisha knew that was a weakness she could exploit. The investigation was sloppy with the kind of reporting errors that make the public howl when a lawyer gets a conviction overturned on technicalities. Fortunately, Tom wasn't the arresting officer and didn't have anything to do with the report. The case looked tailor made for Alisha's calling. She got in to law to defend convicted criminals honorably, fight the BS that corrupted the system, and help any who were wrongly accused. But after visiting Lil' Jo the answer had to be a firm *No*.

The woman had gotten wrapped up in Angelino's scheme. Escaping a charge of transporting a ton of coke in a specially equipped van was like Houdini getting unshackled in a tank of water. How much time would it have taken? She said she could pay. Money was no problem.

Driving to the prison was a four-hour round trip and she could have tackled so many other items on her to-do list. The interview itself lasted less than an hour and the moment that ran through Alisha's mind time and again was when she said she wanted no part of Ojos Negros, and Lil' Jo's eyes burned with fire. It was creepy knowing that Lil' Jo could make a phone call and end a life.

"Don't cross 'em." Lil' Jo growled, sitting in a chair opposite Alisha in a private room. "Serious shit's going down."

"How serious?"

"They're taking over and if you're not with them then you're dead." Lil' Jo stopped abruptly.

"So Arturo's correct, you're threatening me."

"Loyalty is everything," replied Lil' Jo. "You know that."

"So anyone who isn't loyal is—?"

"Taken out."

"What do you mean? What happens?" asked Alisha.

"Do I really have to explain it to you? You're a lawyer, figure it out."

Alisha felt a chill. "Who decides if someone is or isn't loyal?"

"The shot caller."

"Are you calling the shots?" Alisha knew the answer.

"Yes."

"I see."

Representing Lil' Jo would mean involvement with Ojos Negros. There was no way Alisha could do that.

"I mean, someone's got to be in charge, right?" asked Lil' Jo. She relaxed. "You know how Angel got his ass kicked when he tried opening up the pot shops?"

"Yeah."

"I saw he needed help. Protection. He tried going out on his own but got done in by that old-school mobster guy, Frank DeVito. He's nothing compared to Ojos Negros. They're like the devil himself has shown up in town, and they're going to own Los Angeles."

"I'm sure you're aware of the attempt on DeVito's life."

Lil' Jo smirked. "Yeah, too bad he's still breathing."

"Did you have anything to do with that?"

"Next question." Lil' Jo smiled, eyed Alisha, and scooted near.

Alisha felt a seductive energy unleashed, one that was crawling all over her. "The investigation has been taking place and I understand an inmate was killed here recently. Found dead in her cell. Her sister was among those killed at DeVito's house. Is that a coincidence?"

"I don't believe in coincidences."

"Tell me, Lil' Jo. What's next?"

"You don't want to know. It'll spoil the surprise. But don't worry, you won't miss it. You'll know it when it happens."

"I need you to tell me."

"Why? If you're one of us you have nothing to worry about." Lil' Jo leaned against the back of her chair and studied Alisha. "Not sure if I trust you, because I don't think you trust me."

"If you're not open with me, I can't help you."

Lil' Jo smiled and leaned forward, playfully touching Alisha's hand on the table. "Hey, I like you and I want to work with you, but you've got to get me out of here. I don't want you to get hurt."

Nausea engulfed Alisha and she pulled her hand away and stood up. "I've got to go."

"So you going to take my case or not?" asked Lil' Jo.

Alisha looked her straight in the eye. "I can't."

As Alisha walked out of the room, Lil' Jo muttered, "It's your funeral."

***

Mercifully, the freeway was mostly clear as Alisha drew closer to Stone's house. Just a few more exits. The prison system was inefficient, and her own work was now backlogged something awful. Everyone bent to the will of the institution. Inmates who were mostly normal functioning adults understood that they had no bargaining power when they were locked up.

Alisha peered at the freeway signs. *Almost home.* But Lil' Jo was twisted way beyond a normal adult. She had adapted well and, from what Alisha gathered, used her jail cell as a base of operations. But Lil' Jo's last words rattled Alisha who kept her mouth shut and said nothing as she left. Lil' Jo wanted her help but she had refused to provide it. The woman could pay someone else or use a public defender.

What troubled Alisha is now that she had exited the freeway, she could have sworn a black sedan had been following her for the past several blocks. It turned away just as she reached Tom's house.

And then her phone rang.

"Ms. Davidson?"

"Yes?"

"This is Arturo." His voice was trembling and in the background Alisha could hear screaming. "I just heard you're not taking the case." He sounded scared.

"What? How'd you hear that?"

"I warned you. You had to take it. Watch your back. I got to go. 'Bye." There was another unmistakable sound of a scream in the distance right before the phone clicked off.

Alisha's stomach tightened and her arms shook as she pulled into Tom's driveway. She hurried from her car and through the back door, locking it behind her. A *tap, tap, tap* of footsteps surprised her. It was Silver, wagging his tail and greeting her. "I'm glad to see you." She patted him on the head. "You'd be there for me, wouldn't you?" The dog licked her hand. "Yes, that's what I thought."

Alisha went to the front door to make sure it was locked and then boiled water for a cup of tea. It was late enough in the day that she expected Tom to be home, but he wasn't. She poured the water and gave him a call.

"Hello?"

"Tom?"

"Yeah. Alisha? What's up?"

"Just feeling really weird. Where are you?"

"Still at the station. I got bogged down with some information that Kilbraide provided. You sound stressed."

"That's because I am. Look, I'm not supposed to say this but screw confidentiality. I just got back from a meeting with Lil' Jo." Alisha described the discussion and Lil Jo's expectation that Alisha would represent her.

"What'd you say?"

"I told her 'no.' Firmly. She looked angry and said if I didn't take it, I'd be dead. Then I just got a call from Arturo and it really freaked me out. He knew that I wasn't taking the case."

"How the hell would he know that?"

"Who knows?" Alisha paced back and forth across the kitchen. "I swear I could hear screaming in the background, and he said he had to go and the line went dead. He was gone. Tom, after I exited the freeway there was a black sedan following me. I'm scared."

"I'll bet," said Stone. "I'll be home as soon as I can."

"But tonight's game night."

"You still want to go?"

"Of course," Alisha sighed. "I need to get my mind off this. And besides, Andrew's looking forward to it."

"Yeah, he is."

"Tell you what. I don't want to be sitting here by myself waiting for you. Finish up what you're doing. I'll sneak out to pick up Andrew and stop by the store. They're having a terrific sale on pies. At least it's a public place. I'll feel safer. Do your work and then I'll meet you at Jake's."

"Okay. Sounds like a plan. Glad you're back safe and sound, but, uh, bring Silver with you."

"Of course. I'm not leaving without him."

CHAPTER EIGHTEEN

Alisha had grown up with two sisters and a brother, but she had never married and never had kids. She had gotten engaged once, but the guy suffered cold feet one week before the wedding. Thousands of dollars in postage stamps, floral arrangements, bridal gowns, and airplane tickets got thrown away. Alisha's only steady partner since then had been her career which was now wearing her down. So getting mixed up with a family like Stone's, along with Jake and Tasha's, brought a welcome amount of camaraderie and variety into her life.

As she drove along Burbank Boulevard, she realized that Tom was a great find. He was flexible enough to develop a relationship with her because he knew her world—even though he joked that criminal defense attorneys lived on the dark side of the moon.

He had a family that she enjoyed: two girls who seemed content to split their lives between Tom and his ex-wife Kelly. The pair had remained friends and gave the girls a stable life. One was in college nearby and the other heading in that direction. He kept up with their constant barrage of questioning life and fretting over career choices.

And then there was Andrew, a nine-year-old boy from a group home who was placed there early on. Someone that Tom sensed would end up in prison like so many other kids in foster care. So he had stepped in, and very naturally a bond between them grew.

Alisha was as committed to Andrew as Tom was. Silver sat patiently in the back with his nose out the window while she drove west toward the 405 freeway. The streets of the Valley were laid out in grid formation, and she turned right and pulled into an Albertson's grocery store parking lot that was bathed in the red glow of the early evening sunset. She made sure Silver was comfortable.

The store was buzzing with shoppers and she wandered to the bakery aisle and sensed something odd. She quickly turned around. A man in a brown leather jacket, a color that matched his skin, had a cart full of produce and was scanning the shelves. He grabbed a package of hamburger buns and walked the opposite direction, ignoring her presence.

Paranoia. She hated that feeling. Only had it one other time when representing Anthony Angelino. Frank DeVito had his thugs tail her, trying to get information on Angelino. It was a creepy feeling and now she had it again. She finished at the store, tossed Silver a dog treat, and headed to Ivy Acres.

Picking up Andrew for regular outings and visits had become part of her life. And the stop now was quite natural with Andrew bounding from his cottage, across campus, and out to the car.

"Where are we going?" he asked.

"To the moon." She laughed.

He went along with the joke. "You have rockets on your car?" Andrew squirmed and pushed Silver away so he could buckle in.

"We're going to game night, silly."

"Cool."

Ivy Acres was pleasant looking with plenty of trees giving shade and clean up-to-date buildings. But each of the children were there due to trauma. Some much worse than others. Like Andrew. He saw his mother abused by his father during his infant and toddler years. The final fight was when both adults had been shooting up heroin and his dad knocked her down with the force of a heavyweight boxer. Andrew had been pulled away from home and tossed into the uncertainties of a bureaucratic system.

Alisha pulled out of Ivy Acres' driveway, onto the street, and braked hard. She froze.

"Hey!" Andrew lurched forward and fell against Silver who lost his footing.

A black sedan came steadily toward her. And then she relaxed. An elderly couple drove past.

"Sorry about that, little buddy," said Alisha.

"Oh, that's fine. I tried to put my head between my legs just then."

Alisha pulled out and drove north. "You did what?" She laughed.

"You know, like they do when an airplane is going to crash."

Alisha glanced in the rearview mirror. "Were you ever in a plane?"

"No, but I saw it on YouTube. Billy was showing us in the cottage."

Alisha figured that was tame compared to other things the kids could stumble across. The drive to Jake and Tasha's was brief. She exited the freeway and the house was no more than a few minutes away when a car came barreling head-on in her lane. Headlights burned into her eyes and at the last second she braked, it veered away, and sped past.

She was on high alert. She wanted to pull over and catch her breath but in her rearview mirror the car did a U-turn and followed her with every lane change. No pulling over now as she sped up.

"You're driving crazy," Andrew said quietly from the back seat.

"Yeah, sorry about that." She trembled.

Jake's house was only two more streets. She picked up the speed and could tell that the car behind her apparently did the same, gaining on her. She was going to teach the driver a lesson. She braked quickly, hard, and then sped forward again. She gained space but then thought, *My God, what if it hit us?* Images raced through her mind of the men with black eyes jumping out and surrounding her and Andrew.

"I'm scared," said Andrew who huddled against Silver.

"Me, too. Don't worry. We're almost there."

One block to Jake's street. She approached, slowed down, and suddenly another car squealed into the lane and blocked her from turning right. The car that was following sped around on the left and skidded to a stop on the driver's side. Just what she feared. Two heavily tattooed men with black eyes jumped out and rushed to the window. Silver snarled and barked while Andrew screamed and cowered in the back seat.

A man smashed his fist through the window reaching for Alisha's neck. She screamed and recoiled. Silver leaped into action, latched onto his arm, and shook it violently. The man pulled free from Silver's grasp and Alisha gunned the gas pedal, lurched right over the sidewalk, and felt her insides shake as the car slammed from the curb onto the street. She raced to Jake's house and left her pursuers in the dark

She squealed to a stop behind Stone's Jeep. Lights were on in the house. Andrew was crying and Silver was barking out the back window. She blasted the horn several times.

The front door flew open and Tom and Jake came running out.

CHAPTER NINETEEN

Jake peered through the blinds. "It's been a while, guess they're not coming back." He sat down with the others and scooped a handful of chips from a bowl in the center of the table.

"Guys on patrol have cruised the neighborhood and say there's no sign of them," said Stone.

"They're bold and nasty," said Jake. "Just like whoever's shooting down the well-heeled folks around here. Speaking of which, Brannigan, you're saying that picture of everyone on DeVito's yacht wasn't just a one-time event?" He poured a dot of ketchup on a hamburger.

"No." Brannigan chowed down his burger, sitting next to Mary Ann.

"No?" Stone took lettuce from the plate of condiments.

Jake reached for another handful of chips but stopped as Tasha scolded him. "Make sure to leave some for others."

Jake rolled his eyes, grabbed his burger, and bit into it.

Brannigan continued with an air of confidence. "Not at all, Tommy Boy."

"Don't call me that." Stone mumbled and mustard dripped from off the bun onto his shirt. "Dang it."

"They get together every year. Or, in the case of Scott, Cutchins, and Zhuang, they *got* together."

"We followed up the little news article," said Mary Ann, "and found out different people hosted."

"What was the charity that got all the money?"

"They changed each year. One was for kids, another year they raised money for rescue dogs, and the environment. Wild horses like I told you before. All sorts of things." Brannigan spoke as though holding court.

Stone appreciated the atmosphere. Burgers and hot dogs were spread across the table and he sipped a beer just like it was a normal friendly gathering. Chips. They looked appetizing. Tasha got up and took them to the kitchen.

"Hey, where you going with those?" Stone asked.

"Extra calories that no one needs," she said, smiling and returning to sit next to her husband. "You know where they are."

Stone enjoyed a warmth he had seldom known in his career. The kids were in the other room playing video games and chowing down. Andrew's mind was now set on fun. Having them close was comforting. Or maybe it was his arm around Alisha, who was still shaking.

Tasha noticed. "Poor dear. You sure you're okay? Need more tea?"

"I'm fine. Settling down," sighed Alisha. Silver sat next to her and wouldn't leave her side.

The conversation was serious and could turn downright brutal, but Stone liked the open discussion at a family table without the glow of stark, overhead lights that he worked under at the station. "I wonder why they raised money for different causes."

"Oh that's normal, Tom." Mary Ann wiped crumbs from her mouth. "My son and his wife in Sacramento get invited to several different charity events every year. Of course, he keeps getting promoted within CalTrans so he's becoming a big wig." She giggled.

"Oh yeah," said Brannigan. "You ought to see their house up there. Huh, Mary Ann? It's gorgeous—"

Getting distracted was the downside to an informal meeting.

"Focus," said Jake, taking another bite.

"Let's look at the dark side. When you're giving to a lot of different charities, it's easy to hide large amounts of money," said Brannigan. "Especially if you created the organization."

"You mean like what Darlene Cutchins did?" asked Jake.

"That's right," said Brannigan. "Made herself president of the board and funneled plenty of dough into her own family foundation. A killing, an assassination really, seems like it would be done to get her money."

"Which is puzzling," said Jake. "We've spoken to relatives and business associates and so far, nothing. No one knows anything. No one seems guilty. Not with her, not with the others. We've scoured her accounts and there's been no significant money transfers. Her kids will get her insurance but they're totally distraught."

"Same with the others," said Stone. "It was like they were killed for the sake of being killed."

"Was DeVito next in line to be knocked off?" wondered Mary Ann.

"Beats me. With the three victims, all the evidence points to a sniper who did the killing. At DeVito's estate, it was a completely different style of an attack," said Stone. "We know it was Ojos Negros. But who's our sniper?"

"Kilbraide thinks it's someone with a military background. Ballistics show the rifling pattern of the bullets is traced back specifically to weapons with a bore that was originally made for Marine snipers. He looked into it and some of those rifles have been destroyed, or gone missing, while hundreds more have been produced and distributed widely. He said he'll update us."

"Could the sniper work for Ojos Negros?" wondered Mary Ann.

"Why change methods to get DeVito if one bullet worked well on the others?" Stone made a declaration. "What's the motive here? For the last couple of years, I figured Anthony Angelino was interested in more than just operating legal pot shops. They were going to be a front. DeVito tried to muscle in on the operation when he could have gone out and invested in his own stores. We already know there's drug money involved."

"It's more than drug money," said Alisha. "It's control of the drug money. Ojos Negros wants to control people just like they wanted to control me."

"They wanted you because you're a damned good attorney," said Stone.

Jake referred back to the picture from the yacht. "Think about this. Maybe Ojos Negros wasn't after DeVito at all. Harold Mortensen was at the parties. He was on the yacht. His name was on the guest list. And with his wealth he fits the profile of the others who were killed."

"Have you looked at the other guests?" asked Tasha.

"We're working on it," Stone replied. "But here's something strange. Two of the people killed at DeVito's were a man named Frank Banali who was his lawyer. And a young woman who accompanied him that night, Kelsey Johnson. Ballistics tests have come back and their shoulder wounds match up with the shots that killed the other guests, but, and here's the kicker, they also had bullets in the forehead that don't match up to anything else—either the Ojos Negros assailants or DeVito's bodyguards."

"So who shot them in the head, and why?" asked Mary Ann, reaching for a bowl of salad.

"And," said Jake, "here's another wrinkle. Miss Johnson had a sister in prison who was found dead in her cell a couple of nights ago. She was in the same cell block as Lil' Jo."

"I talked to Lil' Jo about that," remarked Alisha, "and, of course, she didn't care and acted like she knew nothing. I know she had something to do with it."

"Then I'll call up there and get the guards to visit her," said Stone.

"A shake down would do her good," exclaimed Mary Ann.

"Makes me wonder, why would she be after DeVito?" asked Jake. "Like they're rivals."

"As far as I know, they are," Alisha was finally calm. "Lil' Jo's calling the shots for Ojos Negros."

"It seems like everything ties back to DeVito," mused Brannigan.

"Why wouldn't it?" asked Alisha. "The picture of everyone was taken on his yacht and they're all dead."

"Is DeVito a suspect?" asked Mary Ann.

"He's always suspected of something," said Jake. "We have to nail down his relationship with each of the victims."

"Let's start with Charles Scott," Brannigan cut in, helping himself to potato salad. "We had a helpful discussion with Shirley Pruitt, the editor of the *Beverly Hills Sentinel.*"

"What the hell's that?" asked Jake.

"Potato salad" said Mary Ann, scooping some on her plate.

"No, I meant the Beverly Hills something or other."

"A community paper," said Mary Ann. "Shirley does a society page. It's more like a gossip column and she says all the people with money want to make sure their friends—and competitors—notice the donations they give."

"Yep, fork over that cash, baby. For the kids, for the animals … for the environment. Right? Hell, no," exclaimed Brannigan. "It's so they keep up their standing and look damned good."

Tasha cautioned him. "The kids."

"They're playing their games. Plus, I was thinking about them," said the salty former police officer. "Otherwise I would have said fuc—"

"Marty," scowled Mary Ann.

"Uh, sorry. But they can't hear me. They're in the other room."

"Yes, we can," yelled Andrew.

"Anyway," Mary Ann took over, "Shirley says the best thing about being an editor is that she covers every charity ball and event in Los Angeles. Free food and drinks. She remembers DeVito and Charles Scott exchanging some terse words. If they didn't keep their distance from each other, then you could really feel the tension."

"Too bad they didn't knock each other out," said Stone. "Scott was in finance."

"Investments," Jake specified. "I wonder if he ever handled DeVito's money."

"Oh, those egos are too much to take," said Tasha. "What about Darlene Cutchins?"

"DeVito invested in a few of her films," said Stone. "Lost some money on one of them. Made back his money plus a decent profit on a few others."

"So he wouldn't have snuffed her out?" asked Mary Ann.

"No, from everything we've found out, they seem more like allies," replied Stone. "If we can figure out the motive then we can begin to sift through *the who* and figure out when the next strike will be. This is all connected to drugs. I know it. Speaking of which," Stone looked across the table at Jake, "Lightfoot called today and apologized for treating us rudely at the beach. Said the DEA's at a dead end and now wants to work together."

Jake groaned. "Lightfoot's a dick."

"Jake," scolded Tasha.

"He is. But whether we like him or not, I guess we're now stuck working with him. Stone, do we really have to?"

"Yes, we do. Anyway," continued Stone, "he said he found an encrypted note on Helen Zhuang's computer referencing DeVito."

"How about that," Alisha spoke up, sipping a cup of chamomile tea. "Tom, I heard in court last week someone mentioning that cocaine use has dropped around here. Did you, or Jake, hear anything?"

"No. What do you mean?"

"A case before mine. This guy was hauled in for dealing. Said he was set up by, excuse me for saying this, law enforcement—"

"Go on," sighed Stone.

Alisha continued. "'He said, 'there ain't nothing to deal right now.' And then some university professor who specializes in this testified on his behalf. It seems like violent crime just spiked and drug use dipped." She paused. "Maybe drug use has slacked off because the money supply is tightening."

"*Trophic cascade,*" said Jake.

"What?" All eyes were on him.

"It's a term describing dramatic changes in the ecosystem when the top predators are removed."

A shout came from the family room. It was Jake's son, Darrell. "Yeah. That was part of my science paper."

"Stop listening to us," said Jake. He turned to the group. "It describes what's happening now. In this case, our victims with their resources have been eliminated."

"It's affecting everyone's behavior. It's brutal out there," said Tasha. "Like the shootings last week. Four people gunned down at Woodley and Sepulveda."

"The top predators have been removed," explained Jake, "and the sniper's impacting everyone down the food chain."

"One gang after another," said Stone.

"It's like LA's going crazy." Mary Ann shook her head and reached for the salad. She spoke quietly so the kids wouldn't hear. "We saw that body mutilated and hung from the freeway overpass."

"And Ojos Negros is running wild in the streets." Alisha sighed and wrapped her hands around the steaming mug. "I'm still in shock. If it wasn't for Silver, who knows what would have happened?" She patted him on the head.

"By the way, I checked under the car and everything looks fine. No damage, except for the window and we'll get that fixed. No worries," said Stone.

Alisha furrowed her brow, upset. "I can't believe Lil' Jo tried to force me to take her case and when I said 'no' she tried to kill me. What's this world coming to?"

"Criminals seemed more respectful back in my day," said Brannigan.

Stone tensed. "What makes Ojos Negros dangerous is that they're a federation of gangs."

"Huh?" asked Alisha.

"There are lots of layers. Like the United States. There are governors and there are central decision makers," said Jake. "Ojos Negros is a network that can operate individually in local chapters or get together and wreak havoc."

"They've been operating quietly," mentioned Stone. "We think headquartered in New Mexico where they can grow and function under the radar. They get recruits and members from across the U.S., Mexico, and immigrants from anywhere in the world. ICE has been picking them up and deporting as fast as they can, but they just come right back in."

Brannigan sighed. "Like killer bees gaining strength."

Jake agreed. "Unfortunately. They're well organized. They've got resources and depth. So now they can swarm a city like Los Angeles. Especially with the right shot caller. Lil' Jo."

Stone expressed his concern. "Now that there's a power vacuum, I'm afraid they're going to try and fill it. What we had before was bad, but if these guys control the streets then it's going to be hell."

CHAPTER TWENTY

Clanging filled Lil' Jo's mind as she tossed one way on her thin mattress and then another. What started quietly built and she half-awakened, turning on to her side trying to stop the noise. A vision of Arturo filled her mind and suddenly she shook with fear that he was seeking revenge on her. She woke from the bad dream as footsteps grew louder. Her cell door slammed open.

She bolted up, eyes wide as guards in full riot gear wearing helmets and wielding batons grabbed her and threw her to the floor. "Hey, what the fuck?" She shouted only to be drowned out by radios crackling. Her face was pressed against the cement and something heavy, like a foot, pressed into her neck, while zip ties were fastened around her wrists and ankles. She lay unable to move and couldn't fight her way out. An overnight raid on her cell. When all was quiet.

An order was shouted through faceguards fastened to the helmets. "Clear it out. Everything. Toss it." Equipment-clad figures reached beneath mattresses and dug through clothing. Magazines and books went flying. So did her stash of ramen, chips, and soap—currency that inmates used to barter with each other. She was dragged outside, guards grabbing her arms and legs. She turned as much as she could to see a guard find her hidden cell phone and another one reach inside a cubby and lift out a pill bottle filled with weed. He pocketed it. *Pendejo.*

Then guards on each side forced her to shuffle slowly backward past the solid metal doors of other inmates who were awakened and looked out the tiny windows of their cell doors. Muffled taunts from Lil Jo's rivals erupted from inside the cells.

One laborious step after another and she was hauled into a brightly lit room where a man she recognized as the warden stood. "We got some questions for you, Lil' Jo."

"And I got some for you." She shouted back. "What the hell you doing invading my space?"

"Your space? It belongs to the good people of California who pay their taxes."

"Bullshit." She mustered her anger and then when the guards got her sitting in a chair the initial shock wore off and she smiled. "You lonely tonight, Warden? Can't sleep? Want to be with a real woman?" She cooed seductively.

"I like you just as you are," he said, sliding into a chair opposite her, "locked up and kept under close guard. Hate to interrupt your sleep if that's what you were doing, but I need some answers. We hear you stay in touch with friends on the outside. And I want to find out more about it."

A guard slid her cell phone across the table. "We found this."

The warden picked it up and looked it over.

Lil' Jo spoke softly. "A girl's got the right to talk to people. Being locked up inside this place gets mighty lonely. Not much to do since you won't let me take classes and I only get an hour a day in the yard."

"I'll go easy on you, Lil' Jo. I'll settle for you getting seventy-two hours in *the Hole*."

Then the phone buzzed in the warden's hand. "Private caller." He gave her a curious look. "Should I answer it?"

***

Nothing. Arturo watched the man put down the phone. Slimy was the name Arturo had given him because he always looked greasy. Slimy called over to another gangbanger, Javier, who was staggering and fondling a woman in tight shorts and a loose T-shirt. "She ain't picking up."

Javier, sporting a new tattoo and unsteady from too many tequila shots, glanced in Arturo's direction. "We'll decide what to do with him. We don't need her approval for shit."

"You don't touch him. Not yet anyway." Slimy took a syringe, getting ready for a nice hit with light reflecting off his bald head that he kept oiled.

Music pulsed through the warehouse. The party started about eleven P.M. and kept going. Bare-chested thugs and plenty of women clacking about in high heels grinded against each other under the faint light and in the darkened corners. They were stupid women, thought Arturo, throwing their lives away for chances to be *thots* in the arms of bad-ass boys. Booze and drugs kept them high and chased away reality.

Arturo watched a good dozen or so foot soldiers aligned with Ojos Negros make their way in and out of the warehouse. Slimy had caught him trying to call Alisha.

"That's what Lil' Jo told me to do." Arturo protested. "Call and threaten her."

Slimy wasn't buying it. "But that's not what the fuck you were doing." He growled as he watched the others take two gang members they accused of snitching, and chained them to a rafter like animals about to be slaughtered. They took their knives, teasing the victims with sharp pokes up and down their torsos, and then slowly cutting them open, giving them time to scream with each slice. Younger gang members took their turns cutting, almost like an initiation ritual.

Arturo never imagined that life could get so sickening and he longed to be back in Zacatecas watching his children go to school and embracing his wife. Regret took him months back and flooded him with guilt for not having stopped Anthony Angelino from smuggling cocaine. He silently begged God's forgiveness and vowed to make things right. Slimy injected himself and sunk into a drugged state while men with black eyeballs explored the women who gyrated and moved to the beats reverberating off the concrete walls.

The smell of weed filled the hazy room, beer cans and liquor bottles clattered on the floor as they fell empty and an open door beckoned Arturo. At this moment, who would notice? His cot was against a far wall but that didn't concern his captors, the *pendejos*. They were steamrolling their way to power, crushing everyone, and now they were celebrating. The party intensified and couples stumbled toward bedrooms made from makeshift partitions.

Javier was nowhere to be seen. Arturo scooped a bottle of Hennessy off the floor and wandered into the crowd. He then turned quickly and stepped out the front door. A younger man with a slight build stood guard outside the entrance. Arturo recognized him. Not too long ago, he was just a kid from the Valley who hung out with the Victor Boyz and got jumped in. "Scooter?"

The guy had the typical shaved head and as many tattoos as everyone else. Scooter inhaled weed and at first nodded to Arturo before awakening with a realization. "Hey, what are you doing? Get back inside."

"Not a lot of friendly faces so I came out for fresh air."

"Got it, dawg. But I can't let you leave." Scooter looked into the warehouse nervously. "I don't want to get my ass kicked, or worse."

"That's fine. Thought you'd like a drink." Arturo held the liquor bottle. It felt about half full and was made with nice quality glass.

Scooter inhaled again. "Cool, dawg."

Arturo quickly lifted the bottle and brought it smashing down on the kid's skull. Scooter collapsed on the ground with a joint between his lips as an onslaught of car engines and SUVs with blinding headlights squealed to a stop in front of the building, blocking the street. Gunfire erupted and Arturo hit the pavement, scraping his arms as he slithered into the shadows of the warehouse with broken glass cutting a hand. He crouched, charged into a full sprint, and looked back to see a swarm of rival gangbangers intensifying their attack on Ojos Negros. As gunfire and screams filled the air, he fled into the darkness.

CHAPTER TWENTY-ONE

Quality information was a detective's best friend and Kilbraide had scanned massive amounts of it. Charles Scott built a financial planning business to more than five hundred clients and then pared those down to eighty individuals worth more than ten million dollars each on average. They provided the majority of his revenue. Sophisticated software and knowledgeable assistants stayed in touch with the clients on the health of their portfolios and offered quarterly updates to give a white glove touch.

In addition, Scott's firm handled financial transactions for several companies. Some had equipment loans with large municipal contracts while others needed funding to import and export supplies to and from emerging markets like China and India. During a personal visit to South Asia, he had heard about the beauty of profits from drug exports. He'd gotten heavily involved and developed an association with Helen Zhuang and her logistics firm.

His operation was run so efficiently that a lean staff of about a dozen people oversaw a business handling over a half-billion dollars in legal transactions every year. He did twice that in illegal activity. Scott himself had plenty of time to live the California lifestyle—golfing at Pebble Beach and hiking in the Sierras were a couple of his favorite pastimes according to associates. So was fine dining up and down the coast.

Kilbraide's eyes were bloodshot from poring over minute details, but he pushed himself just like he was trained to do as a soldier who was decorated in battle. The motivation of finding the missing links fueled him and the answers were found in the hidden financial records that connected the sniper victims together in the drug trade.

One of Scott's clients surfaced from the myriad number of transactions. He and his family lived in one of the most expensive homes ever built in Los Angeles County. The property wasn't in Beverly Hills or Bel Air but in a little-known enclave called Bradbury, a place Kilbraide had never heard of. He wanted the location to sink into his mind and drove to it, nestled in the foothills of the San Gabriel Mountains, about twenty-five miles east of downtown Los Angeles. It had its own mayor and town council who kept a low profile to ensure privacy for the elite residents. Below it ran the major surface streets that paralleled the freeway and passed through the less affluent cities. No driver would casually pass through Bradbury the way they would Monrovia, Duarte, or Azusa.

Kilbraide arrived, parked along the road, and studied the plateau where the estate of Mufqa Khalid was perched. Kilbraide pulled out binoculars. From where he sat, it looked like the property bumped up against the barren foothills. There were no large boulders and few bushes, leaving little cover for taking a deadly shot. A close inspection showed slopes that ran down into a ravine. The hills were at least a few hundred yards away. A gleaming white wooden fence surrounded the property, the kind that homes and ranches had in neighborhoods were passersby could see them.

Down the driveway was a guard house with a security gate and as Kilbraide settled for a look, he noticed a figure step out of the building and glance in his direction. Trees were planted in clumps of three and four around the property. The massive two-story home's main entrance was visible. Wings stretching to the right and left were more difficult to see. Kilbraide noticed a flat area for the swimming pool and tennis court stretching behind the house. It matched what he had seen previously on Google Earth, but in person the area was hidden well by trees and a row of manicured shrubs. This was well-planned and made Charles Scott's mini-estate look totally defenseless.

Documents from Scott's and Zhuang's files had Khalid's name as a developer and investor. Kilbraide dug through files that showed that Khalid, a naturalized citizen, made his money through a commercial real estate empire that included large office buildings and massive condominium complexes. More sprawl to meet the growing demand for housing.

The sound of rotors fluttered through the air and grew louder. A dust cloud rose from behind the estate and after several minutes a small helicopter lifted, passed above horses that were grazing, and headed south toward the freeway before banking west.

Khalid was a successful serial entrepreneur. He also owned a substantial number of advertising outlets and billboards throughout the country and operated a global film distribution company. The man controlled money. His businesses were legitimate and profitable, and yet Kilbraide uncovered a network of offshore bank accounts that were used to launder drug money for Scott and Zhuang.

Another guard emerged, conversed with the first, and walked slowly toward Kilbraide's car. *Time to leave.* He turned on the engine and made his way back toward the Valley. Taking out a man like Khalid wasn't going to be easy. He had a text message from Stone. *Meeting with Lightfoot at three.* Damn. There was another place that he wanted to see. A Catholic church in Burbank.

Khalid was known for promoting inter-faith coalitions. It was one way that he "gave back to the community," as he said once in an interview. He was a Muslim, although from what Kilbraide could tell, the man rarely went to a mosque. An attorney on his staff, though, was Catholic and had close ties to the Los Angeles Archdiocese. The man, John Thompson, lived in a ranch-style suburban house in Studio City. He was a connector and, from what evidence showed, maneuvered between Scott, Zhuang, and Khalid. The attorney was also on DeVito's yacht, according to the guest list. He had Khalid's trust and handled all the finances without question. Maybe he was more key than Khalid. The linchpin.

All these non-profit groups. Kilbraide bristled. Thompson was an officer on the Board of Directors for each nonprofit that was associated with Scott and Zhuang—and he also worked with Darlene Cutchins' foundation. The man even had ties to Mortensen. He was everywhere.

The church that he attended was only a few miles from Griffith Park where Darlene Cutchins had her production office and was killed on the equestrian trail. When Kilbraide arrived and drove slowly around the block, he noticed the church had large windows covered in stained glass with gospel stories. The design created a feeling of safety and comfort.

Kilbraide parked and got out. Cars zipped by and people in dress slacks and shirts bustled about their business. Down the street was a four-story parking structure for the local offices. Kilbraide sauntered over to it and read a sign. *Closed on Sundays.* He climbed the stairs to the top levels and saw that the structure had a clear line of sight to the church. *Possibilities.*

CHAPTER TWENTY-TWO

John Thompson liked the smooth feel of his blue sport coat over his knit shirt and slacks. Neat and orderly as he entered Saint Anthony's Parish. Perfect. He walked along the aisle as mass was about to begin, ushering his six-year-old son and four-year-old daughter to the pew that his family sat in week after week. Traditional. Safe. Normal. A moment in his week he could count on.

His wife, a few years younger in her mid-thirties, walked alongside. Thompson scooted in first. His son, Ryan, stepped in next until his daughter Emily tugged on his jacket and motioned to sit by him.

He smiled. "Sit by your mother," he whispered to Ryan.

The prelude started and the pews were full, surprising since attendance had been dropping steadily during the past few years. But the new priest had a winning personality.

Emily snuggled against her father as Ryan looked bored, but sat and waited. Good kids. Obedient and patient. Thompson credited his wife. Lauren combined a smile with stern eyes to keep the kids in line. He had so much to be thankful for even as the murders of Charles Scott and the other victims surfaced in his thoughts. He recited his blessings. So many shipments and so many under the table dealings. Keeping them hidden was agonizing, but that's what he was paid to do.

He pursed his lips, closed his eyes for a moment, and then opened them. Lauren had glanced over at him as though she sensed his tension.

To his right, a stained-glass window lined the wall. He had grown up at St. Anthony's and had sat in the same spot with his father and mother, just below the image of the Virgin Mary holding the Baby Jesus. He glanced at it and sought comfort in it even as a conversation from earlier in the week surfaced in his thoughts. Another shipment was available. It would take three weeks to reach the addicts who were desperate.

Only he could approve the transfer of funds. This time he would see none of it. Lauren and the kids would be taken care of forever with the profits from that one shipment alone. He was a busy attorney with connections. She would never have to know.

Mass began and he turned to his wife with a smile to get his mind off business. A sensation ran through his neck and shoulders and he looked back. They were there. Faithful. His bodyguards blending in with the crowd near the foyer.

A sad but necessary reality.

He shuddered at recent news.

A headless body tied to the freeway overpass.

Not his fault.

The transfer would happen so seamlessly. All electronic. Hell, he wasn't even needed. Why did he get involved in the first place?

Easy money and lots of it.

The Virgin Mary had a look of longing at her baby, the Son of God, born to die.

"No, please God," Thompson whispered. Emily looked up at him and Lauren glanced over once again.

He leaned back, trying to get comfortable. The beams of the sun streamed through the colored glass, warming his face. Thompson closed his eyes trying to forget why he needed bodyguards. Why he felt the pressure to authorize money and invest in a shipment.

Charles Scott had a firm handshake and easy demeanor. The man could have been governor. Hell, president. But the senseless murders didn't surprise Thompson. He always knew it could happen, but suppressed the reality that it ever would. The market was vicious and the risk went with the territory. He masked it around family and friends with a smile and confidence, despite fear for the lives of his wife, his children, and himself. The seller and financier were as addicted as the poor junkie driving to work, shaking until the next high.

He wasn't invincible. He knew it. Thompson had always thought if someone was going to take him out that he would come face to face with his killer. But the shroud of fear and doubt with the uncertainty of who lurked nearby was too much for him to bear. He could sense it.

No, God. Not now. Not here. Mother Mary was by his side. *Hail Mary full of grace. The Lord be with you. And also with you.*

Thompson suddenly longed for the communion elements. To sip the wine from the priest's chalice and taste the wafer. *Christ's body, broken for you.*

A tinkle. Glass shattered. The stained glass he had known so intimately.

Blessed art though amongst women and blessed is the fruit of thy womb, Jesus.

He has always put his family first—above everything. They're privileged and will never have a need or want. Except the want of a husband and father. His wife is about to be a widow, his children fatherless. Their lives destroyed. Like countless others—lives ruined by his greed to live the good life and provide for his own family.

Holy Mary, Mother of God. He feels the golden glow of the Virgin Mary caressing his face. *Pray for us sinners, now and at the hour of our death, Amen.*

And before he can open his eyes one last time to look at her, a bullet enters his brain. And like shattered glass it explodes out the back of his head, covering his family with the sins of his crimes.

CHAPTER TWENTY-THREE

The shooting transformed the house of worship into a trauma center. Police interviewed witnesses who were still shaking and weeping. Department photographers captured shots of the surroundings while personnel from the coroner's office and forensics went about their methodical collecting of evidence and data.

The tension of working together faded as Stone, Jake, and Agent Lightfoot stood over Thompson's body. His corpse lay in the pew, one arm dangling to the floor. Witnesses who sat behind him said he had slumped onto his daughter. Blood and bits of his skull had splattered over his family and surrounding worshipers.

One shot turned a peaceful Sunday morning into a hysterical arena of parishioners screaming and panicking.

"Where the hell is Kilbraide?" Stone was irritated. He'd received the notes from Kilbraide about Thompson the night before and wanted to question him, but now the man was dead. *Damn.*

"Said he was on his way." Jake sounded impatient while he looked from the pew to the window. "He acts like he's on his own time." He whistled. "That was an impossible angle."

This was the most daring shot yet—into a crowd with an occluded line of sight.

"I can't believe it." Stone was dumbfounded.

Lightfoot repeated what everyone already knew. "Thompson was a powerful attorney. A middleman for a lot of high-powered people, either carrying out their orders or making decisions on his own."

Personnel stepped aside as Brian Kilbraide walked down the aisle and caught up with the others. He paused at the pew and then turned to the window, surveying the shards of glass. "Shit." His eyes were laser focused.

"Thanks for your input," remarked Stone with sarcasm.

"This is a church, watch your language," quipped Jake.

"Sorry, but I don't know what else to say."

"Maybe you'd have more to say if you were here on time," said Stone.

"Hey, Stone. Not now," cautioned Jake.

Kilbraide turned quickly, shoulders tense. "I would have been here sooner. But don't know if you heard that a headless corpse was found lying in the street. Valley Village. Right near the 170. Another gangbanger. About forty-five minutes ago. Slowed down traffic."

"Well, I'm glad you made it, Detective," Stone quipped, feeling helpless. So much was happening on so many different fronts.

"I've been updating things."

"On your own?" said Stone. "We're a team."

"I was at softball practice the other night," Kilbraide joked.

"Glad you got your priorities straight," said Jake. "The season's a wash anyway. We're not going to win any games."

"Yeah, so you might as well focus on the investigation," said Stone.

"I have been," noted Kilbraide. "Each victim has been killed in a highly personal setting. And this is the most personal of all."

Lightfoot looked from Thompson's body and studied the angle from where he would have been sitting to the bullet's entry point through the window.

"The sniper must have known this guy extremely well," said Lightfoot.

"Absolutely," Kilbraide was matter of fact, "to know where the guy was sitting in church."

Everyone related to the victims appeared genuinely clueless and couldn't think of anyone who had a grudge. Nor could the detectives pin down or even get someone to appear to talk about a connection to drugs. No employees, no relatives. It was all hidden in the paper trails and bank accounts.

"Maybe the sniper isn't doing this alone," suggested Stone.

"Possible," Lightfoot agreed. "You could have someone in the church or along the bike path sending text messages. Where the target is sitting, walking, or riding."

"A spotter. Yeah, that's possible," said Kilbraide, glancing around. "Plausible."

"Did you work with a spotter?" asked Jake.

"Of course," answered Kilbraide. "But not always."

Stone motioned to everyone buzzing around the crime scene. "Let's let these guys do their work. Come on, let's check out the surrounding area and get a Big Picture view."

They went outside. Lightfoot looked around. "You guys want to walk the perimeter?

"How about if we start with where the shooter had likely been?" suggested Kilbraide.

"And where's that?" asked Stone.

"The parking structure over there. I scouted it the other day."

"You did?" Stone studied Kilbraide.

"Covering all angles."

Stone locked eyes with Kilbraide. "Do you still have yours?"

"My what?" Kilbraide knew what Stone was thinking. "My Barret? You betcha. Bringing in a nice little side income shooting at tournaments where the gun is checked for proper registration and all the legal crap. I like keeping up with my military skills."

"Give us a demonstration sometime. Let us know when your next tournament is," said Jake.

"I will."

Jake motioned to the parking structure. "Let's go check out the garage. What made you think about the location, Kilbraide? You part blood-hound or something?"

"Chalk it up to extensive military training. Just doing a lot of research, connecting all the dots of people who went to the charity event.

I dug into the files and if there's a hit list, I figured John Thompson would be on it. Again, I took the personal angle and the church was just one of a few possibilities that I thought of. His boy plays Little League baseball. He could have been taken out during a game or practice. I saw family pictures on Facebook hiking to the Hollywood sign with his wife and kids. It said they were also looking forward to a peaceful Sunday and brunch after church. Go figure."

"How about this place?" said Jake, looking at a one-story bungalow. It was a professional office with signs for a dentist, insurance agency, and financial planner. "He could have been on the roof there."

Kilbraide answered. "No line of sight, I'm telling you. It was from the parking structure."

Across the street was a coffee shop with a crowd standing outside, looking toward the church.

The foursome continued to the garage. It had one stairwell and elevator. It was meant for Monday to Friday activity since there were no shopping malls or retail stores in the neighborhood. There was only one ramp, wide enough for cars going up and down. It was simple and basic compared to the structures in the malls.

"All right, we're here," said Stone. "Now what?"

"Head to the third floor."

"Why not the fourth floor?" asked Jake.

"Better angle on the third."

"I'll take the stairs. I need the exercise," said Jake. He looked at Lightfoot. "I don't think you could handle the stairs, you need the elevator."

"Whatever." Lightfoot found no humor in the remark.

Stone said he'd walk up the ramp and Kilbraide took the elevator with Lightfoot. The foursome spread out looking for any possible clues.

At the third level, Stone looked below and observed the layout of the one-story professional building. The roof was typical flat industrial with a central air conditioning unit and vents. The afternoon sun illuminated where the bullet had ripped through the church's stained-glass window and into the head of John Thompson. The angle was perfect.

Stone pointed to the building below. "We need to ask them some questions."

"I'll be there first thing in the morning." Kilbraide sauntered off, glancing right and left.

"This is a great place for a surprise attack on people who aren't expecting a thing," said Jake.

"Hey," Kilbraide called out from behind a supporting column. "Found something."

Stone, Jake, and Lightfoot wandered over. *One Shot, One Kill.* A patch left as a calling card, just like the others.

"Let's get this area closed off and get the teams up here." Lightfoot looked annoyed. "I want this place checked out. Completely. Fingerprints, DNA. I mean, come on. The guy had to sweat, spit, fart or something."

"Remember," said Kilbraide with a straight face, "he's well trained. He's going to hold it in."

CHAPTER TWENTY-FOUR

Finally, the cell door opened. Lil' Jo hesitated. Seventy-two hours with no human contact. No cell phone, no cute bitches to push around and do her bidding, no one to eat meals with.

"Come on out, unless you want to stay. But then I'd have to clear it with the watch commander," said the guard. A bored look on the woman's face. Lil' Jo noticed how her uniform and accessories made the woman's hips look extra wide.

"I'm coming." Lil' Jo stepped forward as two more guards waited and escorted her back to her cell block. It'd take a while to get another phone. She could speed up the process if she could get the guards to look the other way. The ones surrounding her at the moment didn't act like they could be bribed. Their pay and benefits were too good to risk letting an inmate smuggle in contraband.

Her cell block was already high security because of her gang affiliation. Now, after the raid, they were going to keep a closer eye on her. Maybe give her two or three weeks and then do another surprise check.

They went through the motions of putting her in the cell, shutting the door, and leaving. She slumped on to her bunk with the thin mattress and wanted news about the next shipment and what the hell was going on with Ojos Negros. *And what are they doing with Arturo?* She hated this place. Prison really sucked. She had her own little minions, but she'd rather be out. She could do so much more if she were free. Make her mark. Build an empire. Reality gnawed at her gut like a rat chewing on rope.

Sleeping in her bunk that night was itself an awful sentence with no cell phone and no contact with the outside. She had amassed so much power and saw how it could be snatched away at any moment. And there was nothing she could do about it. The thought of feeling like just another inmate was a strange role. Her only privilege was one hour in the yard and a chance to use the facility's phone. Whoever she called would have to be collect and it would be monitored. Breakfast came and went. Boring. Tasteless. And then late morning was her chance to be in the yard. She bummed a cigarette from a gal, a brunette who was in for holding up a liquor store with her boyfriend. The woman wasn't all that bright, thought Lil' Jo. She was good for a few laughs now and then and, overall, was fairly harmless.

No one else hung near her. The realization settled that she was alone. Her homies were still locked up and not in the yard. An uneasy vibe of vulnerability hit her. Suddenly, she wanted to cut her time short and head back to her cell, but a lithe woman who was tattooed along her neck motioned, and followed by a friend, walked over to the wall that Lil' Jo was leaning against.

"Hey. I got news for you," said the tattooed lady. Janah was what she went by. Her friend was only known as Rough Rider.

"Oh, yeah?" Lil' Jo took a drag as Rough Rider stood on one side, too close.

Janah held her arms against her side. "Heard you got a little discipline action, huh?"

Lil' Jo shrugged it off. "Seventy-two hours. Tough shit."

Rough Rider glanced around and slid up against Lil' Jo.

"Want to know what's going down?" said Janah, drawing closer. "Could make you some good money on the outside."

"Oh yeah?" Lil' Jo didn't like how close they were. She got ready to bolt but Janah put a hand on her neck, pulled out a piece of metal, and shoved it halfway up her rib cage. Lil' Jo gasped, engulfed in total shock as the woman pulled it out and shoved it in again. Lil' Jo gurgled, confused. Her knees went wobbly and she fell back against the hard wall.

"This is from DeVito, you bitch. Good luck to where you're going."

The women turned blurry as Lil' Jo slid to the ground, stunned. Her world fell silent and dark.

***

DeVito watched the news copter's Live Cam circling an overpass above the 10 West freeway. Five bodies dangled from the structure. Police reported that three other dismembered corpses had been found the day before in an alley along Robertson Boulevard. DeVito sipped a glass of red wine, a blend from his newly acquired winery that was up the coast near San Luis Obispo. Ryker sat next to him as the large screen TV lit up the room.

"The bastards really got it." DeVito fumbled for his cigars. He pulled the last one from the box. "I need to tell Denise to get me more of these." He turned back to the television. The freeway was stopped in all directions as firefighters and police officers worked methodically to haul in each corpse. They moved carefully so the remains wouldn't fall onto the lanes below.

The studio anchors were careful to point out that the camera was purposefully blurred to not show the bodies clearly since each one had been mutilated and decapitated. The deceased wore black and it was reported that their arms were covered in tattoos. DeVito wished they would zoom in and show the missing pinky fingers, the trademark of his organization.

"Ojos Negros, goodbye," murmured Ryker.

"Good." DeVito chomped on his cigar. "Remind me to pay out bonuses for the nice work that's been done. You did a good job of pulling those other gangs together. Did you tell them they got news coverage?"

"I did." Ryker watched as a second and then third body were carefully hoisted onto the overpass. The news anchors commented on how two of the first responders got sick from what they experienced. "Poor guys. But we're doing them a favor. If we keep this up, then we'll push Ojos Negros back under the rocks where they came from. Done and gone."

"No." DeVito set his cigar down and took his wine instead. "They're like cockroaches. No matter how many we kill, there'll always be more."

***

Arturo sat beneath a blue plastic tarp stretched between stacked wooden pallets, closed in with cardboard walls and engulfed in the white noise of freeway traffic traveling on the overpass. The homeless encampment became a welcome refuge, despite sleeping on concrete and his body aching from very move. Body odor and worse filled the air, but he was thankful. A car blasted its horn in the line of traffic and he jumped, expecting to see Ojos Negros foot soldiers jumping out and scooping him up. But he was free and thankful that he could hide in a community of transient people beneath the freeway. One of them, a guy with a long beard and ripped jeans known as Mountain Man, had a cell phone laying by his side. Arturo eyed the phone and approached the man as he chowed down on scraps from a nearby restaurant.

"Hey?" Arturo knelt beside him.

"Yeah?"

"Can I use your phone? Got to call my wife."

Mountain Man looked at him with amazement. "Your wife?" But he didn't ask any questions. "Yeah, man, help yourself."

It was a welcome relief to talk with Marta. Fear shook her when she heard about the bizarre and heartless killings, but she and the kids were fine. He told her not to worry and promised that he'd be home soon, said he loved her, and then gave the phone back to Mountain Man.

Arturo couldn't hide any longer. He needed information and to get a grip on what was going on. Two men with stringy hair and clothes caked in dirt headed to the public library to wash their faces in the restroom. Arturo joined them, but once inside he slipped behind a free computer and logged on to find out more about the headless bodies covered in tattoos. Ojos Negros had suffered a major defeat in a vicious fight over who controlled the flow of drugs into Los Angeles. Whoever prevailed would control the entire west coast.

He pulled up the news reports. He recognized Slimy's and Javier's bodies and the other headless corpses killed by inter-gang warfare at the warehouse and cut down in ambushes around Los Angeles. A related story mentioned police raids that rounded up a few dozen Ojos Negros foot soldiers and was investigating how they were run from inside a prison. *Lil' Jo was dead.* That came as a shock, but not unexpected. He wondered for a moment who did it. He accepted that he'll never know for certain and the thought soon passed. Now he was among the last of the old school Victor Boyz. A lonely feeling. He actually liked Lil' Jo, well, used to like her. They had some good times growing up together.

He wished it hadn't happened this way but now he was a free man and no one was chasing him. He hoped. He left his two homeless friends in the library and headed north into Van Nuys, into the neighborhood where Anthony Angelino had lived. He hadn't shaved for days and his hair was filthy. He walked past apartments and houses before turning onto the street where Angelino had paid him to transform a two-story bungalow into a marijuana grow house. With the profits he made selling off some of the stolen cocaine, he bought the house.

The grass was getting tall. He stood on the lawn. *What if?* In a flash, he could see his children coming up the sidewalk from school to a home that was a refuge from a world being ripped apart. He could get the house rehabbed and contact his old friends in *the 'hood*, the ones who didn't join Lil' Jo and Ojos Negros.

He turned away from the street and walked to the side of the front porch. He removed a screen, knelt, and felt along the floorboards. There it was. The key. He grabbed it, hurried around to the back door, and opened it.

A musty odor greeted him, but he didn't care. No one was threatening him. He felt like a man dying of thirst who finally came across an oasis. Arturo went to the kitchen, reached below the counter, and opened a cabinet door. He sank to his knees and grabbed a small, nickel-plated handle. He pulled it up and removed a section of the flooring. In between the joists, the bag was still there. He grabbed it, untied it, and counted the bills. Ten-thousand dollars. He heaved a sigh. The money was still there, even after a few months. He set the bag by his knees and reached beneath the flooring again. He felt along and touched the pouch. His heart raced as he pulled out a kilo, one of five-hundred stashed beneath the floor. He saw the logo of the skull with the blood-red tear drop. The cocaine. Safe as well. What he hadn't sold to Charles Scott, he hid in the house. For safekeeping, a future investment. A time like now.

Now that Scott was dead, he'd have to find someone to help him sell it off. Although, it shouldn't be hard since the streets were crawling with drug-starved addicts. He could be swimming in money. It was enough to get out of Los Angeles and out of Zacatecas with his family. To go—somewhere safe and nice where people weren't killing each other. But where would that be? And who would he have to inflict with the misery of addiction to make that happen?

His heart sank. He was just as greedy as Frank DeVito, Slimy and Lil' Jo. He didn't want to end up shot by the cops like Anthony Angelino. The violence and killings had to stop.

A loud knock and rattle on the front door shook him. He quickly shoved the money and cocaine beneath the floor and replaced the boards. There was another knock.

Fear shot through him like an electric current. He moved cautiously, staying to the left of the door and catching a view through the front window. He laughed a sigh of relief. It was the old lady from up the street, and she was alone with her face pressed against the small window in the front door. Arturo opened it. "Hello?"

"I thought that was you," said Mary Ann Bostovich.

"Yes, it's me."

"My God, every time I see you, you're beat up. What happened this time?"

Arturo touched his face which was still tender from the beatings he had suffered. He forgot about the dark bruises beneath his eye turning a yellowish-green as they healed. "Let's just say that life happens."

Mary Ann smiled. "Looks like life's been happening a lot to you. It's good to see you. With all the news reports, I didn't know if you'd still be alive or not."

Arturo was surprised. "Did you think I was in trouble?"

"How'd you get away from them?"

"Wait, what? How'd you know about that?"

Mary Ann was matter of fact. "Nothing gets by me."

"It's a long story."

"I've got time. Want some pie?"

CHAPTER TWENTY-FIVE

A drive up the coast to kayak around Morro Bay and watch the sea otters play around Morro Rock, the volcanic plug in the ocean, affectionately known as one of the Seven Sisters, was the last, enjoyable moment with Brenda.

The memory and knowing it would never happen again made watching the news all the more satisfying. Each body hauled up and onto the freeway overpass was a bonus. More gang warfare erupted, said the reporters. They were killing each other. *Good.* It was like a sign from the heavens that the right path was chosen.

The monsters who made money from other people's misery were dead or would soon be dead. It didn't matter if they lived in a palatial estate or walked around acting repulsive to the rest of society. Staking out where they lived and learning the routines in their ridiculous lifestyles was paying off. No celebrating, though. The battle was still continuing. And it would never be over. Constant vigilance was crucial to ensure that no one else suffered the way Brenda had with the poison running through her veins while gasping for her last breath.

Touching her hair and cracking a joke to make her laugh was the whole reason for coming back from his third deployment. Facing a personal war with a woman who embodied the word *vivacious* was a shock, worse than an enemy ambush. *Don't blame yourself.* Maybe it would be worth burning down the estate where the first party happened, above a private beach in Malibu as the sun set over the Pacific Ocean. *You let your guard down.*

Getting invited by a big-money client to a celebrity's home made his head swim and Brenda was all smiles. Shaking hands with people who had names scrolling on movie credits was itself a rush and would have been enough of a high until someone brought out the cocaine. Brenda did a line and there was a hint of eroticism watching her do something forbidden, like the beautiful side of evil. It was just like college. All in good fun.

And then there was the house party in the Hollywood Hills where he caught her snorting a line with her girlfriends. Seeing her go down that path depressed him. They got into a big fight and she agreed to never do it again, but on the day of their wedding, just before they drove away from the church, she was in the bathroom with a silver spoon.

Not allowing alcohol or drugs of any kind in the home and trying to set other boundaries failed. She craved the high and chased it again and again. Brenda wanted to quit on her own and resisted rehab, but she went to support groups—although she was usually high. Finding and buying the drug was so easy. Too easy.

She dipped into savings, depleting everything, and then came the car accident. The chronic pain around her shoulders and neck opened the door for fentanyl and doctors said her brain feasted on the pleasure. When they would no longer refill her prescriptions, she found dealers popping up like liquor stores on every corner. She started taking it first in tablet form, and when that wasn't enough to satisfy the craving, she crushed and snorted it, and finally turned to the needle – a full blown addict.

She grew distant and then it happened. Injected too much, too fast. The only regrets her dealers had was that a profitable customer was dead. But for them, it didn't matter since others would quickly take her place.

All businesses had a supply chain and drugs weren't any different. The cops were lousy at stopping the flow. They arrested the little people but somehow never made their way to nab the kingpins at the top. The rich and twisted were the ones who had the money and could fund new shipments. They weren't druggies themselves, but they were addicted to cash.

His reasoning was simple. Take out the financiers. Cut off the flow of money and the trail of drugs would slow to a trickle. And that's what he was accomplishing.

Patience was a virtue. It gave him time to build relationships and to get to know lifestyles of so many powerful people. Or, at least they thought they were powerful. He used his intelligence-gathering skills and found their weak spots. That data, coupled with his military training, proved to be a deadly combination.

CHAPTER TWENTY-SIX

Sewing machines buzzed in the hall as women assembled clothing patterns. The laborers had a decent output but Stacy Norhaus, her face framed by the bangs of her jet-black hair, wanted more. Automating the pattern design and more of the production would definitely be worth the investment.

Workers were expendable, especially these. Illegal Mexicans. She walked past the workstations, running her fingers along her pearl necklace. Migrants were like wild dogs running scared, scurrying across the border in search of a better life. So many had no education. The good news, at least for the young women, was that if they didn't perform well here then they could perform well elsewhere, like in a massage parlor.

She stopped by the breakroom where a petite girl with dark eyes and flowing black hair stood with two men near her, sipping coffee. Stacy ignored the girl's frightened look. She was no more than sixteen, maybe seventeen years old, and had been smuggled by Coyotes in from Mexico along with a few kilos of cocaine. Just another mule. But she ruined a few too many patterns. Stacy tried to give the girl a chance but figured she would be better suited to work using her body.

"The van's outside," said Stacy. "Take her."

The girl opened her mouth as though she was going to protest, but the men grabbed her and hurried her along the production floor and through a doorway to a waiting van. White, non-descript. They hustled her in. Stacy took her cell phone and made a call. "Let me speak to Frank. This is Stacy."

The sound of bowling balls filled the air.

"All right. Hold on."

The lanes were busy.

"Go ahead." DeVito's voice was muffled while chewing on a cigar.

"Frank." Stacy smiled. "I'm sending you a new one per our agreement."

"You don't say."

"I do. She's very cute and very young. Terrible assembling jeans but I think her hands are good enough to work a man's body."

"That's good to know." He laughed. "Should I train her myself?"

"She's yours to do with what you want."

"Great. But right now, so much is happening that I don't have time to deal with her so send her over to Bangkok Massage."

"Fine with me. I expect payment in a few hours or sooner."

"I'll tell Denise to take care of it." DeVito was matter of fact.

"Good, Frank. Always a pleasure doing business with you." More pins crashed. "How's your game going?"

"I broke a hundred, but who the hell cares? Anything else?" he asked.

"There's always something else," said Stacy, who was tired of bringing in just a few kilos at a time. She wanted to seize opportunity with a massive shipment and profit from the desperate demand in the marketplace. "Got good news for you. The funding is ready, so within a few days I'll be able to generate a healthy supply for you." Stacy headed across the factory floor, ensuring that everyone was working, and made her way to the parking lot. She had an appointment downtown. About a twenty-minute drive from the little-known industrial city of Vernon that bordered Los Angeles.

"Good," said DeVito. "Keep me up to date."

"I will, Frank. Certainly." She stood near her car, a newer Mercedes SUV. She bought the latest model every year. She wished her daughter would clean out her soccer gear from off the back seat.

Stacy reached for the door handle and never heard the crack of the rifle. The only thing she felt was a dull thud and searing pain as a .50 caliber round exploded through her brain, bursting the driver's side window and lodging in the dashboard of her new car. The impact triggered the airbags. She toppled over dead as they inflated.

CHAPTER TWENTY-SEVEN

Death hung in the station's conference room. Images showed a murdered Stacy Norhaus who wore a blazer and slacks, but her head was obliterated. Other pictures showed a fifty-five gallon barrel with human limbs and remains scattered around it, one of many recently found in non-descript warehouses and alleyways scattered throughout the Los Angeles basin.

The images were gruesome in a different dimension. Gang killings took the lives of more people. The likeness of a tattooed gangbanger with black eyes was spray painted on a wall near the carnage, a sign that Ojos Negros was fighting back. The barrel was filled with acid and investigators found what they estimated were three bodies dissolving inside it, what the police and gangs in Mexico called *Mexican soup*.

"Where the hell's the connection?" mused Stone, glancing between the sets of images.

Lightfoot spoke up. "Stacy Norhaus is well-known in the fashion industry among designers and merchandisers. Several dozen workers have been detained and questioned about tough working conditions. Most of them are illegals and they stayed quiet, afraid to talk to their co-workers, police, and especially ICE about bad treatment for fear of being deported. None of them had gang ties."

"Norhaus made a call shortly before she was killed. The number was traced to Valley Lanes Bowling," said Jake. "A payphone."

"You're kidding. Payphones still exist?" asked Kilbraide.

"Isn't that the place Yaro owns?" remarked Stone.

"A few payphones here and there," said Jake. "He used to own the building, but not sure if he still does. I'm looking into it."

"Valley Lanes is where you said that guy was killed last fall," noted Lightfoot.

"Yeah. Okay, here it is." Jake scrolled through notes on his tablet. "Yaro was leasing it to a guy named Massimo who was shot in the head and his pinky was cut off."

"Shot in the head?" asked Lightfoot.

"Yeah, but different than these killings. Whoever did it walked inside. Reports say it was a handgun used at close range, execution-style. They left his body in the supply closet by a safe but no money was taken. And the lights were turned on and the front doors unlocked."

"And no leads on it?" asked Kilbraide.

"We have our ideas but nothing concrete," answered Stone as his mind raced through mental files. "The missing pinky fingers were linked to other murders at the time, but we don't have anything conclusive."

"The Ojos Negros gang members who were killed had their pinkies cut off, too. Think there's a connection?"

"There's always a connection," said Jake.

"Why would she call a bowling alley?" wondered Lightfoot. "Especially a payphone?"

"Says here in the county database," Jake muttered while studying his tablet's screen, "that DeVito bought the bowling alley shortly after that killing occurred."

Stone sighed and mumbled. "Of course, he did."

Kilbraide scrolled on his tablet. "Norhaus was on the guest list at the big party that DeVito hosted, just like the other sniper victims."

"Everything comes back around to DeVito." Stone glanced at the images.

"So Norhaus was a big money player," Kilbraide wondered, "trying to make deals."

"The sniper must have thought so," said Lightfoot. "We found another one of those One Shot, One Kill patches. It was left at the entrance to an abandoned three-story warehouse a few blocks away. My first thought was the angle seemed nearly impossible, but whoever we're dealing with is pretty damn good."

"Is the patch identical?" asked Stone.

"Yep, exactly the same." Lightfoot continued. "There's a side note that we should be aware of. Witnesses in the shop said right before

Norhaus was shot, a teenage girl was forced into a van and driven away. From the way it was done, sure sounds like sex trafficking."

"She was in the City of Vernon, right?" asked Stone.

"Yeah, just south of downtown LA. Why?"

"We got to ask around. How many massage parlors are there in a five-mile, ten-mile radius?"

"Come on, Stone, it could be a twenty-minute van ride to the San Gabriel Valley, the San Fernando Valley. South to Orange County is quick from Vernon, depending on traffic." Jake sighed. "Let's start with the facts. The Norhaus-DeVito connection. What's the name of the massage parlor DeVito owns? The one we investigated?"

"Bangkok Massage," said Stone. "Check that and all of DeVito's other parlors as well."

"Just got to wade through all the phony companies he uses."

Stone wondered. "Next question. How come DeVito hasn't been brought in to give a statement yet?"

"His lawyer's stalling, buying time. Always typical of someone who has something to hide." Lightfoot shook his head.

"But I also have to ask," Stone continued, "since so much revolves around him how come he's still living? He knows all the victims or knows who they were."

"His estate was attacked by Ojos Negros. I'd say that was quite an effort to take him out," said Jake.

"Yeah, from everything we know it looks like Lil' Jo put the hit out on him. And now somebody shanked her. But I mean, how come the sniper hasn't singled him out?" wondered Stone.

"Maybe DeVito's on the list," said Kilbraide, "and there just hasn't been an opportunity. We should keep a close eye on him. Do a stakeout. Have him followed."

"Captain Harrell would never approve it," said Stone.

Jake suggested. "Okay. Sounds like Brannigan and Bostovich could spend their time slowly cruising the neighborhood."

"That's on you guys," mentioned Lightfoot. "I didn't hear a thing."

"Harold Mortensen wound up dead. He's a big money guy." Stone tapped his fingers on the table. "Was he an innocent bystander?"

"Could be, from everything I've pieced together," said Kilbraide. "I think he was collateral damage and the attackers were definitely after DeVito."

"How do you know?" Stone wondered.

"It's not the same M.O." noted Kilbraide.

"What'd you find out yesterday?" Stone asked him. "You interviewed the businesses next to the church where Thompson was killed?"

"Yeah, but didn't find out anything. Nothing really." Kilbraide hesitated. He glanced and fidgeted in his chair.

"What?" asked Stone. "Come on, damn it. Tell us."

"The dentist didn't have anything to say. The insurance agent was clueless. The last one was the financial planner and he wasn't in. I spoke to the assistant and she didn't know anything, either. Let's face it, everything happened on a Sunday. No one had seen anything unusual the previous week. The dentist was in on Saturday, but, again, nothing. I canvassed the businesses across the street and no one at the coffee shop had seen anything. Everyone else was closed."

"More dead ends," said Jake. "Hey, a pun."

Lightfoot rolled his eyes.

Kilbraide continued. "The financial planner called me and said he'd be in later this morning and that I could stop by."

"Good. Then do it," said Stone. "And let us know what you find. In the meantime, we've got to stop this gang warfare."

"Good luck with that. We should tell them that they're scaring off the tourists," said Jake.

"Not for much longer, I hope," Lightfoot replied. "From the Highway Patrol to Immigration, we've arrested and detained fourteen Ojos Negros thugs just in the last few days. Nabbed them driving in from Arizona and Nevada. Even caught two coming down from Oregon."

"Good." Jake slowly applauded. "Only twenty-thousand more to go."

Kilbraide looked at his phone. "If you don't mind, I'm going to go ahead and take off."

***

Talking disturbed Kilbraide's thinking. He left the station lost in his own thoughts and drove to interview the financial planner. He could have told the guys about the picture he had seen on the financial planner's wall. But he wanted to dig into it on his own. He could tell that Stone's eyes were all over him, trying to figure him out.

Kilbraide arrived and parked outside the small professional building. Less than seventy-two hours after the attack and the church was still cordoned off, but the rest of the neighborhood was busy. People had work to do and a tragedy wasn't going to stop the world. After all, mini-tragedies were lived out every day whether they were fatalities in freeway accidents or loved ones fighting disease.

He walked straight to Suite C where *Live Well Financial Planning Group* was etched on a placard. He opened the door, and the office assistant greeted him.

"Hello. Detective Kilbraide, right?"

Chestnut brown eyes with a waterfall of brunette hair going over her shoulders. *Damn.*

"You got it." Kilbraide took in the surroundings in a split second and the nameplate on the desk. *Janet Perkins.*

A room behind the assistant had a long table and a few chairs. Must be the conference room. Nice paintings were hung. A glass wall separated the space with an office to the left. It had a desk, computer, and phone—and a guy working away. Must be him.

"Bob?" called Janet.

"Yeah?"

Behind the man was the picture Kilbraide had seen, a World War One era photo of a Marine known as Sergeant Major Daniel Daly. Only people steeped in military lore would know about the man who had become a legend in the Marine Corps. And in a corner was a baseball glove, bat and softball.

"Detective Kilbraide is here." She announced him with an endearing smile.

The man got up from behind his computer and stood in the doorframe. He was muscular, in good shape, and obviously worked out. About five-feet nine inches wearing khaki slacks and a blue, long-sleeve shirt. Glasses that matched sandy-brown hair. Business casual, yet he stood sharp and crisp. The only thing missing was a salute. He would have looked right at home in a military uniform. *Marines, no doubt.*

"Hello, Detective, I'm Bob Stevens, what can I do for you?"

They shook hands.

"Got some questions."

"Okay, sure. I have an appointment in about fifteen minutes. But come on in."

Kilbraide stepped into the office and Stevens motioned to a chair facing the desk. "Have a seat."

"Thanks."

A jar of mints was positioned at one corner of the desk. Stevens slid into his seat. "Quite a shock, huh? Sunday?"

"Yeah." Kilbraide glanced around. A university degree and financial planning credentials hung on a wall adjacent to the Marine photo. "Must feel odd coming in to work knowing what happened."

"Weird, for sure. Not every day that a sniper attacks someone in the city."

"Did you notice anything unusual last week?"

Stevens shook his head. "No, sorry. I'm in and out a lot. This is a tough one, huh?"

"Tough?"

"Frustrating. A long process." Stevens folded his hands together for a minute. He wore a wedding ring.

"Tedious, that's for sure." Kilbraide noticed a photo of Stevens rounding third base in what looked like a Metro league softball game. "You got a couple of interesting pictures."

"Thanks."

"Looks like you had a big moment in that one." Kilbraide pointed.

"Hit a grand slam."

"Was that this season?"

"Yeah. A few weeks back."

"I heard about it. You guys are in the Eastern division."

"Yeah." Steven sounded interested. "We're pretty good this year. How did you know?"

Kilbraide nodded. "I'm on a team in the Western division. We really suck. A few injuries. Guys busy doing their work. We plummeted to last place."

"I always liked baseball."

"You play as a kid?"

"Of course. Did well. I got a scholarship to play in college. Shortstop for Pepperdine. Pretty good with the bat."

"Very good. A scholarship, huh?"

"Yep. Got some nibbles from the pros. Saint Louis was interested until I got injured. Took cleats right in the kneecap during a double play."

"Ouch," Kilbraide winced.

"Yeah, cut my legs out from underneath me. Tore ligaments. The pain just consumed me."

"No kidding?"

"Yeah. For months and months. ACL was torn and the meniscus."

"And there went your baseball career?"

"Yeah. But on one hand I didn't mind. I was good, but there were guys better than me. The Cardinals already had good shortstops in Double A and Triple A, so I felt my chances of turning pro really weren't very good."

"So what'd you do?"

Stevens smiled. "I found out that a degree from Pepperdine was something the military appreciated. Made my way to the Marines as an officer. Worked in intelligence."

"No kidding?" Kilbraide smiled. "Jarheads have military intelligence?"

"You bet, we're deadly grunts," laughed Stevens. "But contrary to popular belief we fight as much with our brains as we do with our brawn."

"Good to know." Kilbraide's hunch was confirmed. He pointed to the picture on the wall. "Is that a photo of the *fightingest Marine ever?*"

Stevens smiled. "Sure is. How do you know?"

"I got a thing for military history. I mean, I like sports. I like playing them. Softball, basketball. But the real warriors. The guys who live and die protecting our country. They've always fascinated me."

"Me, too."

"So why the photo?" asked Kilbraide.

"Sergeant Major Daniel Daly. He fought at his best when the odds were against him. He led a counterattack in World War One near the Marne River in France. Battle at Belleau Wood. He charged yelling out, 'Come on you son of a bitches. Do you want to live forever?'"

"Fascinating," said Kilbraide.

"He was quite a man. Fighting was his life. He saw action all over the globe. The Spanish-American war, Haiti, the Boxer Rebellion in China and then World War One. An amazing feat considering how travel was so much slower back then."

"Why do you think he did it?" asked Kilbraide.

Stevens looked thoughtful and considered the question. "That's who he was. A warrior. Fought to save others. To help others."

"You find that inspiring then?"

"I do. You know, one guy against the world type of thing. That's why I do what I do. Running my own office. An entrepreneur. I help people make money. Build their wealth. Preserve their assets. So they can take on the world. And the nice thing is I don't sit behind a desk all day. Like yesterday. I took the Jet Ski out and then saw a client." Stevens lobbed a question at Kilbraide. "So what about you? Army, I'm guessing."

"Yep."

"I understand," Stevens grinned. "Not everyone's cut out for the Corps."

Kilbraide smiled at the jab.

"Always nice to meet a vet. We got something in common."

"I was a marksman," Kilbraide offered.

"A sniper, huh?"

"Call it what you will."

Stevens sounded upbeat. "All kinds of ways to serve our country." He smiled. "Hey, I want to show you something in my car. Things I've collected. You got a minute?"

"Sure do. You were the one short on time."

"My client's always late." Stevens got up. "Come on." He led Kilbraide out the door. "My car's in the garage right over there."

"Do all the businesses around here use that one?"

"Yeah, it comes with the rent we pay. Got something in the trunk you'd like to see. Some memorabilia."

"Yeah?" Kilbraide eyed the structure, unsure why Stevens would lead him there. "Sounds interesting." He patted his gun. Just in case.

Stevens walked calmly. He pointed to the coffee shop across the street. "Good stuff over there. The owner's a Vet, too. Lost his leg to an IED."

"That sucks," answered Kilbraide.

"Yeah. He opened the coffee shop to help other Vets."

"That's what they told me when I was over there. Inspiring, isn't it?" Kilbraide kept pace.

"Absolutely." Stevens led the way to his car, a four-door Nissan Sentra parked halfway up the first level.

Nice middle-of-the-road vehicle, thought Kilbraide. *Not flashy.*

Stevens opened the trunk and inside was a square box, an old *footlocker.* He opened it and showed Kilbraide a variety of patches. "They're all from World War One."

Kilbraide studied them. "They look original."

"They are. Thought you'd like to see them. I had an older client who had them passed down from her father who was in the Marines."

"And she let you have them?"

"I handled her estate after she died. None of her kids wanted them and I've been trying to figure out what to do with them. Out on I-10 is the Patton Museum. Just east of Palm Springs. I've been meaning to drive out there and donate them."

"That'd be a good place for them." Kilbraide scanned the trunk. A pair of dusty baseball cleats and a biking helmet. "You bike, huh?"

"Yeah. I like to get out as much as I can."

"You take the wife—and kids?" asked Kilbraide.

"That'd be nice, wouldn't it?" Stevens closed the footlocker. "Wife passed away not too long ago. We never had kids."

"Sorry to hear that."

Stevens closed the trunk.

"Thanks for showing those to me. Very cool." Kilbraide looked around. "So if there were any people acting suspicious who were walking in and out of here or unusual vehicles would you have noticed them?"

"Possibly. But I'm only in my office about fifty percent of the time. The other time is out seeing clients and networking for new business."

"So nothing put you on the alert?"

"No. Not a thing." Stevens checked his watch. "It's been great talking to a brother in arms, but I need to get back. Sorry I couldn't be of more help."

"That's fine. If I have more questions, I'll be in touch."

"Sure. Whatever you need to ask." Stevens walked with Kilbraide from the garage and back to the building. "I hope you get things straightened out."

"Yeah," said Kilbraide. "It's not going to be easy."

"I'm sure." Stevens stood near the front door of the building. "Looks like my client's here." He motioned to a classic Jaguar parked along the sidewalk. "But you're welcome to come in and hang out if you need to."

"No, thanks. I'm fine for now."

"Okay." Stevens smiled and gave a casual salute. "Good luck, solider. And thanks for what you do."

"Have a good day," said Kilbraide. Stevens started waking inside and Kilbraide called out to him. "Hey, since you did intelligence why do you think a church-going man who was with his wife and kids was murdered?"

"I wish I could explain human nature, but I can't. It's a question for the ages." Stevens walked inside and closed the door behind him.

Kilbraide stared at the closed door. He had interviewed the dentist and the people in the insurance office. They shook their heads in confusion at the tragedy with eyes filled with despair and mumbled about life not being fair as they went about their work. Stevens had a more matter-of-fact air about him and his answers were concise and, as Kilbraide considered, clean and clear. Too clean and no emotion whatsoever to make him stumble over his words.

CHAPTER TWENTY-EIGHT

Marty Brannigan steadied himself on the ladder and gave a thumbs-up to his friend, Luis Gutierrez. Life's twists and turns were funny, mused Marty. A decade ago, he arrested Luis who was a teenager getting in trouble. But the kid had a winning personality and he helped Luis start his own business by mowing lawns. Word got around that Luis was reliable and he quickly matured into the busy owner of a full-fledged landscaping operation.

"I got it. Thanks." Marty was higher than what he had anticipated, about twenty-five feet above the sidewalk.

"You sure?"

"Yeah." Marty took a breath to calm his nerves.

Luis waved, headed to a different ladder, and clambered up the opposite side to trim a network of branches. He grabbed a chainsaw from one of his crew members and started slicing off dead wood.

Retirement from the police force was more exciting than Brannigan had ever expected. Posing as a tree inspector for a university's climate change project, he had dressed in coveralls for the event. He felt like a hero when leaving the house and Mary Ann's adoring kiss remained fresh on his lips.

He had come up with the idea of working with Luis after noticing the oak trees and Chinese elms that had branches dangerously close to telephone wires and hovering above parked cars. In Encino, the newest BMWs, Audis and Mercedes could fall victim to branches downed in high winds. He told his friend that he was working on a sensitive project and needed to access a few trees that just happened to be looking over DeVito's estate. He confided in Luis and mentioned it was a project that needed doing without asking questions.

Brannigan reached in his pocket and took out a few small devices to place at an angle. This was the final installment that he would do with the mini-cameras. Brannigan had been crawling up and down in trees all morning and placed cameras strategically, nearly surrounding DeVito's sprawling grounds. Nothing would go unnoticed. The estate looked back in order, as though a firefight had never happened.

Technology was getting more incredible by the minute. He reached with two hands to place the cameras on a limb and the ladder seemed to shake. An earpiece let him chat with Mary Ann, housed safely at a computer screen back home. She'd be able to tell if the video was coming through clearly and showed the intended target.

"It's off just a bit," said Mary Ann.

Marty never minded heights before and had even rescued cats stuck in trees during his time on patrols. He was surprised how rusty he felt, but it had been a while since he had clambered somewhere high.

"You sure?" he asked.

"I only see DeVito's wall and not above it."

Brannigan's knees felt like jelly. He reached and fiddled with the camera. "How's that?"

"A little better," said Mary Ann.

"What?" Brannigan's voice quivered.

"I still can't see above it."

"Come on, Mary Ann. What about the other cameras?"

"Those are fine, Marty. But they show the house and garage. They don't show the entrance. I thought this would be the easiest one to install."

He wanted to tell her that this project was more tiring than he thought. Hell, he wanted to be a hero. But he also didn't want to fall two stories. "All right, all right." He reached and felt his foot slip forward. Brannigan caught himself and took a breath.

"Still the same."

"I haven't touched it, Mary Ann."

"Oh, sorry."

He looked toward DeVito's estate. Through the tree branches he could see people walk between the house and garage. And then he noticed a reflection in the nook of a small branch. A closer look revealed a lens of a camera that was about the size of a quarter and sat camouflaged on the branch.

Did I do this? An old-age moment crept in and he wondered if he had placed it. Or was it already there?

Brannigan shivered with the thought that someone else was surveilling DeVito. He struggled to take his cell phone from his pocket, trying to snap a picture, and feeling his toes ready to slip off a rung of the ladder.

"What are you doing?" asked Mary Ann.

"Hold on," Brannigan muttered. He took a few pictures of the hidden camera and then carefully picked up the device. The underside had a model and serial number. He snapped a photo of it. Brannigan considered pocketing it to show Stone and Jake, but decided against it. *Who the hell does this belong to?* He set it back, made sure it was secure and shot a few more pictures. *Curiouser and curiouser.* He tried to think of who else would be watching DeVito as he finished his own installing.

"Hey, Marty, you about done up there?" Luis was back down on the ground.

"Yeah, yeah. Just another minute."

A delivery truck pulled to DeVito's gate and he noticed a guard step out and look in his direction as though sensing something. So much could happen at any moment. The fate of western civilization didn't rest on Brannigan's shoulders but if he could get some intel to Stone and Jake—then just maybe there'd be fewer deaths.

The man at the guard gate appeared to sign something and he let the delivery truck through. Within moments it had gone toward the house, stopped for mere seconds to drop off a package, and headed back toward the street.

He adjusted the camera again.

"How's that?" he asked Mary Ann.

"Perfect."

CHAPTER TWENTY-NINE

Video streamed from the cameras that Brannigan had placed in the tree, showing normal activity around DeVito's home. "Nice, huh?" Scratches on Brannigan's neck and forearms along with tree bark down his shirt was the price to pay for his work. The cost was worthwhile as he sat in his kitchen holding court with Stone, Jake, Lightfoot and Kilbraide.

"Good work," said Stone.

"This is a bit illegal and I haven't seen any of this," said Lightfoot, keeping his involvement off the record. "But I do want to know what's going on."

"So what about the other camera?" asked Stone.

"You saw my pictures, right?" asked Brannigan.

"Yeah."

"It's not easy to find." Brannigan hit the search engine on his computer and pulled up the website for his favorite video surveillance supply company. "I've heard about it but, see, this site is so big it even sells to municipal accounts, but they don't have it listed." He scrolled from top to bottom, stopping on various product images. "Mary Ann and I kept poking around and we found it mentioned on a forum on another website."

He pointed to an online discussion of the mini-LRC version 2. The cost put the device in an elite price range and the camera could zoom in and out better than any other model. Its night vision capability was excellent and it came complete with a directional mic and had sophisticated motion and heat sensing capabilities to focus on a subject. Even though the lens was about the size of a quarter, the peripheral range was amazing. Whoever put it in the tree had a nice sweeping view of DeVito's estate.

"Ojos Negros didn't put this up there," said Kilbraide. "They wouldn't need to. Their tactics are swarm and kill. This was a strategic move. Somebody's studying DeVito."

"Our sniper?" asked Jake.

"Could be."

Brannigan scrolled to the bottom of the site but didn't find a "Contact Us" link. This wasn't an e-commerce site set up for ranking high in the search engines. A phone number was listed in the footer, in small print. Brannigan called, got through, said he was a private investigator and convinced the person that he'd like to see a demo of the camera. "He said, 'Come on by.' So let's go."

Stone decided that Kilbraide should go with Brannigan, then report back on what they found. The shop was located in Sun Valley, wedged between two of the dirtiest car parts places in all of Southern

California. The building was one-story with a brown exterior as though it was built to blend in with the frequent dust clouds that hovered over the street.

Brannigan and Kilbraide pulled into the lot, parked, and walked to the front door where there was one simple sign that read *Electronics*. Brannigan pressed a buzzer on the doorframe under the watchful lens of a security camera and after a moment there was a *click*. He opened the door and inside was a throwback to an era of televisions needing repair, old personal computers, and radios. A glass counter ran lengthwise with an old-fashioned silver desk bell on top. Grime was everywhere. "Hello?" called Brannigan. No answer. He tapped the bell. No sound. There was a room in the back, and he thought a noise came from it. "Hello?"

"Coming," came a soft voice from around the corner. A man who was much older than Brannigan shuffled up to the counter. He looked surprised to see actual people. "Can I help you?"

"I hope so," said Brannigan. "I'm the one who called on the mini-LRC."

The man nodded. He wore thick glasses and chewed gum. "Yeah. I forgot to tell you that we're out of stock. I don't carry too many of them."

"Oh, not very popular?"

"They're popular enough. But you can see that I got a lot of older parts to clear out."

Kilbraide spoke up. "Haul it off to those e-waste collection days that the city does."

The man smiled. "Yeah, that's right. Toss it out. Or find ways to make use of things. Which is what I do."

"What do you mean?" asked Brannigan.

"Oh, I tinker a lot. Take old parts, find ways to make them work. I turned an old black and white RCA television into high definition."

"Yeah?"

"Sure did." He laughed. "Sold it to a celebrity for a party they had. They showed old films on it. But I'm not able to say who the customer was."

"Sure," said Kilbraide. "You keep things confidential. I get it."

"Hell, that's not it," said the man. "I can't remember who it was."

Brannigan and Kilbraide exchanged smiles. Then Brannigan glanced around and ideas for new surveillance equipment flowed through his mind until he got back on point. "So how many cameras do you normally sell in a month?"

"Depends on how many people buy them."

Kilbraide pulled out his phone. "We found this one and wanted to see who may have bought it." He showed the man pictures with serial numbers.

The man coughed and took a close look. "Yeah, that definitely looks like one I sold. What do you want with a mini-LRC?"

Kilbraide pulled out his badge. "Police business."

"Yeah, that figures." The man then glanced at Brannigan. "You a cop, too?"

"I was. For about forty years. Now, I do a little private investigating."

"I keep my customer records confidential—when I can remember who they were," said the man.

"Always?" asked Kilbraide.

"I make exceptions, you know, for the right price."

"You want a little cash?" asked Brannigan.

The man smiled. "And get busted for bribery? Right."

"He's the cop, I'm not."

The man looked at Brannigan. "Private eye, huh?"

"Surveillance when necessary."

"Maybe we can cook up something new for you." He looked at both men. "Okay, hold on. I'll be right back." The man shuffled away, banged around in the back, and returned to the counter with a shoebox of receipts. He pulled one out of the box and slapped it down on the glass. "Here's one."

"Rose Pietro?" asked Brannigan.

"Her husband produced a few films, B movies mostly. His life was as cliché as his storylines. You know, hooking up with his leading ladies."

Kilbraide grabbed the slips and shuffled through them. "This is from last year. Well, look at this." His voice rose quickly as he recited the address of Bob Stevens' financial practice, but the customer name was illegible. The purchase slip showed five cameras.

"Do your customers show you ID?" Kilbraide asked the man.

The guy shrugged. "If they've got enough cash or their credit card is approved, I don't bother. I mean, come on, they're buying a camera. Not a gun."

"Let's go," Kilbraide told Brannigan. "Thanks for your help."

"That's it?" The man looked bewildered.

"Yep," replied Kilbraide, "we got what we needed."

Brannigan shook the man's hand. "Marty Brannigan. Don't forget me, I'll be back."

"Sure. Back for what?"

"Never mind," Brannigan hustled out the door after Kilbraide.

CHAPTER THIRTY

After dropping off Brannigan and stopping by the station, Kilbraide once again stood on the hill in Griffith Park overlooking the equestrian trail. Whoever fired had to aim through a tangle of trees, across a road that was popular with joggers and bikers, and busy with cars traveling to the zoo. The round had to be sent at exactly the right moment. Precision was necessary.

The terrain was uneven. The shooter likely worked alone. Where would a spotter be, unless someone was stationed elsewhere giving coordinates and the target's location? *Unlikely.*

Kilbraide was impressed with the self-discipline that was needed to patiently chart individual movements and activities. That alone was a massive task even if the shooter had a lot of time to plan and stalk the pattern of the victim. Each person only had twenty-four hours in a day, and this is where someone like Bob Stevens had an advantage.

Financial planners were a select group of professionals who had access to personal information about a client. They handled money and, depending on how friendly they were, could get to know about their client's desire to make more money, or their financial setbacks. In many cases, they would know personal habits, hobbies, and schedules. Clients could find a quiet office a safe space to open up about their goals and dreams.

Taking out Scott lying by the side of his pool was challenging enough, yet that was easy compared to the other murders. Kilbraide ran each victim through his mind, marveling about how the location of death was intimate. A shot was only taken if it would be a hit; one shot equaled one kill. More surviving family members and co-workers had been interviewed, but still no one knew about any previous attempts on the victims' lives.

A jogging path along the beach at dawn. A warehouse when the victim was getting into her car and the shooter disappeared like a ghost leaving absolutely no trace. Firing into a crowded church and knowing Thompson was sitting near a window, he couldn't even see him. Talk about confidence. And here, in a public park.

Kilbraide was drawn to Griffith Park, the site of the third murder. Miles and miles of trails and roads crisscrossed the area. He pictured where the sniper shot from and a triangle formed in his thoughts. One part of it was the road that came down from the Griffith Park Observatory and led to Forest Lawn Drive and the freeway. The other segment was the road that was at the base of the hill and ran parallel to the equestrian path. The sniper positioned himself on the hillside between both roads.

The vantage point for the gunman was excellent. Kilbraide calculated the time from when the shot was fired to when the shooter fled. An expert marksman could break down the weapon in less than five seconds. He counted with his fingers and imagined the chaos below. *One-thousand one, one-thousand two, one-thousand three.* With people engulfed in confusion and cowering in fear of their own lives, the gunman could easily walk away unnoticed. *Why leave the patches?*

Meanwhile the people on the ground where the victim was murdered would need at least a few minutes to recover from their incredible shock. The first instinct would be to rush to the victim and wonder what the hell happened before calling 9-1-1.

A fast response from the police would be three to four minutes.

Count on ten minutes minimum for the police to start hunting the shooter. And that would be fast.

Kilbraide urged Stone, Jake, and Lightfoot to get more information on Stevens. Why? They had wanted to know.

Because he was in and out of his office with an assistant who worked part-time. She would know his meeting schedule but wasn't around to closely track or know his whereabouts. Kilbraide sought out his own fraternity of fighting men. None of the marksmen that he knew, or had known, lived around Los Angeles. He had driven two hours south to Camp Pendleton and then over three hours north-east into the desert where Twentynine Palms, the largest marine base in the United States, was located. He did a round of extensive interviews that turned up nothing. No one at either base, and no one at the shooting range near Barstow, had ever seen or heard of a Bob Stevens.

A vibe certainly wasn't enough for building a case—*or was it?*

Kilbraide came back to the moment and the surroundings. Parking along the road leading down was allowed, but it wasn't likely the shooter would have stopped there. A car parked for several minutes in a place where there were no restrooms or entrances to hiking trails would have drawn attention. Kilbraide inspected the brush and growth. A bike could fit beneath one of the bushes. Quiet and quick. Just like the other getaways. The rifle could easily have been broken down and fit into a backpack. A man riding these trails and wearing a backpack would look quite normal. Anyone passing up or down the road, either a motorist, a runner, or a walker wouldn't have known about the shooting down below.

If the assailant was in good shape and had used a bike, that person could have flown down the hill in less than thirty seconds, taken a left at the bottom and headed along Forest Lawn Drive and be more than a mile away by the time police arrived on the scene. Given the terrain, it was impossible to detect footprints or bike tracks.

Kilbraide looked up the slope where the road was steep and winding. Someone could have headed that way as well, pedaling hard to the top and coasting down the other side to Los Feliz Boulevard. But that would have been a slower and more difficult route.

Stevens had a biking helmet and cycling shoes in his trunk. He seemed good-natured, which was hardly the personality for a killer. And he was wearing eyeglasses when Kilbraide met him. This shooter had to have perfect vision.

A couple of possibilities existed. Kilbraide knew a friend who wore glasses as a fashion accessory, not because she needed a prescription. Her eyes were just fine. What about Stevens?

Kilbraide got in his car and drove down the road he had been inspecting so closely. With the afternoon sun chasing the clouds away, he drove to the softball fields and parked. He got out, made his way to the diamond, and surveyed the players. This was a deciding game to see who would make the playoffs. He stood near a row of bleachers and turned, surprised, at the greeting.

"Detective, how are you?"

It was Bob Stevens. Hat, glove, spikes. He was fit and looked upbeat, ready to play. He smiled. "Wishing you guys were in the game?"

"Certainly am. I was just in the area and came to watch a few innings."

"Well, I would have bought you a ticket, but the seats are free. Courtesy of the Los Angeles Department of Parks and Recreation."

"Hey, Bob. Let's warm-up." Someone called from the outfield.

"I'd love to chat but got to go." Stevens gave a playful salute with the ball glove on his hand.

"Understood. Go get 'em."

Stevens trotted off and Kilbraide sat in the stands. *A vibe's a first step in building a case.* He watched Stevens toss the ball in the outfield. How deep was his client base? Did he have many friends? And, wondered Kilbraide, how did his wife die?

CHAPTER THIRTY-ONE

The aroma of the bar brought memories back to Arturo. Life was changing and he could certainly tell that by the look in the eyes of his buddy. Johnny Delgado sat across from him with beer mugs between them. Johnny listened. He was another one of the original Victor Boyz.

"I can't believe we lasted as long as we did," mused Johnny.

"Me, neither." Arturo swigged his beer.

"Lil' Jo and Ronaldo, dead. What a shame. And Angel. *Pendejo.* He got careless."

The Victor Boyz did petty thefts and crime when they were younger. Some had immigrated with their families from Mexico while others grew up in the Valley. Angel was the visionary and saw how the gang could operate businesses – some legit, others not – to supply an income stream for years to come.

Life didn't work out that way. Angel wanted to be in charge of everybody, but his vision was too big for his ability and he gave an old school crime network an opportunity to exploit him.

"He wasn't like you, Arturo," said Johnny. "Angel was all talk."

"He tried. Did you hear about it?"

"What? That he got killed in Santa Monica?"

Arturo studied Johnny. "Yeah, on the pier. Do you know why?"

"Some drug deal gone bad."

"That's putting it mildly. That house he was living in, he wanted to turn it into a grow house for his own weed. He had a lot of money to pay me and the crew to set it up. I heard you took over his vending machine route, right?"

"Yeah. I made it profitable. Even though I got to pay a monthly extortion fee to stay in business. Worse than the unions. It's hard work."

"Well, get this," Arturo continued. "Angel was setting himself up with all these businesses and then have other people run them. A network of vending machines for you. Lil' Jo and me were going to take over the cannabis dispensaries once he got them up. It was all evolving. Except he fucked up. Got in with the wrong people."

"It happens."

"But they wanted him. Angel had connections in Mexico that I didn't know about. He worked to get a major shipment of cocaine up from South America and told me about it. I discovered that it wasn't his to begin with. He said he had a buyer and he was going to cut out his boss. He stole it from the people he was forced to work with. Scared the hell out of me. I went along with it, though. We divided up the shipment between Lil' Jo, me, and Angel. Fuck, we each had a ton of coke and we were going to meet at one place. Except I bailed. I had a feeling it was a fucked-up deal."

"You bailed? You did that to your friends? Why the fuck you talking to me?"

"They're dead and I'm not. So that's a pretty good reason. I stashed it at—someplace safe. Spent all night working on it. I was going to tell Angel, but he got dead. So I sold the coke and, believe it or not, did some good with it in Mexico."

"Like what?"

"I built a school. And then came back up and was able to buy Angel's house for next to nothing."

"Dawg, why are you telling me?" Johnny looked around.

"The protection you pay for using the machines goes to the same people that Angel was dealing with. That's what got this shit started in the first place. Angel started smuggling small amounts of coke in candy bars."

"What are you talking about, *vato*?"

"Believe me. They got their fingers in everything. Nickel and dime shit like what you're doing. Massage parlors, bowling alleys. Marijuana dispensaries. Hell, the car dealerships up Sepulveda Boulevard could all be owned by them."

"Again, why are you telling me all this?" Johnny fidgeted.

"I didn't sell all of it. I held a little back for insurance. Dawg, I still have a half-ton of coke, but I want out."

Johnny gave a low whistle. "Half a ton?"

"Yeah, the guy who helped me last time was killed by that sniper dude and I need someone to handle it for me."

"Don't look at me, dawg." Johnny's eyes were wide with fear and he looked sideways like he was ready to bolt.

"I can get a lot of money for it."

"Yeah, you can also get life in prison or gunned down in the streets." Johnny sipped his beer.

"Come on, it's my last deal. People are screaming for it, but it's in short supply."

"I guess that's what happens when gangs murder each other."

"Tragedy creates opportunity. I want to get out and be gone."

"I don't want to know about it. Look, Arturo. I'm getting married soon, my girlfriend's pregnant with twins, dawg. I'm going to be a papa."

"And I got a wife and couple of kids of my own in Zacatecas. I get it. I spoke to her, she's scared to death, and wants me home as soon as possible. I need to move this stuff and then go back to her with a clear conscience."

"I'm selling stupid candy and sodas in machines. I'm going to school at night—you're talking to the wrong person."

"I need your help."

Johnny yanked twenty dollars from his pocket. "I'll give you this. I pay for our drinks and I get the hell out of here."

"Johnny, wait."

He didn't listen. He pushed back from the table. "I don't want any part of this. I don't want to hear a thing. I don't want me and my family to end up as Mexican stew." He stood and walked outside.

Arturo signaled to the server. "Your money's on the table." He followed Johnny outside to the parking lot. "Come on, dawg. I'm not asking you to do anything illegal. Nothing. I just need a name. Come on, we're homies. Get me an introduction and you walk, that's all."

"Really?" Johnny laughed. "On a good week, I collect a thousand dollars from all the junk that people eat or drink. Maybe a little more. Out of that I pay my gas, taxes, food. Rent."

"Dude, I'll pay you. Just give me a name and you'll walk with enough money to put your babies through college," said Arturo.

Johnny thought about it. "A name and that's it?"

"That's it."

"And I get visits from the cops and Ojos Negros comes knocking on my door. And you'll see me on the five o'clock news hanging over the freeway. Or, if I'm lucky, I get locked up until I die."

"Not going to happen. I take all the risk and *I didn't* get the name from you. You know me, dawg."

"Yeah, right. You stole from your homies and you expect me to trust you?" Johnny walked to his car. A Honda Civic.

"Dude, we go back. I'm not going to do you wrong and, besides, I know a really good lawyer. You won't get thrown in prison. Look, I need this, Johnny. Remember the time you hooked up with that guy's girlfriend? He was fixing to kill you, but I stepped in, told him it was me that nailed her, and he beat the shit out of me."

"You're bringing that up?" Johnny laughed.

Arturo smiled. "I saved your ass. You owe me. That guy would've killed you."

"I do this and that's it." Johnny got in his car, gripped the steering wheel, and looked at Arturo. "DeVito."

CHAPTER THIRTY-TWO

Grainy footage blown up to dimensions that were only possible in the digital age showed a figure with what looked like an outline of a backpack hauling a Jet Ski out of the water in Marina del Rey. They checked on who stored that type of watercraft at the marina, but no leads turned up. The lighting was dark and the angle made the video inconclusive. Stills from surveillance footage gathered throughout Griffith Park showed a biker in the distance with what looked like an outline of a similar backpack to the one in Marina del Rey. Angles from Travel Town, the Gene Autry Museum, and the Los Angeles Zoo also showed plenty of cars, joggers and other bikers.

Agent Lightfoot, Kilbraide, and Jake studied it carefully. There was information but not much could be done with it. Nothing unusual came back from Lightfoot's search of public records in Washington, D.C. "Robert Stevens certainly looks like he sat at a desk during his brief career with the Marines," said Lightfoot. "He was born in Topeka,

Kansas and then moved out here and went to college at Pepperdine. Played ball and then joined the service. Just like he said." Lightfoot tapped his fingers on the conference table. "But there's a twist."

"What?" asked Kilbraide.

"The rest of his records are sealed and I can't figure out why."

Kilbraide had done several Internet searches on Robert Stevens and his business, Live Well Financial Planning Group. He was a member of Burbank's Chamber of Commerce and received several positive online reviews about his money management services. Kilbraide had re-visited the shooting range near Barstow, again taking his own gun for practice. He even viewed a list of the most recent members. Stevens' name wasn't on the list. Kilbraide couldn't ignore the gnawing in his gut. There were too many coincidences and something just wasn't right.

"So why would do you think a single guy in Los Angeles would want to murder rich people?" asked Lightfoot.

"Rich people who deal drugs," replied Kilbraide. "I also followed up on that Khalid guy who employed Thompson. He was totally shocked and knew nothing. He checks out clean. In fact, now looking at what Thompson did he would have had the guy charged with extortion. He runs an honest company."

"So why Stevens?" asked Lightfoot.

"Just a hunch," said Kilbraide. "A hunch that won't leave me."

"Then you got to figure out why," said Jake.

"He handles money and lots of it."

"What would his motive be?" asked Jake. "And could he, or anybody, pull off five deaths in completely different locations and only using a total of five bullets?"

"It would take an elite marksman to make it happen."

"But we can't confirm if that's what he was," Jake sounded frustrated. "His service records only say *Intelligence.*"

Stevens was registered with a financial planning society and his name was on file with the City of Burbank's business license and permits. Whoever did the shootings had to be as familiar with the layout of Los Angeles and the nuances of terrain as they were the lifestyle of the victims.

"So you think I'm looking at the wrong guy?" Kilbraide asked Jake.

"Not necessarily. Why would he do it? Like Lightfoot's wondering. Why would a single guy who's making money living in a city full of fun and beautiful women risk getting put away for life?"

"So what keeps you focused on Stevens?" asked Lightfoot.

"He likes the outdoors. He must know Griffith Park extremely well. He bikes."

"Does he Jet Ski?" asked Lightfoot.

"Yeah."

"Is he single?"

"He's a widower. Said his wife died, but he didn't say how."

"Let's dig in to how she died." Lightfoot pulled up an image. "I keep going back to what we know from the beach and how the medical examiner believes Zhuang's right temple got the initial blow from the shot. It's hard to imagine a gunman bobbing up and down on a watercraft."

"That would be tough," Kilbraide acknowledged.

"We tracked down some fishermen who were on the pier before sunrise. One said he heard what sounded like the whine of an engine, like a Jet Ski, but he didn't look around. Said it's not unusual to hear something that early in the morning."

"How about a speed boat?" wondered Jake.

"That'd risk drawing more attention," said Kilbraide.

"The shooter on a Jet Ski?" asked Jake. "Damn. The motion of the water, timing it. Is Marina del Rey the only place it'd launch from?"

"Will Rogers State Park has a boat launch and we asked around," said Lightfoot. "No one saw anything. The other option would be putting it in up north in Malibu, but it'd be in the dark. Marina del Rey to the south makes the most sense. The shooter would head north along the coast with no traffic while Zhuang would be jogging south. The shot is fired, all the attention goes on the victim, and the shooter jets away."

Jake explained how the trip was no more than a couple of nautical miles. He said that if the shooting occurred around six A.M., then whoever did it could have been back in the harbor before six thirty, easily.

He turned on the video again of the Jet Ski being taken from the water, but the camera was filming from a distance. The location was near the Trans-Pacific Yacht Club with docks guarded by locked gates. "Is that the only place in the Marina where there are surveillance cameras?"

"We can check. What's really got me is that when I interviewed Stevens, he offered that he was out on his Jet Ski after the shooting at the church. Like he was giving me information and daring me to ask about it. Then he showed me the collection of patches he had. Seriously, I still can't figure that one out. Seemed odd."

"What I would really like to know," said Lightfoot, "is why his service records are sealed."

"And what I would like to know," mentioned Jake, "is how well he can handle a rifle."

***

After showing his badge at the guardhouse, Stone drove up Frank DeVito's driveway, parked in front of the house and was greeted by a man with wide shoulders. The palatial estate convinced Stone that DeVito enjoyed the profits of drug money along with the profits of his many other businesses, investments, and enterprises. The fact that he had thrown parties on his yacht and the ones who attended were murdered was a damning allegation since each victim was tied to drugs and the last one trafficked humans as well.

The guard wore khaki slacks and a polo shirt that stretched over thick arms. He glared at Stone and behind him was a woman, Denise, wearing a skirt and blouse. "Detective Stone, good to see you again."

She waved and was friendly and acted quite professional. "Denise Everett." She offered her hand and Stone shook it.

"Yeah, I remember." The woman looked like someone who could have handled group tours at a place like the Getty Museum.

"Mr. DeVito is waiting."

"I'm glad to hear it."

She led him along the breezeway and past the pool where maintenance workers were restoring tiles to their original polish. She stepped inside the conference room. "Mr. DeVito, Detective Stone is here to see you. I'll be in my office if you need me."

"Thank you, Denise." DeVito sat holding a glass of red wine and a cigar lay beside him in an ashtray. He stood and shook Stone's hand. The ever-present head of security, Ryker, gave a nod.

"Detective, good to see you," said DeVito.

"I wish I could say the same, Frank."

"Ah, always one with a joke." DeVito sounded like he was meeting a pal. "I'd offer you something to drink, but guess you can't officially down anything since you're on the clock."

"That's correct," said Stone.

"Such a shame," remarked DeVito. "You work so many hours. It must be tough to act like a saint until you get off work."

"Who says I act like a saint?"

DeVito glanced at Ryker. "My friend and I will chat for a while privately."

"Sure thing, Mr. DeVito." He stepped out of the room.

DeVito looked serious when he addressed Stone. "We need law enforcement to uphold high standards just like the clergy and Boy Scout leaders. Otherwise, what would happen to society?" DeVito motioned for Stone to have a seat.

"We'd all become like you?" asked Stone.

DeVito scrunched his face in scorn, like the retort was hurtful. "Detective, detective. Don't think for a minute that I don't care about the law."

"I'm sure you care about it a lot." Stone observed DeVito's demeanor. "For a man whose beautiful estate was attacked, you sure seem relaxed."

"It's the red wine. Has many scientifically proven benefits."

"I'm sure it does," said Stone. "Does it prevent you from getting riddled by bullets?"

"Whatever are you talking about?"

Stone continued. "How'd you escape getting shot? A gang of foot soldiers from a drug cartel stormed your compound—"

"My estate—"

"—and sprayed the place with gunfire and you came out alive."

DeVito laughed. "You sound disappointed."

"You had a few guests who lost their lives."

"Yep, the deadliest dinner party I ever hosted." DeVito stayed straight faced. "A party to die for."

"It's funny?"

"Not at all. A little gallows humor is in order, otherwise being hunted while innocent can make one feel quite grim and morose."

"You sure know how to pick 'em, Frank. You seem to attract death wherever you are. Your dinner party here and that event you held on the yacht. You're aware that five of the individuals who were murdered by the sniper were all guests at your fundraising event?" Stone glanced around and said in a mocking tone. "I'm scared to be sitting here."

"Are you close to bringing anyone to justice?"

"I'm sure you're anxious to know."

"I am."

"I'll let you know the minute we do. But, first, since you haven't made the time to come down to the station and give your statement, I decided to drop by and review a few things with you."

"Wonderful."

Stone was getting ready to ask a question when Ryker came back into the room and whispered in DeVito's ear. He listened and for a moment, his eyes widened and then he shrugged. "Just say we'll call back in a bit."

Ryker nodded and left.

"Got business to take care of?" asked Stone.

"It can wait. Continue."

"Why, thank you. Someone ordered the assailants to attack your property. Correct?"

"Someone must have told them to." DeVito laughed. "It's not like they would have taken the initiative on their own. They just follow orders."

"Do you know who ordered it?"

"No, enlighten me."

"We suspect it was a woman who was being held in state prison. An associate who was in the warehouse with Anthony Angelino when it got raided."

"You going to follow up with her? Investigate her?" asked DeVito.

"We can't because she's dead. She was killed in the prison yard during exercise time."

"That's sad."

"It really is. And that young woman who was killed the night of your party, her sister was in the same prison and was also killed. Coincidence?"

"Strange world we live in," DeVito sounded wary. "Glad I'm not in prison. Lots of people getting killed in there."

"You see, as much as I hate to say it, I'm concerned for your well-being, Frank. I hate to see you murdered before I can put you in jail."

"You have a big heart, Detective."

"That's why I do what I do. And why I wanted to ask you about your fundraiser. Are you sleeping well at night?"

"Just fine. Thank you."

"You're not scared about being a target?"

"Should I be?" asked DeVito.

"You tell me," said Stone. He looked at DeVito. Each of the victims clearly had ties to smuggled drugs. Zhuang and Scott's logistics operation connected North America, Asia and South America with enough fentanyl to supply the globe. "Someone doesn't like what's going on."

"Apparently not," said DeVito.

"You had a connection to each of the victims."

"Yes, they came to parties I hosted. We've already established that. Detective, it sounds like you don't know who you're dealing with. Maybe you're in over your head."

Stone was annoyed. "And you did business with Darlene Cutchins."

"Very good. You've done some homework. Yes, I financed a couple of films with her." DeVito drank his wine. "Detective, I'm concerned about why a private citizen like myself has to undergo such scrutiny."

"Believe it or not, Frank, I don't want to see you get taken out by the *One-Shot Sniper.* So we're looking for motives. Any type of motive. With the kind of businesses you own, you've certainly angered and pissed off a lot of people. Jealous husbands or ex-boyfriends angry that their women are working in one of your massage parlors? Or serving at your bars? What about the drug dealers who hang out at those places?"

"You make it sound like I'm standing at the door checking IDs. And don't forget, Detective, I own fancy restaurants as well for the suit and tie crowd. I even own a winery." He took a sip from his glass.

"I know, you're an innocent man, Frank, and it's the rest of the world that's corrupt and out to get you."

"That could very well be the case," said DeVito.

"It could be," said Stone. "But I don't think it is." Stone paused. "So where's your wife? You concerned about her well-being?"

"She's fine. She's trotting around the globe like she always does." DeVito looked Stone in the eye and smiled. "Detective, I think you're pretty good at what you do. But when are you going to quit all this goody-two-shoes shit and come work for me? I can double or, hell, triple what you're currently making."

Stone was unimpressed. "Frank, I'm a cop. That's what I do. I arrest people like you."

CHAPTER THIRTY-THREE

Brannigan studied the feed from the camera while Stone was meeting with DeVito. He sat in the comfort of his lounge chair while the images streamed on to his laptop.

"Apple or cherry pie?" Mary Ann called from the kitchen.

"Toss me a beer."

"Marty, be serious. If it was evening that'd be fine, but we're on duty."

"Who's going to know? I thought that was a benefit of working from home." Brannigan chuckled. "Come here, Mary Ann. Look at this." He showed her the image of the driveway and the cameras zooming in and out around DeVito's property.

"What? Everything looks fine."

"Exactly. So a little beer isn't going to impair my vision. Or our vision. And neither is this." Brannigan reached and pulled Mary Ann onto his lap, giving her a passionate kiss. She met his lips but then pulled away.

"Marty." She got up and smoothed out her blouse and skirt.

"Oh, come on."

She giggled. "Apple or cherry?" She hurried to the kitchen.

"Cherry." Brannigan enjoyed the little bits of work that Stone and Jake sent his way. He and Mary Ann were keeping busy with requests from store owners wanting to protect their inventory, suspicious Hollywood-type spouses and even a boy down the street needing to locate his bicycle. Doing a stake-out at home with video streaming was definitely the way to go. And the best part was that the toilet was only a few steps away which was important for Brannigan when his prostate was acting up.

Mary Ann returned with a slice of pie.

"Hey, where's the ice cream?"

"I asked you to buy it. Remember?" Mary Ann settled next to Brannigan and downed a forkful of pie.

"Oh, yeah."

The video continued as it had for hours and hours with nothing unusual coming across the screen. Suddenly, the easy chair felt like it had Brannigan in its grip and he needed to escape. "I got to pee."

"Again?" Mary Ann was bewildered.

"What do you mean 'again?'" Brannigan answered. He set his pie aside and struggled out of the coziness of the chair. "It's already been—"

"About fifteen minutes," said Mary Ann.

"Oh, come on. A lot longer than that." He hurried to the bathroom that was just off the kitchen.

"You missed your physical last month."

He didn't like what she was implying. "I'm fine. There's no rush. Besides, I'm eating raw pumpkin seeds and it really helps my plumbing." Brannigan turned on the light, closed the door and started doing what he needed when Mary Ann screeched like she had just witnessed something terrible. He finished in a hurry, making a mess across the toilet seat and stepped out. "What was that?"

"There's a face." She nearly choked on her slice of pie.

"A face?" Brannigan hurried back to his chair. "What?" The video stream was exactly as it was when he left. "What face?"

"It was there."

"Where?"

Mary Ann sounded annoyed. "Up close. Right into the camera."

Brannigan took another bite of his pie. Several seconds went by and nothing. The video was as boring as ever. After a couple of minutes, he set his pie aside and figured he should clean up the mess in the bathroom.

"You're going again?" Mary Ann sounded concerned.

"No, I'm not 'going again.'" Brannigan stood and turned as Mary Ann gasped and pointed.

"There."

He whipped back around in time to see a face looking at the camera with a puzzled look and then moving in so closely that the face completely blocked the lens. "Holy smokes." The picture jiggled as Brannigan glanced around his chair. "Where's my phone?"

"I don't know."

And then the image stopped moving. Whoever was fiddling with the camera in the tree put it back, except the lens was now at an awkward angle. DeVito's estate looked cock-eyed.

Brannigan panicked at the fear of another attack with Stone in the compound. "Shit, Mary Ann. My phone."

"Use mine." She nearly dropped her pie as she grabbed her phone and punched a few numbers. Jake answered.

"Yeah?"

"Detective. Mary Ann Bostovich. There's someone in the tree outside DeVito's. We saw him looking in our camera."

"You what?"

"We saw someone looking into the surveillance camera in the tree overlooking DeVito's estate."

"When?"

"Just now," said Mary Ann.

"Who was it?"

"We don't know yet. Got to rewind everything."

"Damn, I'm just heading back to the station. Call Kilbraide."

"I don't have his number," said Mary Ann.

"Wait," yelled Brannigan, reaching beneath the chair's cushion and pulling out his phone. "Got it."

Suddenly the face appeared again, but just for a second and then it was gone. Brannigan punched Kilbraide's number.

CHAPTER THIRTY-FOUR

DeVito watched a closed-circuit monitor on the wall showing Stone leaving the property. He turned to Ryker who was standing near. "Okay, now tell me what the hell's going on."

"That guy who worked with Anthony Angelino wants to talk to you." Ryker held a smart phone.

"Great timing. Right in front of law enforcement. Why didn't you just deal with it?"

"It sounds urgent. He says you'd be interested in hearing what he has to say since it could solve the mystery of missing inventory."

"No kidding?" DeVito smiled. "Sounds like a call worth taking."

"I'll put him through."

DeVito settled at the conference table as Ryker punched a few numbers. "Go ahead. It's on speaker." Ryker set the phone down, scribbled notes, and pushed a pad of paper in front of DeVito.

"Mr. DeVito?" Arturo's voice was clear.

"That's me. And you are?" asked DeVito, glancing at the paper.
"Arturo."

"How are the wife and kids? I hear you're expecting another."

"You hear a lot."

"I do. So you were a co-worker with Anthony Angelino? And you have important information for me?"

"You can say that."

DeVito struck a cautionary tone. "Now don't bullshit me, just tell me what you got."

Arturo went to the point. "You hired him to transport a few tons of coke up here—"

"Whoa. Hold on, are you nuts saying something like that over an open line? I don't know what you're talking about."

Ryker interrupted. "Don't worry. The line's secure." He smiled. "That's why you pay me the big bucks."

"Okay, Mr. Arturo. Continue," said DeVito.

"I wanted you to know that the Feds didn't get all of the inventory that Angelino had."

"No kidding? What does that have to do with me?" DeVito asked, getting annoyed.

"Because I don't want it and I don't have any use for it."

"What do you mean, 'you don't want it?' Where is it?"

"It's safe with me. I'm not in the business, so I thought maybe you would like it."

DeVito got angry. "Maybe I would like it? That's very thoughtful of you. You could have sold it and kept the money for yourself and never said a thing. You're a real Good Samaritan," DeVito said sarcastically. "So you want to drop it by or do you want me to come pick it up?"

"Not so fast. We need to talk about it."

DeVito laughed. "You little prick. You want money? You want to sell my own coke back to me?"

"There's enough here that you could still make a good sixty to seventy million, but If you're not interested, I can find someone else."

"All right, smart ass. Sure, I'd like it. And what do you want for finding it?"

"A finder's fee. Say, ten percent."

DeVito liked the tone in the guy's voice. He sounded honest, if such people actually existed. "How do I know it's any good?"

"It's your coke, *dawg*. You only deal in the best. I sent a sample via courier to your front gate."

"When?"

"About thirty seconds ago. I just got confirmation it arrived."

"Hold on." DeVito motioned to Ryker who was scrolling through computer records. "Go check it out." DeVito was impressed with Arturo. "We'll do a little inspection here and I'll let you know what I think."

"I don't have time for games," said Arturo. "I'm a motivated seller and I know you don't like playing games, either."

"You act like you know a lot about me," said DeVito.

"I know enough. I don't need much to make me happy in the deal," said Arturo. "Here's what's important to me."

"I don't care what's important to you. So how do you want to do this?"

"I'll call you back this afternoon with details, but let's meet tomorrow. Not too far from your home at the Sepulveda Basin and I'll have the coke loaded in a van, all ready for you."

"You mean where the golf courses are?"

"And the lake and the wildlife reserve. Lots of places to have a quiet meeting for a few minutes without getting noticed. You give me a definite yes and plan on being there. Or else I hang up and there's no way in hell you're going to find me or ever see the product. Like I said, I've got plenty of buyers to choose from. I'm giving you first dibs."

"So how much of a fee do you want again?"

"Like I said, a mere ten percent, just like agents here in La La Land get for helping out their actors. Nothing extravagant."

"So you want to be a rich man?" mused DeVito.

"You probably got that much stashed under your bed."

"You're definitely a smart man."

"Do you want it or not?"

DeVito spoke slowly. "The answer is yes."

Ryker rushed in with a sampling of coke and gave DeVito a thumbs up.

"Just so you know, if something happens to me," warned Arturo, "the coke will vanish for good. Don't fuck with me or it's all gone."

"There's no need to play tough with me, Arturo. In fact, I've taken a liking to you during our conversation."

"Good to hear. Under-promise and over-deliver is what I like to do."

"Let's meet up and get this transaction taken care of."

"I'll be in touch."

The phone went dead.

Ryker looked at DeVito. "Do you want me to tell Denise to get the funds ready for transfer?"

"What are you talking about?" smirked DeVito. "I'm not paying that asshole a dime."

***

Brannigan hunched over his laptop, studying the voice levels on the screen. He ripped off his headphones and jumped out of his chair like someone had jolted him with electricity. He scrambled for his phone and called Stone.

"Yeah?" the answer was crisp.

"They're meeting tomorrow."

"Who?" asked Stone.

"DeVito and that Arturo guy."

"But I just left DeVito's," exclaimed Stone.

"Yeah, I watched you leave. And somebody was in the tree. Didn't you get the messages?

"No. What tree? What're you—"

"Never mind," Brannigan interrupted. "Just check your texts. Sounds like some exchange will happen."

"God, I hate texting. Marty, what do you mean an exchange?"

"Keep up, Stone." Brannigan spit it out. "Drugs, damn it. DeVito, Arturo. This is what you've been waiting for."

"You sure?"

"Yeah, I listened to their whole conversation."

"You what?" Stone was puzzled. "What are you talking about? How'd you—? You never cease to amaze me, Brannigan."

CHAPTER THIRTY-FIVE

Through his earpiece, Stevens listened to DeVito and Arturo while driving back to his office. *Work to do.* He pulled in front of his office, dashed inside, and hooked up his laptop. He kept an eye on Janet who was answering phones and sending emails to clients. A trusting young lady wanting a career in personal finance. But it was time to leave and do what he needed.

DeVito had been on his list for a long time and Balboa Park was as good a place as any to check him off. The speech-to-text translator captured the conversation and Stevens printed it off along with a map of the location and set the papers on his desk, inside a journal. He deleted the interaction from his computer and then used a program to wipe it out as cleanly as possible. Destroying the papers would be much easier than trying to hide a digital trail. A match to light it on fire was all that was needed.

Getting out of the office would be easy. Have all meetings cancelled. He pulled everything together and was ready to go when an older woman walked in. She stood at the receptionist desk, looked over to him, and waved.

***

Mary Ann felt quite accomplished. It had been over two years since she patrolled her neighborhood and called Detective Tom Stone and Jake Sharpe to investigate a shooting at Anthony Angelino's house. Then teaming up with Marty when he left the force gave the two of them the chance to play a part in Angelino getting busted and stopping a large shipment of cocaine.

She was determined to find out what Stevens was up to. Marty told her 'no,' but she protested. She swatted fear aside like a common house fly and snuck out while Marty made another all-too-frequent trip to the bathroom. She would be fine and he wouldn't stay upset too long, especially after a little kissy-face. The gleam in her eye faded as her thoughts came back to where she was standing. Murder and drugs, they went together. Only a short time had passed since the man they believed was Bob Stevens had scrambled down from the tree outside DeVito's estate.

"Hello?" Mary Ann said to the receptionist.

"Oh, hi." Janet glanced toward the desk where Stevens was shuffling through papers. "How can I help you?" She looked puzzled.

"I wanted someone to look over my finances. My schedule suddenly opened up today and I've heard so many good things about Mr. Stevens that I decided to stop right in."

Janet smiled. "That's nice. Did you have an appointment?" She opened a calendar.

"I won't take long." Mary Ann eyed the office. There was the photo of the Marine that Kilbraide had mentioned.

Stevens got up with his things, walked toward the front, and set his papers on Janet's desk. He greeted Mary Ann. "Hello."

"Hi. You're Bob Stevens?" She shook his hand.

"Yes."

Mary Ann noticed that he acted annoyed and not like the calm presence that Kilbraide described.

"Is Janet getting you what you need?"

"What I needed was just a few minutes with you."

"I'm afraid that's not possible right now."

Janet reached for a pen and accidentally scattered the papers.

Mary Ann picked one up that fell at her feet. It was a printout of a map showing the area around the 405 freeway and 101 freeway. "Here go."

As Stevens took the paper, she noticed a fresh scratch ran the length of his arm. "Wow, looks like you got a war wound."

He shuffled through the papers. "I was at home trimming bushes."

"Oh, I see. Anyway, I had questions about retirement accounts and wondered what you know about Roth IRAs." Mary Ann smiled.

Stevens looked agitated. "I'm sorry. I really don't have time right now. Janet can schedule your appointment."

"This won't take long."

He hurried back for his laptop and grabbed a jacket. "I've got to run."

"Something I should know about?" asked Janet.

"I forgot that I had a networking meeting." Stevens looked at Mary Ann. "Take my card and let's see if you can come back next week." He slid his laptop into a computer bag, headed out the door, and called back to Janet. "Hold my appointments."

"Yes, Bob."

He was gone.

Mary Ann noticed another paper sticking out from beneath the desk. Scribbled on it was *DeVito. Balboa Park*. She handed it to Janet who thanked her for it.

"What time next week would you like your appointment?"

Mary Ann thought. "You know, I need to check my schedule. I'll call you later." She stepped outside. Time to call Marty.

CHAPTER THIRTY-SIX

Arturo's bet that DeVito would go for the coke was a safe one. The man couldn't pass up tens of millions of dollars. He looked in the alley behind the house where a handyman was finishing painting the words *Vic's Window Washing* on the side of a white van. He sold a brick of coke on the street to a small-time dealer he used to hang with. The money paid for the vehicle and its paint job. He got a new phone, wired some cash to Marta, deposited some in his dad's account, and pocketed the rest.

Getting back to Mexico was all worked out. He would use the low rider that his dad had stored for him and then drive south through Imperial County. He'd head east to Arizona, and then cross the border below Yuma. Soon the long nightmare would be over, and he'd again wake with his wife in his arms and his children scampering across the floor. He was grateful that she had no interest in drugs or the lifestyle that came with it.

That was his goal, and this was the last obstacle to get through. The thought of DeVito paying him a fee was actually less appealing. He just wanted to get out of this deal alive. He thought of what Angel had told him about DeVito forcing him into a helicopter, and then fighting for his life before killing and tossing out the three *pendejos* who tried to throw him to his death.

But that was Angel. He attracted high stakes drama and even seemed to thrive on it. Arturo felt that he kept a level head with people. *What if DeVito tries something?* He assured himself it wasn't likely, but he had carefully mapped out the park to make a safe exit.

Now that he had the rest of the coke loaded in the van, he'd lock the house up until he could return with his family. That was in the future, but now he had to focus on this moment since that was all he had.

He replaced the flooring in the kitchen and thought about everything that could go wrong. What if DeVito tried to cheat him or kill him?

That's not going to happen. Stop being paranoid, dawg.

But DeVito had a reputation and he wondered how many men and women had been flown on a helicopter and kicked out over the High Desert; bodies that were never recovered, beautiful people who became food for coyotes, vultures, and the occasional mountain lions that wandered down from the north-facing slopes of the Angeles National Forest.

And then he felt it. A pang of guilt. Here he was, ready to make several million dollars but for what? Addicts desperate for the drug to transform their minds and bodies into something they couldn't control.

Damn, the money would be so nice. Life would be easy. But who else would have to die? Would anyone try to get in DeVito's way and meet their own terrible fate?

Do it. Go through with it. This one last time.

Arturo walked through the house to make sure everything was in order and then his phone rang. The number looked strange. It rang again and he tapped *answer*. "Bueno?"

"Hey dawg, got news for you."

"Johnny?" It was Johnny Delgado.

"This ain't no conversation. Got it? Listen carefully and then I'm hanging up. DeVito wants you dead."

"What? How do you know?"

"Man, I heard things. You know, whispered, but I heard enough. I'm out of here. Taking the wife and going away for a couple of days. I hate this shit, man. I told you. I told you. Watch your back."

The phone went silent, so that was it. His vibe was right. DeVito knew where the house was. *Shit.* He could scramble and start selling brick by brick to whoever he could. But then he stopped, and in a moment reviewed what he wanted and what he knew. Construction. Building homes, working on cars. A tradesman and fucking proud of it. That's how he'd make his money. Several million in his pocket from drugs would be nothing but a curse hanging over him and his family for the rest of their lives. But he did good deeds with the last chunk of money and he'd make it work again.

Or, he could just leave and head back to Mexico. Since DeVito knows about it, and Johnny heard shit talked about, then others must know he's sitting on a treasure of white powder. And what if the cops found out? He could never return to the U.S. Ever. He'd be as much a crook in the law's eyes as DeVito. But he didn't have a whole organization to evade arrest and not get captured or killed.

Face it head on. Look the lion in the mouth and then rip its jaws apart before it devours you. Strike first and strike fast. *Fuck it. I'm going home to Mexico. Family's more important than money.*

He needed a good lawyer, grabbed his cell, and punched in Alisha's number. The phone rang.

"Alisha Davidson, may I help you?"

Arturo skipped the small talk. "I hope so."

CHAPTER THIRTY-SEVEN

Text messages rolled in furiously on Stone's phone.

"Hey, Jake. Can you check that?" He kept his eye on the road.

Jake looked at Stone's phone. "Since you didn't read the first texts, Brannigan's just resending and updating us on Arturo and DeVito's meeting."

"What's happening?" asked Stone.

"It's confirmed that they're going to meet tomorrow at Balboa Lake in the Sepulveda Basin."

Jake's phone lit up with a call.

"It's Lightfoot," said Jake. He put it on speaker. "You're on."

"Where are you?" asked Lightfoot.

"With Stone. We're heading to his place."

"We've just gone through all the surveillance video that came in from Marina del Rey. It certainly looks like Bob Stevens lifting a Jet Ski out of the water."

"How can you tell?"

"It's real grainy and from a distance, but we ran it through a facial recognition program and it came back as an eighty-six percent match with Stevens."

"Kilbraide's hunch was right on," said Jake.

"We got a lot of planning tonight," Stone said. "I don't know what the hell Arturo thinks he's doing but we're going to nab DeVito once and for all. Sounds like we're going to get Arturo as well. Let's get everybody together."

"You hear that?" Jake asked Lightfoot.

"Yeah. Where?"

"Let's do my place. Pizza," said Stone.

Jake cringed. "I'm so tired of pizza. There's this great Mediterranean place—"

"Okay. Pizza and Mediterranean."

Lightfoot chimed in. "And fry bread tacos. It's like a comfort food—"

"Get what you think is best." Stone's phone rang and it was Alisha. "Hey there, what's up?"

"I just got a call from Arturo," she said. "We need to talk."

***

Kilbraide got copied on all the messages and then drove to Stevens' house once he got the text from Mary Ann. *He left the office.* She reported he seemed distracted and that he had dropped a paper with DeVito's name and Balboa Park written on it.

DeVito's the next target. Kilbraide believed it made sense based on the connection that DeVito had with the other victims. He was betting that Stevens would go home first, so staking out the house made sense. Several minutes passed and then Kilbraide saw the Nissan turn into the driveway and pull into the garage.

Kilbraide climbed out of his car and watched the garage door close. A screened breezeway connected the garage and the house. His premise was that if Stevens was indeed the shooter then he'd be leaving again to survey the park where Arturo and DeVito were going to meet. Kilbraide scanned the property as he walked up the driveway. There was no movement from inside the house. He paced toward the garage and noticed a bike leaning against the breezeway.

A window opened, startling him.

"This is a curious place to meet." It was Bob Stevens. "I'm quite surprised to see you here." Stevens looked like he was wearing a biker's outfit.

"I just came by because I had a few more questions for you. You going out?"

"Sure, nice day for a ride. I'd like to get going, but you obviously have something on your mind."

"I do."

Stevens looked calm. "Come on in." He opened the side door.

Kilbraide made a mental note of the layout.

Stevens noticed the hesitation. "Come on, I don't bite."

"Thanks for the invite." Kilbraide stepped into a spacious kitchen.

"Want something to drink? Some water?"

"No, I'm good," said Kilbraide. "You do a lot of riding?"

"As much as I can." Stevens filled a water bottle. "You look like you stay in shape."

"I try."

"Got a gym membership?" Stevens asked him.

"I had one. I prefer spending time outdoors."

"Just like in the service?" asked Stevens.

"What do you mean?"

"It's what you get to know, isn't it?" Stevens leaned against the kitchen counter. "Did you like it or not?"

"The military?"

"Not just the military. What you did?"

"A sniper?" Kilbraide stood near the kitchen pantry. He ran a hand over his jacket, feeling the gun underneath.

"Yeah. Impressive record. A hundred and one confirmed kills. You're in an elite club," said Stevens.

"You checked up on me?"

"Why not? You were checking up on me. I was just curious."

"And gathering intel?" asked Kilbraide.

Stevens laughed. "Absolutely. I'd like to get a few more retirement accounts from you law enforcement guys."

"We have our own retirement plans."

"You'd be surprised what I can do for you."

"Or maybe I wouldn't be surprised." Kilbraide looked around. "Did you like your military career?"

"It was so-so. Some decent leadership training but not much excitement."

"No kidding?"

"Lots of desk work," remarked Stevens.

"Is that what you call those overnight flights to Colombia?"

Stevens didn't respond.

"And to Pakistan?"

Stevens paused before he answered. "I did what I was told to do. That's classified."

"Taking out strategic targets. How many confirmed do you have?" Kilbraide kept his eyes locked on him.

"You're here to ask about my military work?" Stevens smiled. "Mind telling me how you found out?"

"Lots and lots of networking and a little bit of hacking." Kilbraide was direct.

Stevens was calm.

"You're the One Shot Sniper, aren't you?" asked Kilbraide.

Stevens smiled. "And you're an ex-military guy who cares about peace and justice. We got a lot in common." Stevens looked Kilbraide up and down. "Is that why you became a cop?"

"Why'd you do it?" Kilbraide kept a hand close to his side and the gun.

"Because justice is limited," Stevens stared at him.

"Really? Just brother to brother in arms. Tell me more."

"I found it out the hard way when I watched my wife die from an overdose. She was a beautiful woman who convulsed and shook violently when she finally succumbed to the drugs. The cops never did a damn thing. I hate seeing people being torn apart. I wasn't going to stand by idly. I'm a patriot. I love my country."

"Oh yeah? In that case you know we have laws and, being a patriot, you need to uphold those laws."

"I'm going to do what the law never did, and that's take out all the top dogs and let the rest fight for scraps."

"So you became a vigilante and kill people?"

"Oorah." Stevens gave a sarcastic sneer. "God bless America."

"Are you on your way to kill DeVito?"

"He's next on the list."

Kilbraide spoke casually. "I'm going to arrest you."

Stevens was matter of fact. "Come on. You looked at my military record. I'm untouchable."

"You know as well as I do that no one is above the law."

"No one?" Out of nowhere, Stevens exploded with a roundhouse kick to the side of Kilbraide's head.

Kilbraide collapsed and everything went black.

CHAPTER THIRTY-EIGHT

"You're sitting on a half-ton of coke and expect me to let you off?" Stone drilled his gaze into Arturo.

Alisha's office was a smart place to meet with its mini-conference room. It was also a neutral location. Arturo looked to Alisha with eyes that asked her for input.

"Come on, Detective," said Alisha, taking on her professional role as a defense attorney, "he told you his story."

Stone scoffed. "You're as innocent as Angelino was."

"Look, Detective. I admitted what I've done. I had second thoughts the whole time about riding along with Angel. That's why I got out. Give me some points, okay? I've done some good stuff."

"Riding along? You transported a ton of cocaine. That's a hell of a lot more than just riding along." Stone saw regret and vulnerability in Arturo's demeanor, qualities he had never seen in Angelino and certainly not a hint of it in DeVito. He grabbed a water bottle from the table and sipped it. Late afternoon was passing by fast.

"Tell me," said Stone. "At what point did you join Angelino in getting the shipment in?"

"Yeah, it was all Angel. I had nothing to do with that part. It was already across the border and secure, just waiting for us to pick it up."

Stone glanced at Alisha and he had questions for her, but kept it professional. It was in Arturo's favor that she was representing him as far as Stone was concerned. Here was a man he liked who was confessing to a crime. Stone was undecided on the best action to take.

"Look, I came here for one reason," pleaded Arturo. "I want to get rid of the stuff and, like I said earlier, I can help you get Frank DeVito. Without me, you've got nothing on him."

Stone pursed his lips like he was going to make a speech and then stopped to ask Arturo a question. "Why didn't you just sell the stuff?"

"Right now, I thank God I'm alive. I could have been killed Halloween night like Angel or be in prison like Lil' Jo. Or Ojos Negros could have me hanging from one of the overpasses with my head cut off. But I'm sitting here talking to you both." Arturo was composed. "Detective, I want to see my wife and kids again. And I want to do it with a clean conscience."

Stone felt like he was at an intersection of two paths in the deep, dark woods and he wasn't sure which one to take.

"You know, Detective. I could have walked away from everything this afternoon. Just give DeVito the keys to my house and say, 'Help yourself' while I was driving to Mexico. Or just leave and forget about it. But that's the problem, I wouldn't have been able to forget about it and that's why I didn't drive to the warehouse that night with the others. I'll be honest. I want to do good and I don't want to go to jail for doing it."

Stone had heard dozens and dozens of bullshit excuses and stories of false remorse from men, and women, that he arrested over the years. But Arturo wasn't lying. He was smart enough that he could have dumped the coke a whole lot earlier and the LAPD would never have known anything.

"I had to wrestle with myself," Arturo continued. "I mean I'm staring at millions. You got to understand that's some pull and tug."

"I gotcha," said Stone. "You sold off a little, though, didn't you?"

"A little bit here and there." Arturo took out a few pieces of folded paper. "I wrote this down to help you out. I've already called him and set everything up. Here's my plan for DeVito." He handed it to Stone.

"Why do you care about nabbing DeVito?" asked Stone.

"I don't, except that he's ruined a lot of lives and I've heard that he's going to kill me. I just can't play this game." Arturo looked Stone in the eye. "No disrespect but why is he still a free man?"

Stone nodded, not offended in the least. "It's tough getting to the top guys. People on the streets are easy to arrest. He's built a legal fortress and has such a tangled business web that he'd make a spider proud."

Arturo smiled and then turned somber. "So what are you thinking, Detective? Do I help you out and go through with this or do you put me behind bars?"

Stone thought long and hard. He looked to Alisha and she gave him a shrug that said, *Your choice, make the right one, but it better be the one to let Arturo go.*

Then Stone turned to Arturo and said, "All right, you have the right to remain—"

"What?" Arturo looked shocked.

"Just kidding. Call your wife and tell her you'll be home soon."

CHAPTER THIRTY-NINE

Stone surveyed the map of Balboa Park laid out on his dining table and muttered, "Where the hell is Kilbraide?"

Jake glanced at his phone. He had sent a volley of text messages but there was no reply.

"Didn't he tell you what he was doing?"

"You know Kilbraide," Jake sighed. "See a lot. Speak a little."

Lightfoot wandered into the dining room from the kitchen carrying a plate of fry bread tacos and a slice of mushroom and sausage pizza. "This is our big chance, Stone. By the way I heard that your friends in vice found the massage parlor where that girl had been sent to. Freed her and six others. Good work. Sounds like a happy ending. Let's see if we can pin anything on DeVito."

"It's been a dream of mine for some time."

"So what do I need to know about tomorrow?" asked Lightfoot, taking a bite of pizza, the cheese dripping from his chin.

Jake spoke up. "Balboa Park is a patch of wilderness in the urban jungle." He pointed out the features. "Here are the entrances. Then the picnic areas." He hovered over a legend showing the tables. "Over here is a lake with paddle boats for rent and it's real popular. Then to the east, this part, is a wildlife refuge and marshland. That's near the Sepulveda Dam. You can kayak it when there are enough winter rains."

"No kidding?" Lightfoot wiped his mouth and chewed away.

"Plus golf courses, sports fields, and landing strips for those radio-controlled airplanes."

"When I'm not busy busting drug smugglers, I'll check it out for fun."

Alisha came into the room along with Brannigan and Mary Ann.

"And Captain Harrell's giving you plenty of back up?" asked Lightfoot.

"Yeah, we've updated him and we're coordinating." Stone laid out the details. "Captain Harrell is setting up a team, and patrols will be stationed around the perimeter. We'll also have department helicopters on standby if necessary."

"So what if DeVito doesn't show?" asked Lightfoot. "And what makes you think you can trust this Arturo guy?"

"DeVito will show. He likes money more than oxygen and he can't hide out forever. He's got his fingers in a lot of shady operations and we'll eventually get him for something. As for Arturo, he's a good guy and he's willing to put his life on the line. Anything can happen, of course."

"Where's Kilbraide?" asked Lightfoot.

Jake had a concerned look. "At this point, I'm not sure. I'll go find him."

"Just check in with us," said Stone. "All the time."

"You got it." Jake grabbed his things and left. He got in his car and drove into the evening.

The plan in motion was for Kilbraide to trail Stevens after Mary Ann had left the office. Jake decided the most logical place to follow up was at Stevens' home.

Take a drive by. See what was up.

Jake got there and nothing was obvious. Kilbraide's car wasn't anywhere on the street. He got out and walked carefully down the driveway. The house next door was dark. Across the street, a jogger made her way along the sidewalk.

Jake peered through the windows into darkness. Nothing. Everything looked orderly. No reason to call a unit. Jake wished his inner vibe could just jump out of his body. He felt like a kid playing *hot and cold*. Standing near Steven's window he felt a presence like he was in a warm area. Now, walking back to the car he felt detached and a bit cold. A nagging wouldn't go away, so he slowly walked back down the driveway, studying the house. Nothing. He circled the property and then climbed the steps to the side door and listened.

All quiet. He messaged Stone. *Not here.*

***

The first thing Kilbraide noticed as he regained consciousness was the throbbing in his head. His knees were tied up against his chest and he was engulfed in darkness. The walls were tight like he was scrunched into a box. He took a breath to maintain composure, and then waited. Step one was a decision. It wasn't a moment of panic. Yell. Find out the situation. It's not likely anyone would hear him.

"Hey!" he shouted. The sound didn't carry. That's what he thought. He was stuffed in a dark space like a sack of potatoes. Stevens could have killed him but decided not to. *There's enough oxygen.* Kilbraide ran through the possibilities as to why Stevens let him live. Fellow patriot and respect for the military connection? Possibly. But the brotherhood had its limitations. Because Stevens likes cops? Could be. But each murder said something about the man's character. He needed to concentrate and pour himself mentally into each killing. High-value targets required extra special care. Kilbraide smiled. *A white glove treatment.* Stevens was after DeVito so he tossed Kilbraide aside for now, but maybe he'd come back and finish him off.

Kilbraide struggled, but the ropes held him taut. *Now what?* His plan was simple. Wait and think.

CHAPTER FORTY

Evening descended as Stevens retreated into the soggy grass in Balboa Park. The marshland made it easy so he could hide and yet observe the area where DeVito and Arturo agreed to meet. He could tell from the back-and-forth conversation that the deal was going through. Too many details were arranged. He studied the park bench where they agreed to sit and measured the distance from his position. Doable. More so than Thompson in the church. That was an accomplishment, one for the record books. *Good job.*

This would be as easy as the killing in Griffith Park, easier than the ones along the boardwalk and at the warehouse. Scott was in many ways the least complicated pick. Sure, the wind and terrain created a challenge, but the man loved entertaining poolside like a king holding court. It was fitting that he die first. His arrogance was obnoxious.

Stevens took pride in undertaking this thankless job, just like the other assignments that he had done for the agency throughout the world.

Never a thank you. He smiled. And certainly no heroic parades down Main Street. But he was used to it. Working without recognition and for the good of his country. A long-suffering patriot.

As the sun set, he shut out his everyday life and transformed into the warrior that he really was. He smudged dirt across his face and pulled reeds from around the water, using them to cover himself and blend in with the surroundings. He took a small shovel and dug a few feet into the dirt for his pack. He pulled out a camouflage tarp to stay covered during the night. Everything checked out. Change of clothes, his weapon with one round, and his calling card—the patch that read *One Shot, One Kill. No Remorse. I Decide.*

Do this and leave. He had been found out, which was disappointing but not totally surprising. He was always ready for anything and had his passport stamped with an alias and his ticket punched for Vanuatu, the South Pacific island nation. He would settle into the resort community and let several years pass by.

He heard deep breathing. A jogger running near the marsh in the dusk. He slipped beneath the tarp and the person passed by unaware.

Kilbraide should have known better. Cops talk tough. They act tough and despite so much power with the law they often fail to bring anyone to justice. Kilbraide should have thanked him. But no. Stevens appreciated the role that he made for himself as a hero that no one knew about. The lack of coke flowing into the streets was the reason he should be thanked. It grated on his nerves that no one would thank him. Yet, he would press on. He could just leave the country and not engage the enemy in any more fights. Transfer his personal assets and let that be that.

Instinct told Stevens he knew better. His deal with the CIA was lifelong and they would never let him go. When needed, he would have plenty of wealth and be flown from one assignment to the next and treated like quiet royalty. For a moment, he thought of a short story that he had read and that was written around the Civil War, *The Man without a Country*. A U.S. Army Lieutenant in the early 1800s was on trial for treason and announced that he never wanted to hear the name of the United States again. He was sentenced to spend the rest of his days at sea without his country's name ever being mentioned in his presence.

Stevens clenched his teeth. That wasn't him. He loved his country and fought for it. But it was choked in its own ability to fight abuse and crimes against its people. His wife died from a drug overdose and no one was even taken to court over it. No one was ever tried. The financiers just kept lining their pockets and filling their accounts with the misery of others.

Rustling was in the bushes to his right, north up the stream. A shadow moving through the grass and weeds, and then continuing. Someone without a home, struggling to survive. Los Angeles was full of them and the number seemed to grow by the week.

Stevens lay on his back and glanced at the sky, and in this tiny section of wild that wasn't covered in concrete a person could actually see some stars. That was freedom. Love of America. Always faithful. *Semper Fidelis.* He closed his eyes and visualized how DeVito and Arturo would meet. The points they would walk from and how close they would be to each other. He would wait and breathe, getting in the rhythm and then aiming for DeVito.

Arturo would react and likely hit the ground. Stevens counted on the cops knowing that the meeting was going to occur. Contingency planning was his strength. After the kill, he would retreat further into the marshland and wade up the stream, out of view and gone forever. A ghost.

CHAPTER FORTY-ONE

Janet noticed a client account lying on the desk. This was the transfer for three million dollars that Bob had talked about. *Needed by Monday* was the note scribbled on the paper. She scooped it up and called her boss. No answer. A strange uneasiness settled over her. He had seemed out of sorts and didn't look like his normal self. He looked worried when he left yesterday afternoon and that lady had come in to talk with him. He seemed far away, mentally.

Janet picked up the note and drove to his house, making another call en route. Still no answer on his cell or home phones. Traffic was light and she pulled up to the street and got out. His car wasn't there. She looked in the little front door window and knocked. Nothing. She jiggled the handle, but it was locked and still no response on her phone.

The windows along the side of the house were too high for her to peek inside. She had been to his home twice before. Once to deliver documents and the other for a casual barbeque he had before his wife had died. The side door was unlocked, and she stepped inside. "Hello?" She called. "Mr. Stevens?"

No answer except for what she thought was a quiet *thump*. "Bob?" She walked through the kitchen toward the front door. "Hello?" Nothing. She was worried and walked back into the kitchen. "Bob, are you here?"

And there it was. Another thump. A dull sound like something was muffled. She opened the pantry but saw no one. Just cans on a shelf. "Bob?" She felt panic and confusion. The thump hit again. It was a hollow sound from within the wall. She held her breath and knocked. The knock came back and startled her. "Bob?" She shook.

"Hey, somebody out there?" The voice was low and deep.

"Bob, is that you? Are you okay?" She touched the wall, glanced around, and pressed her hand against the wood panel. "Hold on." Nails held the section in place. She banged a fist, and it vibrated but didn't give way. "I'm trying, okay?"

"Okay."

That wasn't Bob's voice.

"Hold on." She remembered the utility closet near the back door where she pawed through an assortment of tools, nails and what looked like a box of bullets. Strange looking ones. Much larger than she ever would have expected ammunition to look like. Then she found a hammer and ran back to the closet. "I'm working on it."

"Good." The voice was weak.

She pressed the claw of the hammer against the nail. Nothing. "I'm going to pound on it, all right?"

"Yeah."

She was in such a panic that she didn't even think about calling 9-1-1. She gritted her teeth and slammed the hammer against one nail. The wood gave way enough that she could tuck the claw underneath, pull, tug and loosen the nail. "Hey, we got one. Hang in there, please." Then there was the second nail. Slam the hammer, tuck the claw, and fight to pry it up. She did. She pulled back on the wood but needed one more nail free to get it open. Slam the hammer, tuck the claw, and fight, fight, fight. *Got it.* She pulled the paneling free.

And inside was a man who sat trapped in a homemade crawl space with his knees tied up against his chest. A combination of panic and adrenaline made her skip around. She was fidgety and scared. "Don't worry."

"You're the one who looks worried." His eyes were half open.

She worked hard but the knots were too tight. She ran to the kitchen for a knife and started sawing with the teeth against the nylon. It finally sprung loose. She was alarmed as she realized, "You're Detective Kilbraide, aren't you?" She continued cutting until he was free and then grabbed him a glass of water.

He gulped it down. "That's me. Expecting someone else?" He groaned. "Help me out." He weakly lifted an arm and she took it.

"Oh my God. What happened?" She held on to him as he stood.

He groaned, grabbed the wall for leverage and finally stretched his legs. "It's like this—"

"I'll call nine-one-one."

"No. Don't." He was embarrassed about being cold-cocked by a knuckle-dragging jarhead and he didn't want a patrol to slow him down with all their questions.

"Okay. I'm sorry."

"I know."

She pressed against his side as he got his balance.

"Oh, man." He stepped out and rubbed his legs.

"What happened? Where's Bob? Is he okay?"

Kilbraide was taken aback. "So you don't know?"

"No, what?"

"He's not a nice man."

"What? Bob did this?"

"He sure did." Kilbraide walked past the kitchen, turned on the faucet and stuck his mouth beneath it, guzzling more water. He grabbed an apple and granola bar from a fruit basket on the counter and chowed them down. He looked around the living room.

"I can't believe it," said Janet, following close.

He headed back down the hallway, searching past a bathroom where he quickly stepped in to relieve himself. Once finished, he scanned the hallway and ducked into the next room. Maps covered the walls along with a store of ammunition. Kilbraide's badge, cell phone, and weapon were sitting on a stand. His gun was dismantled. On a desk was a sheet of paper with a line drawn through the handwritten names of the victims: Scott; Cutchins; Zhuang; Mortensen; Thompson; and Norhaus. The last name on the list was *DeVito*, circled in red. *So this was it. Command Central.*

He turned to Janet. "Don't talk to anyone unless it's us. Do this. There's an In-N-Out up the street. Get something to eat, sit down, and don't move until the police show up."

"Am I in trouble?" she gasped.

"Maybe. Maybe not. But we're going to ask you a lot of questions either way." He dialed.

"Hello?"

"Stone?"

Stone sounded confused. "Yeah? Kilbraide?"

"That's me."

"Where've you been?"

"Visiting with Bob Stevens, but unfortunately, I got a little tied up." He reassembled his gun. "I've been trapped in a closet since last night. Lost a battle but I sure as hell don't want to lose the war. Stone, listen. Stevens is the One Shot Sniper and DeVito is his next target."

CHAPTER FORTY-TWO

Arturo stopped along the northern end of the park, got out of the van, and walked toward the spot where he would meet DeVito. The park bench was only a football field length away and yet his body was stiff like he was filled with lead. Arturo had no regrets. This was the right thing to do instead of fleeing the country.

A clean conscience was worth more than the money that cocaine would bring and so was being able to move freely between the United States and Mexico, the two countries that he loved. DeVito was the prisoner. He was a man who was stuck with bodyguards, a complex business network that was nearly impossible to manage, and filled with fear that he could be toppled any moment from a rival's bullet.

About fifty yards from the meeting spot, Arturo stopped. Across the field, Frank DeVito stood surrounded by four men, the outlines of their weapons were visible under their jackets. He motioned to them and they stayed behind as he continued alone toward Arturo. They waited out of earshot but never let their boss out of sight. No doubt other bodyguards were stationed around the perimeter of the park.

Arturo walked up to DeVito who met him by the agreed-upon bench.

DeVito smiled and shook hands. "You looked like a statue over there."

"I just wanted to make sure we followed our agreement." Arturo unbuttoned part of his shirt and patted along his waist. "I've kept my part. No wires, no weapons."

"I know. You're not that dumb," said DeVito. "Shall we?" He motioned to the bench and sat. "I figured we could have a little chat and get to know each other."

Arturo hesitated. "A friendly visit, huh?" He smiled to hide his tension as he sat down.

"Why the hell not? I like working with people who impress me."

Arturo wanted the deal done and finished, but DeVito had this strange way of chatting like he was an old friend, even when the stakes were high.

***

Stevens lay in the marsh like he had through the night, welcoming the water and mud, alert with a familiar sense of excitement and duty. It wouldn't take long to finish DeVito. He saw them head towards the target area and silently congratulated himself once again for getting the intel correct. Few had his skills. Perhaps no one else did.

He watched them shake hands, sit, and get into the mode of a friendly conversation. Stevens had DeVito in his sight with the crosshairs neatly focused on the forehead. He breathed in slowly and out rhythmically. In and out while the two men chatted. Stevens stayed steady and focused, slowing his heart and counting the beats. A child and adult passed by in the foreground. *Wait. That's it.* The grown up and child served to inspire him. That's who he was doing it for. The innocent ones. And now. He could feel it. DeVito was oblivious. Totally unaware. Nothing else mattered. Stevens heard no one else. Saw no one else. *Now.* His finger tightened on the trigger.

"Police!"

The shout broke the stillness and made Stevens jerk ever so slightly as he fired. The bullet flew off course and a tree across the field took the hit. Its branches shattered. First time he had ever missed. Stevens was enraged. Furious. He turned to see Kilbraide through the weeds standing and aiming a handgun.

DeVito and Arturo hit the ground. His bodyguards ran toward them with guns drawn, creating total chaos and trying to protect their boss from an unknown assassin. The ant mound got kicked, but the target got away.

Stevens, clutching his weapon, scrambled away through the murky swamp, disappearing from Kilbraide's vision. Marine training at its best. Become invisible, blend in, and slip away. He stayed low and zigzagged through the undergrowth, a rare place in Los Angeles that was as green as a swamp in Louisiana. He was racing toward a bridge with a thick grove of trees beneath it and his escape out of the park.

"Stevens. Give it up. It's over."

As much as he wanted to respond, he couldn't betray his position. He stayed silent as he disappeared into the brush. The bridge was near. He glanced back toward the park and could see DeVito brushing himself off and being whisked away. *Kilbraide's wrong. It's never over.* He would regroup to fight another day. It was up to him since the police had proven they couldn't stop the flow of drugs.

Cops poured in, surrounding DeVito and his thugs while police helicopters rattled the skies. DeVito was going to walk free. Like he always had.

Stevens ran through the weeds, choked with emotion that he had failed his wife. *I can't believe I missed.* Trees and bushes grew even thicker and he dodged in and around the trunks. He knew Kilbraide's background and could sense the detective waiting for the right moment to take a shot. Police were closing in from all directions.

He was getting closer to the bridge. A sewer pipe hidden in the grove of trees below it was his objective, his Plan B, his escape.

Out of the corner of his eye he spotted Kilbraide running and heard him shout a warning. Then came a crack of a weapon and a blast into his left shoulder. Shot. Stevens tumbled to the ground, engulfed in intense pain, scraping his face on briars and pebbles. Blood flowed, his fingers went numb, and he lost his grip on the .50 cal as his arm seemed to melt into nothing.

"Don't move."

Stevens groaned. "I'm not."

Maybe he could just raise the barrel, suicide by cop, and join Brenda in paradise. The trigger was inviting but his fingers didn't work. He screamed when a knee jammed into his lower back and rough hands patted him down, handcuffed him, and turned him over.

Kilbraide's face, framed by the sky with its blueness and layer of wispy clouds, burned with anger.

Stevens smiled. "I can't believe I let a Ranger shoot me."

Kilbraide held his gun steady as other cops arrived, grabbed the rifle, and secured the area. Radios crackled and a paramedic's siren wailed. "Yeah, it was a hell of a shot, you're not an easy target. The Corps trained you good."

"You don't know the half of it."

Kilbraide holstered his service weapon, knelt, and applied pressure to the shoulder wound.

Stevens grimaced. "You proud of yourself?"

"Just doing my job. What I'm trained to do."

"Problem is that you let a bad guy go free." Stevens took a pained breath.

"No, I stopped a bad guy. But if you're talking about DeVito, we'll get him. Legally."

Stevens wasn't impressed. "You guys have a piss poor track record."

"Oh, yeah? Then I'll change things."

"You do that. Stop 'em dead in their tracks, man." He started breathing hard as the ambulance rolled to a stop and medics jumped from the truck.

"Just like you did, huh?"

Stevens gave a weak smile as the EMTs tended to him. "You'd be good at it, man."

"I'm good at what I do now. Stopped you, didn't I?"

"Yeah, you did. For now, but it doesn't matter."

"What are you talking about? Of course, it does."

Stevens was matter of fact as his shirt was cut off and gauze wrapped around his wound. "You don't get it, do you?"

"Get what?"

Medics lifted him on a stretcher, carried him to the ambulance, and got ready to slide him in. "I told you before. I'm untouchable."

"Nobody is."

"You'll see." As the doors were closing, Stevens lifted his head and winked at Kilbraide. "Oorah."

CHAPTER FORTY-THREE

Valley Medical Center sprawled for several blocks with enough cars to make it look as packed as a shopping mall on Black Friday. Kilbraide drove past the *Emergency* sign and parked. He met Stone and Jake inside the sliding glass doors and the trio made their way in the elevator to the third floor trauma unit.

Kilbraide's eyes were red and bleary like Stone's and Jake's from writing reports most of the night. They had been receiving continual updates on Steven's condition. He had surgery to remove Kilbraide's bullet and was then returned to his room where he was handcuffed to the bed's railings and guards were posted outside. The last communication said his vital signs were stable and he had slept comfortably.

Stevens viewed himself as a crusader, but fought with a warped vision of righteousness and revenge. He was a hunter tracking down people who had enriched themselves through the misery of others. What was puzzling was that Stevens had the skill to ruin his victims by siphoning off their assets, but instead decided to stop them cold through murder. Kilbraide wanted to know why he made that choice.

Stepping off the elevator and into the glaring lights of the unit, the detectives passed silently by nurses and doctors in scrubs, showed their badges at the nurse's station, and walked to Room 326. But a call came from behind.

"Excuse me, may I help you?"

Jake turned first as a charge nurse came walking toward them. "Room 326."

"Oh?" The nurse glanced at her tablet. "The authorities already transferred Mr. Stevens."

"Transferred? What authorities?" asked Stone who hustled with Jake and Kilbraide to a spacious private room with a window and a bed—that was empty with sheets and a blanket pulled neatly and tightly.

Stone's response was simple. "What the hell?"

CHAPTER FORTY-FOUR

"It's not fair," Kilbraide protested. "He arms himself and shoots others, but he's hands-off to us."

Lightfoot stood with Stone and Jake on a ridge in front of a spectacular view that went from the hills of Malibu to the calm of the Pacific Ocean. Malibu Creek State Park was a fascinating blend of rural and urban worlds with hundreds of miles of hiking trails. "We don't make the rules, but we do our best to enforce them."

"Son-of-a-bitch," grumbled Kilbraide. "He told me he was untouchable."

"You're confirming the CIA ordered him transferred?" Jake asked Lightfoot.

"C-I-A or some other alphabet soup name. Who knows? A black op with more pull and authority than any of us has."

Kilbraide was worked up. "And that gives them the right to snatch him away from the law?"

"They are the law."

Stone picked up a pebble and dropped it down the slope. "Come on, Lightfoot. Off the record. Tell us what you know."

Lightfoot laughed. "I would if I could."

"Who else could it be if it wasn't the CIA?" asked Kilbraide.

"I don't know."

"Yeah, right, Lightfoot. You're a Fed."

"I'm one of many. The government with all its ways of protecting people is like standing down there and looking up at these hills. You have no idea that all the valleys or the twists and turns exist until you take a closer look and then an even closer look. And then you still don't know."

"I can't even imagine," said Stone.

"So a guy like Stevens gets to knock off people and go free?" scoffed Kilbraide. He kicked at a clump of dirt.

"I wouldn't call him 'free.' Whoever grabbed him is watching him closely, every moment. The truth is, I'd bet the man has no freedom."

Jake shook his head. "I can't believe our own government would let American citizens be assassinated."

"Seriously? Don't be so naïve," said Lightfoot. "This is my theory. Idea number one. The more we've dug into Scott and Zhuang's relationship the more we see a connection that fueled drugs and terror around the globe. Stacy Norhaus had ties in Central and South America. And the same with Thompson and Cutchins."

Stone interrupted. "He wasn't as good as he thought. Ojos Negros beat him to Harold Mortensen, and he missed DeVito."

"Hold on," said Jake. "Ojos Negros did him a favor and he missed DeVito because of us. Really, because of you, Kilbraide."

Kilbraide shrugged off the recognition.

"So Stevens was taking down an international ring," said Jake.

"Who knows?" wondered Lightfoot. "Each of the victims had some illicit connection to another part of the world. They created some kind of problem for the governments of those countries. Some havoc. And the rulers of those countries didn't like it and threatened America's interests unless we took action and got them out of the way."

Jake couldn't believe it. "Dude, you're speculating so damned much. You sound like a conspiracy nut."

"Hear me out," Lightfoot continued. "The government didn't sanction what Stevens did, but he wanted revenge for the death of his wife so they let him take out some troublemakers. They still had to protect who he was and so they came and grabbed him. And our foreign interests are protected, and everyone's happy."

"Our interests? Like what?" asked Jake.

"A military base put on notice. Some multinational corporation's facilities getting threatened." Lightfoot raised his hands like he was guessing. "This is just my simple theory."

"Do you have an idea number two?" Kilbraide shook his head.

"Yeah. Stevens was a rogue agent who was distraught over losing his wife to an overdose and took it on himself to deliver justice. Even simpler. But like I said, the CIA, or whoever, snatched him up so he wouldn't divulge classified information."

"We still don't know for sure. And if that's the case, then why would the CIA do this?" asked Stone.

"Stevens' is an incredible asset. They don't want their boy locked up. He has great skills and a motive for taking revenge. No family ties. Let him loose and he could be a real menace. But keep him focused and he can be strategic. Popping off one bad guy after another, just like hunting turkeys. Coming up with an alibi is tricky, so make him disappear and let the murders grow cold. That's about as realistic as it gets since most homicides in Los Angeles go unsolved."

"But it's not unsolved," said Kilbraide. "I know what happened."

Lightfoot shrugged. "And how are you going to prove it? Stevens' house was scrubbed down well. Cleaned out quickly and all of a sudden, he doesn't exist."

"Is he actually a financial planner?" wondered Stone.

"He had legitimate clients from what I've been able to tell," said Jake. "So what about them? What're they told?"

"Whatever they want to hear," said Stone. "They don't care about their advisor, only about their money. Somebody will fill Stevens' shoes."

"What about his assistant?" asked Kilbraide.

"She checks out clean," replied Lightfoot. "Says she didn't know anything about his other life. Right now, she's got her hands full dealing with Stevens' clients and, who knows, maybe it'll become her business.

But I'm thinking Stevens' set up the entire operation as a front so he could get access to the big dogs and take them out."

"That makes sense," agreed Stone.

Jake looked at Lightfoot. "It sounds like you know a whole lot."

"I listen and learn, and I won't, or can't, say any more. Except this. Keeping America safe and making sure the world doesn't fall apart is a messy business."

"My head is spinning," said Jake, taking in the view as he lightened the mood. "Any of you ever try hang gliding?"

"Nope," said Stone. "I like my feet on the ground."

"I hear it's peaceful. Real quiet. Floating on the wind like a bird."

"Then you should try it," said Stone.

Jake laughed. "Does this look like a bird's body to you?" His phone buzzed and he read the text. "Speaking of my body. Tasha says the food is almost ready and that it's time for me to grill."

Stone was ready to eat. "Let's head down."

The picnic site below was in full view. Alisha and Tasha were chatting away while Andrew played with Jake's kids. Monty Tusco sauntered from the parking lot to the picnic area, looked up, and waved to them.

As they braced themselves going down the trail, Kilbraide spoke up. "I'd still feel better if Stevens was in a cell awaiting trial."

"And with DeVito as a cell buddy," said Stone. "I know what you mean. It seems like that guy's untouchable, too."

"Old Frank *is* just a good chess player," said Jake, "but, *Zugzwang*."

Everyone gave him a questioning look.

He continued. "What? Come on guys. Zugzwang! Learned it playing Scrabble. It's where the chess player is forced to make a move...usually a bad one that weakens him. DeVito will make that move, and when he does, we'll be there for the endgame."

"And *check*!" Stone interjected as he crept down the steep grade.

"Checkmate!" Jake corrected.

"You guys are strange," said Lightfoot. "I'd like us to grab DeVito, but he's invested in a strong legal team and, like magic, everything's been swept away."

"He came out on top," said Jake, "consolidated power, and now controls the gangs. I hate to admit it, but quiet has come over the Valley. Though it's an uneasy peace."

"It was so weird walking in the hospital and seeing an empty bed," said Kilbraide. "How do they get away with that? I'm still in shock."

"Remarkable, huh?" said Stone.

"A one-man militia. Sounds lonely. I'll bet that's why he left the patches."

Jake agreed. "I guess in his own way he wanted some connection and recognition for the job he was doing. Crazy, huh? But it doesn't change our mission and our jobs." Jake steadied himself.

"But still," moaned Kilbraide. "The murders are unsolved."

"No, they're solved," said Jake. "We know who did it. There's just no justice. But we can feel good that we kept a half-ton of coke off the streets."

"Jake's right," said Stone, close to the picnic area. "Arturo took a huge risk and is going to be looking over his shoulder for a long time. He's a good guy we can be thankful for. Not everything is wrapped up in a neat little bow, it really sucks. But I won't give up on DeVito. I never will. I'm patient. I've got time. And I'm not going to let him bring me down. I'm not going to give him that control." He turned to Kilbraide. "Don't let Stevens do that to you, either."

And there was a lot of good to celebrate. Jake's kids were patiently showing Andrew how to throw a Frisbee while Silver tried to get in on the action, prancing and waiting for a toss. Brannigan was holding Mary Ann's hand and Alisha stood over the grill.

"Hey, I said I'd do the hot dogs and hamburgers," said Jake in a near panic. "No offense, Stone, but your girlfriend doesn't know how to cook." Jake scampered to the grill.

"She admits it," Stone yelled. "Between the two of us, we barely know how to open a can of soup and order a pizza."

"I've got higher standards," Jake shot back. "Let's eat, drink, and be merry today. For tomorrow, there will be bad guys who won't get away."

AUTHORS' NOTE:

We hope you enjoyed the adventure. Please leave a review on Amazon, Facebook, Goodreads and other outlets so more readers can discover us.

"Fast-paced page turners with suspense that starts at the beginning and keeps building right to the end."

Visit our blog to join our Detective Tom Stone Reader's Group for sneak previews, special offers and fun contests.

Find us online:

Facebook: www.facebook.com/tomstonedetectivestories/

Blog: www.tomstonedetectiveblog.wordpress.com/

Website: www.carvedinstone.media/tomstonedetectivestories/

Email: dettomstonestories@gmail.com

***

READER REVIEWS

A Nitty Gritty Christmas

"Enormously engaging and captivating. Read the book. You won't regret it."

"I am a sucker for suspense and this was loaded with it. I really got into the well-developed characters. Looking forward to the next one! By the way, would make a killer movie!"

"'Nitty Gritty' is a brilliant way to describe it. I felt like I was stepping into the Los Angeles underbelly and living the life of an L.A. police detective."

Sweltering Summer Nights

"The story is realistic, brings about the relevant drug issues and social inequalities that comes with it. Tom Stone is a well-rounded man, one hell of a detective with a big heart. Strong family values such as love and compassion despite the non-traditional family setup."

"I loved the LA Medical Dispensary concept. Tom Stone is quiet a perceptive and intuitive detective with a great partner Jake. Angelino brought a touch of Tony Montana, from Scarface as the villain"

"Great action thriller! A gripping story of police work and urban life. The plot is intriguing and kept us in the book. Highly recommend!"

Day of the Dead

"Drugs, violence, women all play a part and with Halloween fast approaching things are starting to get messy. This is a fast paced page turner with suspense that starts at

the beginning and keeps building right to the end. Action all the way through it is a great read."

"I enjoyed reading this story! Don and Lon kept the pace moving. It was quick read, I felt comfortable with the characters and places in the book. I recommend 'Day of the Dead' to all looking for a quick detective story!"

"This book had a great pace and it took me straight off on a brilliant ride to the fantastic ending! I was hooked right from the beginning and I read it in a few hours as I didn't want to put the book down."

One Shot, One Kill

"Gripping. A study in what drives a killer into madness. It was an edge of the seat page turner. I couldn't put it down, and I can't wait till the next in the series."

"I like the way Stone and his friends interact with each other, like a family, bringing community to the otherwise fractured city of Los Angeles."

"The story launches with and intense beginning and keeps a suspenseful pace that leads to a surprise ending."

A Deadly Path

"The BEST little story I've read in a long time. If you haven't read any of the other Tom Stone Detective Stories start with this one. It'll intrigued you... I loved it."

"4 Stars for 'A Deadly Path.' Action fills the pages; a father's frustration swiftly turns into protectiveness and sacrifice; and a series of murders in the city comes to a chilling conclusion. 'A Deadly Path' is filled with thorny family dynamics and hair-raising suspense."

"A realistic look at a dad, Detective Jake Sharpe, trying to bond with a son he doesn't understand while they're on a hike. A serial killer lies in wait to shoot them and in the tragedy that ensues, Jake is proud of how his son responds. A quick read that celebrates family and justice."

***

TOM STONE DETECTIVE STORIES

Tom Stone: A Nitty Gritty Christmas (Novella – Book 1)

Cocaine stuffed into candy bars are appearing throughout Los Angeles. A child's overdose at Christmas pulls Detective Tom Stone and his partner Jake Sharpe into the seedy, underground world of drug smuggling. The duo races to stop whoever's responsible before another innocent life is lost. They piece together clues and close in on the criminals until Stone finds himself trapped, facing certain death at the very hands of the men he was hunting.

Tom Stone: Sweltering Summer Nights (Book 2)

Two murders and a cocaine trail threaten dreams of riches for Anthony Angelino, owner of the High Tide marijuana dispensary in East Hollywood.

Once arrested by Detective Tom Stone on suspicion of smuggling cocaine, the courts set Angelino free and offer a second chance. But the drug cartel that he tried to double cross has a different idea, and when Stone's high school-age daughter is found browsing in the High Tide, Stone starts tracking Angelino and uncovers the ruthlessness of betrayal.

As Stone fights for justice and confronts Angelino's attorney, he finds himself enamored with her strength and beauty—and admires her principles of right and wrong.

Healing his fractured family and keeping Los Angeles safe makes for a long, hot summer.

Tom Stone: Day of the Dead (Book 3)

Multiple murders with one grisly connection have Detectives Tom Stone and Jake Sharpe pursuing every lead. Their main suspect, Anthony Angelino, fresh out of prison, dreams of building a new empire, but his past quickly catches up to him and once again he is on the run from the police, and the drug cartel that tried to ruin him.

The head of the cartel, Frank DeVito, using his vast resources puts a tail on Stone hoping the Detective's investigation will flush out Angelino. Then he can exact his revenge and claim what he says Angelino has stolen – a large shipment of pure cocaine.

Angelino's girlfriend, Sara, caught between right and wrong, pleads for him to escape the deadly lifestyle. As the body count rises, Stone, grappling with his own questions and answers, confronts the challenges in his relationship with Alisha Davidson, Angelino's defense attorney.

Tom Stone: One Shot, One Kill (Book 4)

A vigilante sniper terrorizes Los Angeles with perfectly-timed assassinations, picking off the ultra-wealthy who finance the flow of drugs into the city. As each one falls, a power vacuum is created and a ruthless drug cartel moves in, seeking control of the streets through intimidation, mutilation, and brutally murdering anybody who gets in their way.

Detective Tom Stone and his partner Jake Sharpe suspect mob boss Frank DeVito has a role to play in the carnage after the cartel's shot-caller, a woman in prison named Lil' Jo, orders an assault on DeVito's estate.

Gang violence escalates while the sniper extracts his revenge, eliminating the elite one shot at a time. Stone turns to a new detective on the force, Brian Kilbraide, who had served as a sniper with the Army Rangers.

Stone and his team must race to stop the bloodshed and bring DeVito to justice before the sniper's powerful bullet cuts him dead.

Tom Stone: A Deadly Path (Short Story)

Detective Jake Sharpe pulls his son Darrell away from video games and on to a hike in the foothills above Los Angeles. A father and son jaunt becomes a fight for survival when they take a turn on a little-used path. Tom Stone and the boy he's befriended, Andrew, journey with them in this action-filled short story.

Find us on FACEBOOK, Amazon, Barnes & Noble, iTunes, and Kobo

Sign up for our Tom Stone Detective Stories Newsletter.

***

ABOUT THE AUTHORS

Don Simkovich – Don would like to give a shout out to his wife, Cindy, for her support during the writing process. Storytelling has been part of Don's life and career as a journalist, author, and ghostwriter of blogs and books.

Fiction grabbed his interest at an early age and he has returned to the craft in the past several years, enjoying the mishaps, emotions, and happy endings his characters experience.

He lives with his family and dogs in Pasadena, California.

www.donsimkovich.com
Twitter: @donsimko
Facebook: www.facebook.com/don.simkovich
Amazon author page: www.amazon.com/author/donsimkovich/

***

Lon Casler Bixby – Lon is a published author in various genres: Fiction, Poetry, Humor, Photography, and Comic Books. He is also a professional award-winning photographer whose work has been featured in a wide variety of magazines, art & coffee table books, and has also been displayed in Art Galleries throughout the world.

Lon lives out of his photography studio in Burbank, California where he shares his living space with his wonderful, albeit spoiled, Silver Lab named Silver.

Twitter: @LonBixby
Facebook: www.facebook.com/lon.bixby
Amazon author page: www.amazon.com/author/loncaslerbixby/
Portfolio: www.neoichi.com
Portfolio: www.whileyouweresleeping.photography

ABOUT THE COVER ARTIST

Benjamin Southgate – Ben is best known for visualizing and bringing to life ideas through fully crafted and detailed artwork. As a freelance artist Ben utilizes Photoshop alongside traditional mediums to create character and environment illustrations straight from pen to canvas.

Familiar with a multitude of genres, Ben has experience working with dark fantasy, urban environments, science fiction, and creature designs. He is always keen to explore new ideas and find fresh ways of representing creative projects.

Living beside the Norfolk Broads in England, you can find Ben drifting into the depths of imagination on his Wacom Cintiq 24HD or you can contact him on his webpages.

Twitter: @Benvsouthgate
Facebook: www.facebook.com/BenjaminSouthgateArt
Portfolio: www.artstation.com/benjaminsouthgate

***

Made in United States
Orlando, FL
06 December 2022